TO RULE IN HELL

AN OMEGA THRILLER

BLAKE BANNER

The characters and events portrayed in this ebook are fictitious. Any similarity to real persons, living or dead, is coincidental and not intended by the author.

ISBN-13: 978-1-63696-338-9

ISBN-10: 1-63696-338-2

Cover design by: Damonza

Printed in the United States of America

www.righthouse.com

www.instagram.com/righthousebooks

www.facebook.com/righthousebooks

twitter.com/righthousebooks

THE OMEGA SERIES

Dawn of the Hunter (Book 1)
Double Edged Blade (Book 2)
The Storm (Book 3)
The Hand of War (Book 4)
A Harvest of Blood (Book 5)
To Rule in Hell (Book 6)
Kill: One (Book 7)
Powder Burn (Book 8)
Kill: Two (Book 9)
Unleashed (Book 10)
The Omicron Kill (Book 11)
9mm Justice (Book 12)
Kill: Four (Book 13)
Death In Freedom (Book 14)
Endgame (Book 15)

ONE

I WAS IN THAT PLACE BETWEEN WAKING AND SLEEP, where everything is feeling. You do not imagine in pictures: Your mind is dark. There are no voices: your mind is quiet. And in the dark silence, you feel. I could feel Abi's back, pressed close against me. I could feel her hair on my face. I could feel the fresh linen of the bed, a cool breeze from the window on my face. For the first time in my life I felt I was home and safe. So I kept my eyes closed and held on to the feeling.

Slowly sounds began to filter in. Outside, March was melting the winter snow and the birds were celebrating loudly. A transmission complained in low gear as a truck moved down Main Street toward the farm. Across the road the doc told somebody it was a fine morning—if you wanted to freeze to death. There was laughter and that made me smile. I felt Abi chuckle and I opened my eyes, raised myself on one elbow to look down at her. She was smiling but still had her eyes closed and spoke in a sleepy voice.

"He's such a grouch."

I kissed her shoulder. "You seen the time?"

"It's Sunday."

"Tell that to my stomach."

She opened one eye to look at me sidelong. "Your stomach?" She began to turn. "Come here and let me explain something to your stomach..."

I should have ignored it. I should have let it ring. But it had been too many years of training and conditioning and I had turned and reached for my cell before I knew what I was doing.

"Yeah..."

Marni spoke and I went cold inside. "Hi Lacklan, it's been a long time..."

For a moment I felt sick. I could feel Abi's eyes on me, curious. I said, "Yeah, where are you?"

"Not on the phone. I'm where I was." She was still in Oxford then. A wave of relief, then shame. She went on, cold and efficient. "I'm afraid this isn't a social call. I need to be quick."

"Sure, yeah."

"I need you to do something."

A spot of anger and resentment in my gut. "What?" I felt the bedcovers move, looked and saw Abi walking to the bathroom. Marni was talking again.

"I'm on a secure line, but I can't stay on long, so I need you to trust me and not argue, OK?"

I took a moment to answer. Finally I said, "Yeah, OK..."

"I need you to go to Seattle, 5508 B, 26th Avenue South, Beacon Hill. There you will collect something."

"Collect what?"

"Shut up. When the guy, you can call him Ernst, opens the door to you, you'll tell him you need an extension. He'll tell you to come in and look at some drawings."

"Are you serious?"

"Shut up, Lacklan! He will give you some items and some instructions. Have you clearly understood everything I have told you?"

"Yes, of course I have. But, Marni...?"

"Be quick. I'm running out of time."

"When this is over, we need to talk."

A moment's silence, then. "Yeah, when it's over."

The line went dead.

I sat a moment, staring out at the snow melting on Main Street. I could hear the shower going in the bathroom. The hot pellet of anger in my belly turned into a wave of rage and frustration. It welled up to a peak inside me. I closed my eyes and breathed. It passed, and I swung out of bed and joined Abi in the shower.

Downstairs we made breakfast together in silence. We were alone. I had got Primrose an apartment in Boston, where she was applying to universities, and Sean had joined her there for Easter. Abi and I had been going to spend the Easter on our own together. It was the first time we had been alone.

I put the coffee pot on the table, she set down two plates of bacon and fried banana, and a dish of pancakes. We sat and I watched her while she stared at her plate for four long seconds.

"You're leaving, aren't you?"

"I have to go to Seattle."

"Will you come back?"

"Yes. I don't know how long. It may be a couple of days, or it may be a week. I won't know until I'm there. But I have told them I need to talk to them. This is my last job, Abi."

"Please don't lie to me."

I shook my head. "I am telling you the truth. I've had enough. I'm through."

She reached over and took hold of my hand. Her eyes told me she wanted to believe me. They also told me that she didn't.

After breakfast I packed up the Zombie, kissed Abi and told her I would call her from Seattle, and drove down the long track to Blood Canyon Road. There I turned north. I picked up the I-80 at Mill City and settled down to a thirteen hour drive. The Zombie was actually a 1968 Ford Mustang Fastback. But it had been modified by some crazy geniuses in Texas. Now the twin electric engines delivered eight hundred bhp and one thousand eight hundred foot-pounds of torque direct to the back wheels. It could do 170 MPH over a mile without breaking a sweat, went 0 to 60 in just over one and a half seconds, while spreading your face across the back of your seat, and did it all without making a sound.

I settled at a steady eighty, shook a Camel from my pack, lit it with my battered, brass Zippo and put the Eagles on the sound system. Desperado seemed somehow appropriate, as I thought about what I was leaving behind me and wondered about what I was heading for.

Marni had made it clear it wasn't a social call. That meant just one thing. It was about Omega, and that meant that after the near catastrophe at the United Nations in New

York[1], they were done licking their wounds and now they were ready to join battle again. I knew that while I'd been trying to live a normal life with Abi and her kids in Independence, Marni and Professor Gibbons had not been sitting on their laurels. They had been planning, preparing for when Omega resurfaced. It had always been a matter of time. Now that time had come. They were back, and so were we...

We?

I thought about the word.

All my life there had been two constants: my love for Marni and my hatred for my father. On his deathbed he had made me promise that I would protect Marni in her mission to bring down Omega. It had not been a hard promise to make, back then. But now things had changed. Marni had walked away, and she had not looked back. I had found Abi, and a home in Independence. Now it was a promise I was preparing to break.

If they wanted me to collect something in Seattle, then they would want me to deliver it somewhere too. I would do that. And then I would tell Marni and Gibbons that it was over. I had no future with Marni, that much was clear, and the only future I had fighting Omega was more killing. Killing was something I was good at. I was the best of the best. But nothing wearies, destroys you, nothing drains your soul as much as killing. And I had had enough.

As Don Henley kept telling me, I wasn't gettin' no younger.

I crossed into Oregon as the sun hit noon. I crossed the Black Rock Desert at speed and stopped for a late lunch at

---

1. See *The Hand of War*

Prineville. Then I took US Highway 26 toward Portland, and as evening began to close in, I started to climb, through ever denser pine forests, toward Mount Hood. Finally, at shortly before eleven that night, I stopped at Tanglewild, outside Seattle, because I liked the name, and booked into a Best Western for the night.

As I lay, staring at the dark ceiling, preparing myself for sleep, Independence, the Pioneer Inn and Abi seemed suddenly to be a very long way away.

BEACON HILL IS NOT the most exciting place in Seattle. It is a dormitory for the people who work downtown and in the Eliot Bay area. There is nothing there but houses, thousands of them—not quite identical, but close enough—in endless, almost identical rows.

26th Avenue South was not hard to find. I came in on the I-5, followed Beacon Avenue north to South Orca and turned left into 26th. The house I was looking for was on the right, about halfway up, and about as boring and inconspicuous as Beacon Hill itself. I pulled up, climbed out and slammed the door. It echoed down a street with no people in it. I took a moment to look at the house. It was a red brick with very straight, modern lines and a path that wound up through a huge rockery, covered in pines and cypress trees. The path ended at a front porch that was more like a terrace.

I climbed the path, rang the bell and then hammered for good measure. The door was opened after a moment by a man I guessed was in his early sixties. He wore heavy, horn-rimmed glasses like the ones Michael Cain used to wear back when the world was young, and a gray cardigan like the one his grandfather used to wear before that. He had it buttoned up and I could see a pipe poking out of one of the pockets. He smiled at me and said, with a hint of reproof, "I came as fast as I could. Can I help you?"

I raised an eyebrow. "I hope so. I need an extension."

"Oh, well then, you'd better come in. I'll show you some drawings."

I thanked him and he led me through a spartan, minimalist living room with a stone fireplace, furniture with bare, polished wooden legs, and five cats, to a kitchen in tubular metal and black and yellow Formica. A sixth cat followed us in and I saw six dishes on the floor with cat food in them. Each dish had a name, so I guess the cats could read. He waved a hand in their direction and said, "Don't mind the gang. I was just about to make tea. Will you have some?"

"Thanks. I need to be on my way. I'd rather get down to business if you don't mind."

He gave a small, private smile as he prepared two mugs with tea bags. "How do you know you need to be on your way?" he said, then glanced over his shoulder as he switched on the kettle. "I haven't given you your instructions yet. Sit down."

I sat at the Formica table. He took a large manila envelope from on top of the toaster and dropped it in front of me. From the pocket that did not contain his pipe he took a pair of latex gloves and pulled them on. Then he opened the envelope and extracted an ID card. He handed it to me.

"Do me a favor and get lots of fingerprints on that, would you? Nothing alerts the intelligence agencies like an ID card with just two fingerprints on it. You are Joseph O'Brien. I thought you had a bit of an Irish rogue look about you. You live in Chicago. Your job, address and other details are all in the envelope. None of it will stand up to close background checks, obviously, so try to avoid drawing attention to yourself. Here is your driving permit and a credit card for any expenses you may have to incur as Mr. O'Brien. Give them a good maul too. When you are done with them, burn them thoroughly."

I looked at the two documents and the card, then up at Ernst. "What the hell is this? What do I need these for?"

"Don't shoot me, I'm just the messenger." He said it into the envelope, fishing out a couple of sheets of A4, which he handed me. I looked at them. They were just biographical details that went with the ID documents. He went on, "Now, at twelve noon you will take your car to the SP Parking at First and Colombia. You will go to the very top floor and there you will meet an old friend of yours..."

"Who?"

"I have no idea. All I know is that he will be waiting there for you. He will deliver an uninteresting saloon car to you, and tell you what to do and where to go, so to speak. He will then take your own vehicle back to Boston." He smiled. I didn't. I had decided I didn't like him.

"Who gave you these instructions?"

"Even if I wanted to, I couldn't tell you because I don't know."

The kettle had stopped boiling, but he made no move to make tea. I guess he had decided he disliked me as much as I disliked him. I said, "Are we done?"

He nodded and waited. I took the documents and stood. "Thanks for the tea. Say goodbye to Mr. Tiddles for me."

"Goodbye. Close the door on your way out."

I made my way to my car, aware of him watching me from his window.

It was a short drive along Beacon Avenue and over Holgate Bridge, up to the Waterfront. All the way I was asking myself who the 'old friend' was that was going to meet me at the parking garage. I wondered briefly if it might be Marni or Gibbons, but I was pretty sure they were still in Oxford.

I arrived with a couple of hours to spare, but drove the Zombie to the top floor anyway. There were only a couple of other cars up there, a Ford Focus and a Dodge Charger. I climbed out and was immediately buffeted by the wind coming in off the bay. The view was spectacular and I took a moment to look out over the dark stretch of Puget Sound. When I turned to make my way to the elevators he was standing there behind me. I should have known it would be him. I smiled.

"Kenny."

"Good morning, sir. I have your car. May I say what a pleasure it is to see you?"

I laughed out loud, partly at his old-world formality, and partly at the sheer, unexpected joy of seeing him. "It is a pleasure to see you, too, old friend. It's been a long time, too long."

"Indeed, sir. Almost two years. Rosalia sends her best wishes. You are missed at home..." For a moment I didn't know what to say. I was overwhelmed by feelings that confused me. He must have sensed it because he smiled and held out a key. "It's the Dodge, over there, sir, a nice V8.

Miss Marni said to get something inconspicuous, but I thought you'd like something with a bit of grunt."

"It's a perfect choice." I took the key and handed him the ones to the Zombie. Then I laughed again and slapped him on the shoulder. "Let's go and have coffee, Kenny, and you can tell me about Rosalia and the house... Has it really been two years?"

We rode down in the elevator and walked up to 3rd Avenue, where we found a café with tables in an internal patio. We ordered coffee and I sat watching the man who had been my father's butler for two decades; who had in many ways been more of a father to me than Bob Walker ever had. He was now my butler, though it was hard for me to think of him as such, and since my father's death I had barely set foot in the house. Listening to him now, filling me in on the state of the lawns and the gardens, of the woods, the house and Rosalia's health (Rosalia—my surrogate mother—my cook!), I realized, almost with a sense of panic, that what he and Rosalia wanted most from me was for me to take my place in that house, and bring order back to their world. To fill my father's shoes.

He fell silent and I realized he had finished his coffee and I had barely touched mine. He hesitated a moment, then said, "Miss Marni gave me a message for you, sir."

"Yes," I said. "I had almost forgotten. It has been so good to catch up..." Even as I said it I was aware that it was both true and hypocritical of me. Though I loved Kenny and Rosalia, every fiber of my being wanted to run from my father's legacy, and they were a part of that legacy. And yet, I could have sat all day listening to him and his stories about rosebushes and the falcons that were nesting on the chimney pots.

"The message is, sir, that she wishes you to drive to Spokane, to leave the car in a side street there and to purchase, cash, a ticket on the Empire Builder, which I understand is a train, to Chicago. And, once there, to purchase a ticket to Washington, D.C., in the name of Joseph O'Brien. Again, she advises that the ticket should be bought cash. There is a room reserved for you, in the name of O'Brien, at the Hotel Hive, on F Street. It is a... um... *modest* establishment, but I do not believe you will be staying there very long. Today is Monday. On Wednesday evening, at six, you will be met in the bar by a gentleman. He will ask you how your extension is progressing, and you will inform him that it is a work in progress. He will then take you to meet somebody. I am afraid, sir, that I do not know whom you are to meet."

I nodded for a long time. I was thinking that things wouldn't even get started until Wednesday, but I had told Abi I'd be away a couple of days or a week. It was going to be considerably more than that. I sighed. "Thanks, Kenny." I looked at my watch. "I guess we had better get going."

On the way back to the parking garage Kenny said suddenly, "Sir, may I ask a question? Two, questions, in fact."

"Of course, Kenny. Anything."

"Can we..." He hesitated. "Can we expect you home at some point, sir?"

I smiled. It was a good question, and I wasn't able to answer it until we were stepping out of the elevators onto the roof. I walked him to the Zombie and as he opened the door I said, "It's a question I have been asking myself a lot lately, Kenny, and I'm beginning to think that the answer is yes. I don't know when. Maybe I'll know more after Wednesday."

"That is good news, Rosalia will be very happy."

"What's your other question?"

"Will Miss Marni be with you?" I guess he saw by my face that there was no simple answer to that one, because before I could reply, he said, "Ah, I see, sir. Well, I'd best be getting back then. Perhaps we should leave a few minutes between my departure and yours. We'll be hoping to hear from you in due course. Goodbye, sir."

And with that, he climbed into the car and slipped silently away.

TWO

The drive to Spokane should have taken six hours but it didn't. The four wheel drive Dodge, with its V8 growl, is not a car for cruising or looking at the scenery. I hit the I-90, crossed the two bridges, and after Issaquah I was out of the city and burning rubber at 100 MPH, headed east in the afternoon sun. Both me and the Dodge were happy.

I arrived in Spokane at five PM, dropped the Dodge in a side street and, according to Kenny's instructions, bought a one way ticket to Chicago on the Empire Builder. I discovered then that there was only one a day. It departed at twenty-five minutes past one in the morning and arrived in Chicago thirty-six hours later, at three fifty-five in the afternoon. It would have been faster by ten hours to drive, but I guess Marni, or Gibbons, was trying not to leave a trail. At some point, I figured, I might find out why.

Premium was extortionate, but for once in my life I took a leaf out of my father's book and went first class, because I got a room, a bed and food, all of which I was going to need.

I called Abi from a pay phone and told her I was going to be at least a week, maybe two, but that I was more certain than ever that I was coming back. She was quiet, like she was trying to believe me, which made me wonder whether I believed myself. I was pretty sure I did, but I was also in uncharted territory. Family were things I had been running from as long as I could remember. Now, suddenly, I found I wanted to create both.

After I had hung up, I killed eight hours by getting lost in the city, buying a book, having an early dinner at a restaurant and then downing some drinks and watching TV in a late night bar. At one AM I made my way to the station and boarded the train.

The rest of the journey was a kind of interminable blur: the relentless rhythm of the train on the tracks, and the endless spectacular scenery of the north, interspersed with chapters from a futuristic dystopian thriller about a guy fighting an unwinnable war against an all-powerful organization that controlled world governments. I wondered if the author knew how close he was to the truth. But eventually, after thirty-six long hours, we arrived at Chicago, and I shoved the book in my bag.

From the railway station I took a cab direct to O'Hare and managed to get a seat on a flight departing that evening at seven forty-five, arriving at ten thirty. I called the hotel and told them I'd be arriving earlier than expected. I could have booked in at the airport Hilton, stayed the night and caught a morning flight, but it felt like I had been traveling all my life, and getting nowhere. Now I just wanted to arrive, get the job done and go home.

I finally climbed out of the cab at the Hotel Hive at just

before midnight, sixty hours and three thousand miles from where I had started, with still no clear idea of what I was doing there, or when I would be able to go back to Independence, Abi, and the life I was trying to build. I checked in at reception and discovered that Marni had had the good sense to book me a king-sized attic. I rode the elevator up to my room, poured myself a large Bushmills and collapsed on the bed.

———

I SLEPT in late and had brunch in my room while I showered and shaved, and wondered what the hell I was doing in D.C. So far all the instructions I'd received had been aimed at one single thing, ensuring that nobody followed me. And the only items I had collected had been documents to conceal my identity. Now I was here, in D.C., as Joseph O'Brien, and whoever I was due to meet in the bar would presumably tell me why. But the fact that I was in a hotel in Washington, rather than a dive in the Bronx or a hamlet in the Mid West, could mean only one thing: that Gibbons and Marni were trying some kind of political power play. This clearly involved Gibbons' political 'connections', but what I was struggling with was how it involved me.

As I thought about it I realized there was a second possibility, and that was that I had been duped and I was here to meet Ben. D.C. was Ben's turf, and twice already I had been brought here to his office at the Pentagon. But the last time I'd met him here had resulted in the deaths of several senior members of Omega, and one former president. I was pretty sure that next time I met Ben, he'd be trying to kill me, not talk to me.

It was unlikely, I decided, to be a trap set by Ben, but I was also pretty sure that he would be making an appearance sooner or later.

I spent the afternoon in my room working out and killing time, and at five thirty I went down to the bar. There was a lot of red brick, dark wood and artsy elegance. I ordered a martini very dry and found a table near an open fire. There I sat to wait. My contact arrived at five fifty-nine with a luminous sign on his head that said 'Navy Seal'. All six foot two of him stood in the doorway in his Italian suit and his Ray-Ban shades, assessing his immediate environment and seeking his target. I sighed and looked at the small flames in the hearth. After a moment I heard his large feet cross the floor to my table.

I looked up at him and smiled. "Hello."

He spoke with no inflection at all. "How is your extension progressing?"

I nodded. "Well, you know, it's a work in progress. Sit down and order a drink, will you? And try to stop looking like a damn Navy Seal."

His right eyebrow twitched. "Sarah asked me to hurry. She has the roast on. We can have drinks when we get there."

I shook my head, drained my glass and stood. As I grabbed my coat I asked him, "You ever consider a career in Hollywood? There is something so natural and believable about your delivery."

"You ever consider a career as a comedian? You're funny."

Outside it was getting dark and there was a bite in the

air. He started across the sidewalk and I saw he had a black Grand Cherokee Laredo waiting with its hazards flashing. As he moved around to the driver's door, he said, "In D.C., this is blending in."

I sighed for the second time. Maybe he was right, at that. We spent the next hour driving all over the District of Colombia, as far north as Fort Slocum Park and as far south as Wesley Heights by way of the White House. All the while he seemed to have his eyes fixed more on the mirrors than on the road. I decided he was thorough, and made up in attention to detail for what he lacked in innate intelligence. He was a well-trained gorilla.

Eventually he seemed to relax and we headed, by way of many side streets, toward Trinidad. On Montello Avenue he turned right into Penn Street and stopped outside a slightly dilapidated, double-fronted red brick that looked like it might have been new in the 1890s. The front lawn was running to seed and the Georgian gabled portico was shedding its white paint. He glanced at me. "This low-key enough for you?"

I nodded. "Yeah, your ninety grand Cherokee fits right in here."

"Quit griping. She's waiting."

"Who is?"

"Go and find out, hot shot."

Just for a moment there was hostility in his eyes. Resentment? Hurt pride? I climbed out and made my way across the lawn, along the cracked concrete path toward the front door. I heard the big engine whine and watched the red taillights move away into the dark.

The door was plain wood with peeling varnish. I tried the

bell. It didn't work, so I rapped with my knuckles. After fifteen seconds the door opened. The hall inside was dark, but I could make out the form of a man holding a gun. He said, "Step inside, put your hands on your head and face the wall."

I didn't move. "How about I break your neck instead?"

"I wouldn't do that. You're covered on three sides. Besides, I just want to check you for weapons. Quit being an asshole and step inside."

I went in and put my hands up. He kept his distance, closed the door and snapped on the lights. I was in a dingy hall with a staircase opposite, and a door on either side. There were two men, both with the same Special Ops look: short hair, expressionless eyes and shirts that didn't fit across their chests. The guy holding the gun on me was in his fifties, the other was twenty years younger, with dark hair and dark eyes. He said, "Face the wall."

I gave him the dead eye and said, "No."

He frowned, like the moon had just risen in the west. "Face the fucking wall!"

I spoke to the older guy. "No. Frisk me if you want, but I'm not turning my back on you until I know who you are and why I'm here. And if you try to take my weapon I'll break your arm. Now I came to D.C. because you asked me to, so let's get this fucking circus over with or I'm going to walk out that door and go home."

His frown deepened. "You have a weapon? You came here with a weapon?"

"Sig Sauer p226, I have a knife in my boot. And make no mistake, I'm serious. Touch them and I'll break your arm. I don't know who the hell you are or why you asked me to come here. And frankly, your reception stinks. Start explaining, pal."

The older guy hesitated. He wasn't prepared for the unexpected. Few people ever are. When people hesitate, that's when you take charge. I said, "I gather I am here to meet somebody?"

His face said I was right.

"Keep me covered. Take me to them. If I am satisfied that I am not in danger, I'll put my weapons on the table."

He sighed and jerked his head toward the door behind me. "Through there, and keep your hands where I can see them."

His young pal pulled his Glock and opened the door. I followed him in. The older guy stayed behind me. I was in a long room the stretched from the front of the house to the back. There was a fireplace that was cold and black with ash. A coffee table stood in front of it with a seedy sofa and a couple of threadbare armchairs. Heavy, sage green drapes were drawn across the windows at the front and the rear, and the light, which was dull, was from a couple of old lamps with flyblown shades.

There was a woman sitting in one of the armchairs, watching me. I recognized her. She was younger and more attractive in the flesh than on TV. I guessed she was in her late thirties, with densely curled copper hair and dark blue eyes. Her clothes were expensive, as you'd expect, but understated and elegant.

I nodded. "I should have guessed, Senator Cyndi McFarlane." I turned to the older guy. "I'm going to put my weapons on the table. I'd appreciate it if you holstered yours.

We're friends here."[1]

McFarlane looked at them and nodded. "Major Hawthorn, Lieutenant Garcia, this is Captain Lacklan Walker. He is a friend. I would like you to leave us alone now."

They left reluctantly and she turned back to me. "Please, leave your weapons where they are. The drinks are on the sideboard. Mine is bourbon. May I call you Lacklan?"

I spotted the bottles. As I poured I said, "If I can call you Cyndi."

When I handed her her drink, she was smiling. "Well, as it seems we may be spending some time together, I don't see why not."

I sat and raised an eyebrow at her. "Does it? Are we?"

"Yes indeed. Your instructions are to..."

I was shaking my head and interrupted her. "I'm sorry, Cyndi, there has obviously been a misunderstanding somewhere along the line. I don't work for anybody, and nobody gives me instructions. I was asked to come here by an old friend, and I am here because I am doing her a favor. Let's be clear about that right from the start."

She stared at me for a long moment. Then she raised her eyebrows and stared into her drink. "I see. Well, I stand corrected, but this poses a problem, because now you are privy..."

I shook my head again and interrupted her for a second time. I could see it was getting on her nerves. That was OK with me. "I am privy to nothing so far. I was asked to come and see you by a friend. So I came. I don't know the details

---

1. See *A Harvest of Blood*

and for now nobody has used the magic word. I'd like to keep it that way."

She was staring at me hard now and looked like she might be about to get mad. "I have to say, Captain Walker..."

"Mr."

"*Mr.* Walker, that I am not accustomed to being interrupted constantly *or* being spoken to in this way."

"I can see that, Cyndi, but if you want my help you had better get used to it. Now, how about we start again from the beginning, and this time you tell me what it is you would like my help with. If I agree, then you can make me privy to any details."

Her cheeks had flushed and her eyes were bright. There was an edge to her voice when she said, "Yes, *sir!*" I waited, and after a moment she went on, "Without making you privy to any details: I need to travel to a given destination to meet with your friends. You can imagine what we are going to discuss, so I needn't tell you just how important it is that I get there in one piece. Your friends suggested that you were the man for the job."

I jerked my head at the door. "What about Major Confusion and the Subtle Boys?"

"Do you *have* to be so insulting?"

"Sometimes, yes."

"Your friends, both of them, said that you were the best there was. Professor..."

"Don't!"

She sighed. "He said that my security team were no match for..."

"I hear you. He's right. They may as well go around with neon signs on their heads. The people you are up against are very well funded, well trained and professional. But you know that. You work with them every day."

"Will you help?"

"Do we need to leave the country?"

"No."

"And the meeting is with my friend and the professor?"

"Yes."

"How long will this take?"

"Well, that depends to some extent on you, but I would imagine it will be three or four days. No more than a week."

"OK, I'll do it."

She didn't look overjoyed by the news. After a moment, she said, "About your fee..."

"No fee. I told you, I don't work for anybody. But there are conditions."

"Why am I not surprised?"

"I am in charge of this operation, and you make Major Hawthorn and his boys aware of that. We do things my way or I am out."

"Very well. Anything else?"

"Yes, who else knows about this?"

"Nobody."

"What about your husband?"

"My... Now *come on!*"

"How much does he know, Cyndi?"

"He is my husband! We have no secrets!"

"That changes as of now. People's lives are at stake, not least mine. You tell him nothing until you get back. If that is a problem, we are done here."

"Mr. Walker! I have had just about *enough...*"

I stood. "Thanks for the whiskey."

She was on her feet. "Now you wait just one goddamn minute, mister!"

I shook my head. "No. I am not prepared to have people's blood on my hands simply to pander to some silly notion of the sanctity of marriage. You want to play nice, get out of politics. My father murdered his best friend because they told him that if he didn't they would slaughter his family. When he'd done the job, they promoted him to one of the highest positions in the organization—the organization you are up against. That is the kind of people you're dealing with. If we do this, the operation is hermetically sealed. And that includes your husband." I took a step closer to her and looked her straight in the eye. "Put this operation in the hands of your band of clowns, and you'll all be dead before the end of the week. And that would be a shame, Cyndi, because I have always admired you a great deal. They need you, but they don't need Major Hawthorn—or your husband."

I could tell she really wanted to slap me, but I could also see she knew I was right. After a moment she took a big, deep breath and said, "Mr. Walker, Lacklan, will you *please* sit down."

I sat. She sat. I took a sip of whiskey and pulled a pack of Camels from my pocket. I showed it to her and said, "Do you mind?"

She held out her hand. "I'll join you."

I flipped the Zippo and lit her cigarette, then I lit mine, inhaled deeply and sat back. "Now, make me privy to the details."

She sipped and took a long drag. As she let out the smoke she said, "I need to get to New Mexico, Albuquerque, for a meeting with Marni Gilbert and Professor Philip Gibbons. They both say you know Omega better than anybody, and you have hurt them badly in the past."

I nodded. "They're right. OK, Cyndi. Here is how we are going to do this. You are going to go home, and you tell your husband that you have to go out of town for a few days. If he asks you where, or why, you tell him that it is confidential and you can't discuss it."

"He won't believe me. We have never..."

"That's not important. The only thing that's important is that he knows you are going voluntarily and you don't want to tell him about it. All we need is that he doesn't alert the cops because he thinks you've gone missing."

She spread her hands. "Fine!"

"What is your normal routine in the morning?"

"Oh, um..." She shrugged. "I rise at six, breakfast, work in my study, then at nine Charles, that's Major Hawthorn, drives me to the office..."

"OK, you're going to do that as normal, but tomorrow you are going to take a detour and you're going to go to the public parking garage on 9th Street. Go to the topmost floor. There you get out and you get into my car. I'll be waiting for you. You tell the Major to wait half an hour before leaving. Then he goes on to your office. He goes to the parking garage there. Waits ten minutes and then continues with his usual daily routine. Have you got all of that?"

She nodded. "Yes."

"Repeat it to me."

"*What?*"

"Repeat it to me, Cyndi."

I made her repeat it twelve times until she had it verbatim. Finally I made her tell me her address and stood. "OK, get one of your boys to drop me on Florida Avenue. I'll get a cab from there. And Cyndi? I am serious, you tell Hawthorn the bare minimum that he needs to know. Anybody else you tell absolutely nothing. That includes Marni and Gibbons, and especially your husband."

She stood. Her face flushed red. She'd had about as much of me as she could stomach. "Why *especially* my husband?"

I stepped close to her. "Because if I was out to find you, to assassinate you, the first person I would target would be your husband. If he doesn't know where you are or what you are doing, he may just have a chance of coming out alive."

She went white.

I said, "The people you are going up against are very bad people, Cyndi. You need to have assimilated that by tomorrow morning."

She stared at me for a long moment, her eyes making small, darting movements over my face. She was asking herself if she had made a smart choice or the worst mistake of her life. After a moment, she called, "Charles, come in please." The door opened and the major came in. "Please take the captain to Florida Avenue..."

THREE

It was another Jeep, pretty much like the one I had been brought in. Maybe she'd got a discount on a job lot. We crossed the front lawn under a black, starless sky, climbed in and slammed the doors. As we pulled away, he glanced at me. "So what's the story?"

"No story."

"What does she need you for?"

"That doesn't concern you."

We turned into Montello Avenue. "Everything that affects the Senator's safety is my concern."

I studied his face a moment and decided he was either in love with his boss or working for Omega. I said, "That is an admirable sentiment, Major, but unless you're going to put toothpicks under my nails, forget it. This doesn't concern you. Period."

We didn't speak again till he'd dropped me at the corner of New York Avenue. There, I stopped with the door half open. "Don't share this with anyone, Major. Not your colleagues, not your wife, not even your dog. Do you understand? Don't let her share it with her husband either. Are you hearing me?"

He didn't say anything, but he nodded. I got out. I waited till he'd disappeared from sight, then I crossed the road and hailed a cab. I got it to drop me at the Veteran's Park on G Street, by way of the CVS on K Street, and walked the block to the hotel. I ran up the six steps and pushed into the lobby. There was a young man on reception.

"I need to hire a car for a week or so."

"No problem, sir, we can arrange that for you."

He rattled at the keyboard on his computer and I handed him Joseph O'Brien's ID, driver's permit and credit card.

"For tomorrow morning, sir?"

"Eight AM or sooner."

"Seven thirty?"

"That's fine."

"And will you be dropping the car off here, sir?"

"No, I'm checking out tomorrow at six AM. I'll drop the car off at O'Hare in Chicago, a week from tomorrow, on Thursday 22nd."

"Very good, sir." He tapped in my card details and handed me back my ID and credit card. "It will be out front seven thirty tomorrow morning. Enjoy your evening."

I had a pizza at the hotel pizza restaurant and went up to my room to sleep and prepare for the next day.

The senator lived in an elegant, understated, five million dollar, red brick house on P Street NW. I was there at eight thirty the next morning, parked in the shade of some elegant plane trees fifty yards from her door, in an anonymous Ford Focus. I was wearing the latex gloves I had bought the night before at the drugstore, and waiting for her to show.

At nine, just as she had said, the Black Jeep rolled up to the door and Major Charles Hawthorn climbed out and rang the bell. Two minutes later, she stepped out of the house and he opened the back door of the Jeep for her. He checked the road, climbed in behind the wheel and took off. I followed them east, staying about seven or eight cars behind them, watching in front of me and behind me to see if they were followed—or if I was being followed.

Eventually they turned onto Pennsylvania and then I Street, and from I Street they turned onto New York Avenue and made for the Technoworld Parking Garage. I closed in, just four or five cars behind them, and followed them through the barrier into the dark maw of the entrance. As we spiraled steadily up toward the top floor, their tires echoed mine in a weird rhythm of sqeals, like wounded pterodactyls chasing each other, screaming in the cavernous half light. We finally came to the top floor. I saw the red lights on the black Jeep up ahead and stopped a few paces behind it. The major got out and I got out to show him it was me. He opened the door for the senator, spoke some urgent words to her. She shook her head and came to the Ford at a half run. He carried her case to the trunk and put it in next to my shoulder bag. As I closed the trunk he eyed me.

"She better come back in one piece, Walker."

I didn't bother to look at him. "Save it for your memoirs, Major. Wait half an hour before you leave." I climbed in behind the wheel and handed her a pair of surgical gloves.

"Put these on, don't take them off until I say you can."

She took them and stared at them. I turned the car around and headed back down the ramp. She was still staring at the gloves, frowning.

I said, "Do it now."

"Is this *totally* necessary?"

"Yes. Do it. Then turn off your cell. The GPS makes it trackable."

She sighed and pulled them on as we came out of the garage and into the morning sunlight. Then she turned off her cell, like it was the most boring thing she had ever done.

We crossed the Potomac via the 14th Street Bridge, as though we were headed south. After Springfield we joined the I-95. I kept one eye fixed on the rearview mirror all the time, drove fast and changed lanes a lot. At one point the senator said, "What are you doing? What's got into you?"

I said, "Don't talk till we get to Montclair."

Her cheeks may have flushed. I wasn't looking.

By the time we reached Montclair I was pretty sure we were not being tailed, or at least not in a car, and I pulled off onto Dumfries Road, headed west. Pretty soon we were in semi-countryside. She gave me what was probably meant to be a withering look and said, "Can I talk now, *sir?*"

I still had one eye on the mirror. "Wait till Manassas."

She didn't talk again until I took Route 15 out of Warrenton, headed toward Culpeper. Then she couldn't contain herself any longer, narrowed her eyes and shook her head and said, "Have you *any* idea where you are going? Are you lost?"

I smiled at her, which made her frown, and said, "Not at all, Cyndi. We are on our way to Charlottesville."

"And in what universe is that on the way to Albuquerque?"

"In the one where you want to get there alive."

"And if possible this year!"

Satellites I couldn't do anything about, except hope Omega didn't know yet that I was Joseph O'Brien, and therefore what car I was driving. There were no choppers above us and I was certain by now that we were not being tailed by a car, so I allowed myself to relax, settled to a steady seventy and said. "You know time is relative, right?"

"*What?*"

"I aim to get you to Albuquerque in three to five days."

"*Three to five days?*"

"But that is going to seem like five years if you don't stop griping." She drew breath but I kept talking. "Tell me something, were you an only child or an older sister?" She turned in her seat and stared at me with wide, angry eyes. I glanced at her and shrugged. "My money is on elder sister. Am I right?"

She turned back to the road. "I do not intend to have this conversation with you. You are rude, boorish and insulting."

I shook my head. "I'm not being insulting. You are a good, caring person who wants to do the right thing and look after people weaker than herself. I think that's admirable, and it is something you often find in elder sisters."

She frowned at me for a while. There was suspicion in her eyes. “You’re serious, aren’t you?”

“Yeah.” I looked at her and smiled. “You’re also bossy and certain that you know best all the time.”

She sighed.

“Most of the time you probably do. But in this case you don’t. I do.”

“So were you an older brother or an only child?”

“I was the younger brother. Hated my father and wanted to rebel. It was either sex, drugs and rock’n’roll or the army. I chose the army.”

She was quiet for a while. “You don’t seem the army type.”

“Yeah, well, the Regiment isn’t quite like the regular army.”

“Your father was in Omega?”

I nodded. “One of the top three.”

She considered me for a while. Outside, the world passed in a steady flow of trees, occasional houses and farms, and the steady throb of eastbound vehicles passing on my left.

“You must know a lot about Omega.”

“I know more than most people who are not members.”

She looked curious. “Why aren’t you more involved with Marni Gilbert and Professor Gibbons? Seems to me you could be a real asset.”

I shrugged. “It’s a long story. They have their way of doing things. It isn’t my way.” I studied her face a moment. She didn’t look away. I said, “They are a bit like you, Cyndi. They believe that they can tackle Omega by following the rules. They believe that Omega is like the Mafia, or a drugs cartel: a problem *within* society, that can be dealt with in the same way as other problems, by applying the usual solutions, and that life, society, the world will just keep right on going." I shrugged. "But it isn't like that."

She gave a lopsided smile that was half humorous and half skeptical. "It isn't? OK, maybe they are more powerful than the Mafia, and the corruption goes to a very high level, but it is still within society, and we still have to deal with it by following our own rules." She shrugged. "That's why it's called the Rule of Law."

I waited a moment, watching the long, straight road ahead, sucking my teeth. Finally, I shook my head. "Cyndi, if you had gone to this meeting with Gibbons by plane, which would have been the logical thing to do, by tonight you, Marni and Gibbons would have been dead. If we had taken the main east-west interstates—the obvious route—by tonight we would have been dead. You are a United States congresswoman, but you are forced to take an elaborate, secret route across America, in a hired car, because Omega is hunting you down. I have been twice to their office—in the Pentagon..."

She leaned forward, frowning. "*What?* They have an office in the *Pentagon?* You cannot be serious!"

I raised an eyebrow at her. "As I recall, the Mafia have no offices in the Pentagon. You have no idea yet what you are up against." I waited a moment, wondering how much to tell her. "You remember the Federal Agent who helped blow the nuclear bomb at the UN about a year ago? They thought at first he was Agent Harrison McLean, then it turned out not to be. In the end they never traced him, right?"

"Of course I remember, it was what started my campaign."

"That was me. I defused that bomb. It was intended to trigger a war with Europe."

"*What?*"

"And as an incidental bonus take out Marni and Gibbons. You kept asking on TV, how could terrorists get hold of a U.S.-made tactical nuclear device? Well, now you know. The terrorists were a front and the bomb was supplied to them by Omega. Omega owns people in Congress, in the military, in the courts and in law enforcement."

She had gone very pale. "Is this true, what you're telling me? I can't believe it. It's science fiction."

"You once described them as a cancer, on TV. They are not a cancer, Cyndi. They are a symptom of a sickness that goes much deeper. When I tell you they have an office at the Pentagon, and that former president Hennessy was a senior member, I am just scratching the surface."

She stared at me for a long time. Then she said, "Hennessy... He was killed, in a bomb blast at the Pentagon, just a few days after..." I glanced at her, but I didn't say anything. She put her hand to her mouth. "That was *you?*"

I shrugged. "Was it?"

"But... *you're a terrorist!*"

"Don't get carried away, Cyndi. Right now I am the guy taking you safely where you need to be. Don't lose your perspective."

"You can't go around just murdering people willy-nilly because you don't agree with their politics!"

I burst out laughing.

"*What* is so funny?"

"Your belief in your system. It is actually refreshing. I

wish you knew how many men, women and children were murdered by the people who died in that office. And not because they disagreed with their politics, simply because it was expedient to kill them. Marni's father was one of them."

"What proof have you got of that?"

It wasn't so much a challenge as a plea. "Proof? Proof I could put before a committee, or a court of law? None. My father told me on his death bed. Gibbons and Marni, they have some proof we have accumulated over time: recordings, video..."

We were quiet for a time as we approached Charlottesville. I turned onto the I-64 and started heading west.

"But if you plan to challenge Omega through the courts or through committees, you better be damn careful about what judges preside, and how those committees are constituted."

She shook her head. "Dear God, I hope I haven't made the biggest mistake of my life here. What will you do to me if I refuse to cooperate with you?"

I considered her for a moment, then sighed. "Nothing, and to be honest, Cyndi, that is the least of your worries. You have been very vocal about your belief in the existence of a government within the government, and Omega must be acutely aware of you as a threat. By now they will have studied you and they will know everything about you and your family, and about your associates and friends. Chances are very high that they know about this meeting."

"How could they?"

"That depends on how careless you have been. Your security team is sloppy, overconfident and arrogant. So are you. There are a number of people they might have got to, and a dozen ways they might have found out. We have to assume they are looking for you right now." I gave a small laugh. "You don't need to be afraid of me. Right now is probably the safest you've been for the last year." I grinned. "I'm like the good Terminator. I won't let anything happen to you, but you do need to trust me."

She didn't look amused or convinced, and we drove on in silence, toward the George Washington national forest.

FOUR

THE REST OF THE DRIVE WENT WITHOUT INCIDENT. We followed the I-81 as far as Beckley and then the I-64 in a big loop through the forests and into Kentucky as far as Mt Sterling, a small town outside Lexington. Before we got there, at just past five PM, I pulled in to a small, seedy looking motel at the roadside, told Cyndi to stay in the car, and went in to reception pulling off my gloves.

The guy behind the desk was in his forties, overweight and didn't look at me when I walked in. He was watching a small, portable TV that was more interesting than I was. That suited me fine.

"I need a room for the night."

"Single or double?"

"Me and my wife."

"Sign here. ID and credit card."

He shoved a book at me. I gave him Joseph O'Brien's ID and card and put an illegible signature in his book. He gave me a key and told me where the room was, all without raising his eyes from the TV.

I pulled the latex gloves back on, parked the car outside the door to our room and carried our luggage inside. Cyndi closed the door slowly, staring at the double bed. The room was dingy and unattractive in a functional way, with melamine and vinyl furniture and walls that could have done with a lick of paint five years back.

"What the hell is this?"

"Don't worry, I'll sleep on the chair."

"Not good enough."

I looked at her and felt a flush of anger in my belly. "You want separate rooms?"

"*Of course* I want separate rooms!"

"OK, you want to go to reception and book a second room, be my guest. While you're at it, call Major Charles Hawthorn to come and drive you the rest of the way to Albuquerque."

"What?"

"*Wake up, Cyndi!*" I pointed in the general direction of reception. "You book a room and the first thing he is going to ask you for is ID, and after that your credit card! The minute they go into the system, red flags will go up all over the Omega IT system! Within three hours you'll be dead!"

Her face went crimson and for a moment I thought she was going to stamp her foot. "*This is intolerable!*"

"I am getting tired of arguing with you, Cyndi. I am going to get you to Albuquerque alive, and that means being inconspicuous and not leaving a trail." I pointed at her. "Keep fighting me and you will cause a problem."

"Are you threatening me?"

"I am *telling* you, that if you keep fighting me at every step you are going to attract attention. And if we are spotted by Omega, they will come after you. Get that into your damned head!"

Her jaw dropped, not figuratively but literally. "I have *never* been spoken to like that!"

"I told you, get used to it, because for the next five days, unless you shape up, you're going to get a lot of it!"

"I am a United States Senator, goddammit! You cannot treat me like this!"

I picked up a leaflet on the bedside table. It advertised take out pizza and hamburgers. I studied at it a moment. "I have heard you say some real smart things over the last year, Cyndi. But what you said just now was about the stupidest thing I ever heard anybody say. Political office does not make you worthy of respect. Your actions make you worthy of respect." I handed her the leaflet. "We don't leave this room till tomorrow morning. Choose something to eat. I'll call out."

She threw the leaflet on the bed, then slammed into the bathroom to have a shower. I chose for her, made the call, poured myself a stiff measure of Irish and sat and thought about the only weak link in our security so far. It might be nothing, or it might prove to be a problem the closer we got to Albuquerque.

Unless she had told her husband, the only person who knew that Cyndi was with me, in that car, was Major Charles Hawthorn. At least, that had been true this morning. Now it was anybody's guess. I had taken an eccentric enough route coming out of D.C. to throw any tail off our scent, but the closer we got to our destination, the smaller the search area was going to become. I had no particular reason to believe that Hawthorn was in the pay of Omega, but I had no reason not to, either. And logic dictated that over the last few months Omega would have been pulling out all the stops to get somebody in Cyndi's inner circle. Her husband and Hawthorn would have been prime targets for them.

Whether he was in their pocket or not, I had to assume that he was, and that meant that within the next few hours I needed to find a new vehicle: either rent one or steal one. Both had drawbacks in terms of being traceable, but for the moment I figured renting as Joseph O'Brien was the safest bet, because Omega would not yet have made the connection between the Focus and the fake ID.

Cyndi came out of the bathroom in a robe with a towel wrapped around her head like a turban. She sat in a chair on the other side of the room, with her elbows on her knees and seemed to examine her thumbs for a moment. She still had her gloves on.

"I owe you an apology," she said. I didn't say anything and after a moment she looked up. I was watching her. "What I said about being a senator was stupid and you were right to slap me down. And it is also true that I have been on your case all day. I guess I am scared and my go-to response to being scared is to become aggressive."

"It's not the worst go-to response to fear. Just make sure you focus your aggression in the right direction. Apology accepted."

She smiled. "You are also a big pain in the ass when you get going."

I lit a Camel, then tossed the bottle of Bushmills, the pack of cigarettes and my lighter across the bed, where she could reach them. She poured herself a drink and lit up.

After a moment I said, "There is a threshold."

She frowned. "A threshold?"

"When people are trying to kill you. At first there is a sense of unreality as though your brain cannot accept that this is really happening. A lot of people die in that state. If you manage to survive it, you cross over a threshold, where the full impact of the possibility of death hits you. Then your autonomic system kicks in and takes over and you panic. Because as a species, at least in the West, we have forgotten how to deal with death. Your heart rate goes off the scale, your blood pressure goes through the roof and, worst of all, you stop thinking. A lot of people who didn't die in the first stage, die in a state of panic."

"And then?"

"Then you realize that if you want to live, you need to focus and think. You can't give in to panic. And you can't pander to emotions, fear, good manners or sensibilities. You focus on what you need to do to stay alive."

"Is this a master class from the master?"

"You'd better believe it."

"And I am in the first stage?"

"Yes."

She sighed. "I guess you're right. I do find it hard to believe that anybody could be that crazy."

I sipped my drink and took a long drag of the cigarette. As I let out the smoke I said, "I am not sure that they are crazy, Cyndi. I have known two of them very well. Psychosis is being unable to distinguish between reality and fantasy. They haven't got that problem. The big difference with them is that, what for most people would be fantasy, for them, is reality." I paused, frowning, thinking. "It's hard to explain. Having somebody killed, triggering a war in which two hundred thousand people die, children are slaughtered or become homeless, families are destroyed..." I shrugged. "To the men and women who constitute Omega, who inhabit that level of power, that kind of inhuman atrocity is their daily bread. It's not a fantasy. It is their reality."

I heard the engine of a small bike or a scooter entering the parking lot outside. I pulled the Sig from my waistband, cocked it and told her, "Get into the bathroom, take your drink and your cigarette with you. Close the door."

She did as I said and a moment later the doorbell rang. I peered out the window. It was a kid of maybe sixteen holding a couple of bags of food and beer. I shoved the pistol back in my waistband and opened the door. As I took the bags and paid him, I had a look at the parking lot, and glanced up and down the road. Nothing had changed. There were no new vehicles parked nearby. Nothing suspicious at all. But my gut told me that was wrong.

I closed the door and put the food on the chest of drawers. Cyndi came out of the bathroom, saw the food and smiled. It was a nice, natural smile. I studied her face a moment and somehow knew that that night she would cross the portal. I just hoped she crossed it alive.

After we'd eaten I put the packaging into the trash and checked the time. It was midnight. Outside, on the edge of hearing, I caught the whine of a big engine. I peered out of the edge of the drapes and saw a large, black SUV parked at the gas station across the road. It hadn't been there before. Now it was.

I switched off the light and went on line on my laptop to rent a car from the smallest car rental I could find in Lexington, while she brushed her teeth. Then I stood and took the sheets and covers off the bed. She saw me and spoke through her toothpaste. "Wha ewe hooing?"

"I'm being cautious. You're going to have an uncomfortable night, I'm afraid."

She spat, rinsed, and wiped her mouth with a towel while I began making her a bed in the bath.

I gave her my most charming lopsided smile and said, "At least you're not six foot two."

"What are you doing?" she said again.

"I think we might have visitors. I want you to sleep dressed and I want you to be packed and ready to leave at a moment's notice. And I do mean a moment. I say go, we go."

She followed me into the bedroom where I put three pillows in a line on the bed and covered them with the eiderdown. She looked sick.

"Are you sure?"

"Pretty sure."

"What are you going to do? Where are you going to sleep?"

"I'm not going to sleep tonight. But I need you rested." I shrugged. "You won't sleep, you'll be too stressed, but lie down and close your eyes. Get as much rest as you can. Try to relax." I tried to look reassuring. "You never know. I might be wrong."

She didn't answer. She was standing in silhouette, backlit and framed by the bathroom door. I went and stood close to her. She looked up into my face and I could see that there was real fear in her eyes. "It's real, isn't it?"

I nodded. "Yes."

"They want to kill me."

"Yes." I looked at my watch. It was twelve fifteen. "After you switch off the bathroom light, they'll give us at least an hour to get to sleep. If they come tonight, it could be any time after twelve. Get dressed, get packed up, then get as much rest as you can. Keep your gloves on. Do not leave any prints. Once I've closed the door, do not come out again until I call you."

She nodded and went into the bathroom. I closed the door behind her and moved one of the chairs into the corner, so I was facing the entrance and the window at an angle. The drapes were not heavy, and the light from the streetlamps outside made enough of a glow that a body would be visible as a silhouette against them. I screwed the silencer onto the Sig, and settled to wait.

They came at ten minutes after three. The first thing I was aware of was the scrape of a heel on blacktop across the parking lot. Then another. Then a muttered voice. That meant at least two of them. They were not trying to be quiet. Some shuffling outside the door. I thought I made out three or perhaps four bodies. Then a shadow up against the side of the window, beside the door. When they came in I would be invisible to them. I was in deep shadow in the corner. I raised my weapon and steadied my breathing.

There was a soft rattle, then a click and the door eased open. The thin beam of a small flashlight penetrated the gloom, focused down at the floor. Two of them stood in the doorway, looking at the bed. Past them I could see another, on the left of the jamb, keeping watch. The shadow of the fourth was still visible against the drapes.

One thing was clear so far. They were not pros. The use of the flashlight was stupid. It not only risked waking their target, it cast the rest of the room into deeper darkness. They inched in closer a couple of steps, then directed the beam of the flashlight at the bulk of cushions under the eiderdown. I waited for his first shot. I had guessed it would be silenced, and it was. His weapon spat once. Then mine spat four times, two double taps, one into the shooter's chest, the next into his pal's.

It took the two guys outside a while to register that something was wrong. They heard the repeated spit of the weapon and assumed it was their man being thorough. They heard the grunts of pain and the thump of bodies on the floor. I guess they assumed it was the victim, falling out of bed. By the time the guy on the left of the door had turned to look in, I was right there, looking into his eyes. He wanted to shout. Actually he wanted to scream, but he couldn't because he had the blade of my Fairbairn and Sykes fighting knife stuck through his trachea. I pulled him inside and let him drop with the knife still in his throat. In the same movement I stepped outside and put the Sig to the last man's head. He was frowning, still wondering what the hell just happened.

I looked him over. He was holding a bargain basement 9 mm Taurus PT 111. He was forty-something, had a belly and stubble. He looked rough. He also looked scared. I said, "Hand me your weapon. Get inside."

He nodded and did as I said. As we moved in, I closed the door and switched on the light. He stared down at his pal, the one with my knife in his throat. He wasn't dead yet. His eyes had rolled up and his feet were jerking. I reached down and pulled the blade out of his throat. The blood flowed freely and he slipped away into oblivion. I wiped the blood on his pants and slipped the knife back in my boot.

The guy with the stubble and the gut was trembling badly. I said, "What's your name?"

He tried three times before he could say it. "Joe. I'm Joe. Look, pal, I didn't mean no... I mean if I'd known... We thought, we was told..."

"Shut up, Joe."

"Yeah, sure..."

I looked down at his three colleagues. They weren't wearing Italian suits. The guy who'd done the shooting was wearing jeans and cowboy boots. He had shoulder length blond hair and a denim shirt under a black leather jacket. His weapon was a 9 mm Smith & Wesson SDVE, three hundred and fifty bucks. The guy who'd come in with him had black hair in a ponytail almost down to his waist. He was also wearing jeans and boots, just like the guy whose throat I'd cut. He was unshaven, in a sweat shirt with a brown leather jacket. These clowns were not Omega. They weren't even pros.

I pointed at the chair where I'd been sitting. "Sit down. Help yourself to a glass of whiskey, have a cigarette."

Now he looked really scared. "Why?"

"Because we're going to talk. Tell me what I want to hear and you go home. I might even give you some money for your trouble. Piss me off and I'll cut your throat, like your pal."

He held up his hands. "OK, man. I'll tell you anything you want to know. I ain't no hero. I ain't about to give you no trouble."

He edged over and lowered himself into my chair. I sat on the end of the bed and watched him. "Drink. Smoke."

He nodded. "Yeah, OK. Whatever you say, pal. I'll do whatever you say."

"Who did you think you were going to find here?"

"A woman. They said there'd be a woman. They said there might be a guy, but we was to get rid of the woman. And the guy, obviously. If he was here. I didn't know... We didn't know it would be you... obviously..."

He tried three times and managed to light a cigarette.

"They?"

"The people who paid us to do the job..."

I smiled. "I got that, Joe. Who were those people?"

He swallowed hard. His hands were shaking so badly he could hardly hold his drink. "I don't know. They don't... They never... It don't work that way..."

"Relax. How did they get their instructions to you?"

He pointed his trembling cigarette hand over at the first guy I'd shot. He was almost weeping. "Hank. They talked to Hank on the telephone."

I shook my head. "Hank is not a hit man. Neither are you. You're amateurs."

"No, no... No man, we ain't hit men. No way. We's, like you might say, enforcers. Hank has killed a couple of guys. Me, I never, you know? I'll break an arm, maybe a leg. Usually I just help to hold the guy."

"You're enforcers? Who for?"

"It's just a small outfit in Glen Burnie. We do a bit of this, a bit of that..." I waited. He swallowed. "Irish kid. He's a bit crazy. He sells crack. Sometimes people don't pay, so we go and see 'em."

I nodded that I understood. "So what the hell are you doing in Kentucky?"

"Sometimes Hank freelances, you know what I'm saying? He'll do anything. He ain't squeamish. So he has some clients, sometimes they call him, you know, to do a job."

"Who are the clients?"

"I dunno, man. Honest to God, man. He never told us. He'd just say, 'OK, boys, we got a job.' And that was it. We'd go and do it..."

"Kill somebody?"

"Sometimes, mostly just hurt them or put a scare into 'em."

I thought about it. It didn't make a lot of sense. Actually it didn't make any sense at all.

"Glen Burnie? That's outside Baltimore."

"Pretty much, south of the river."

"When did you get the call?"

"I dunno, Hank called us about five, five thirty. We was on the road by six."

Just after we'd stopped. I nodded. "That your black SUV in the gas station across the road?"

"Yeah."

"Who's the driver?"

"Me. I always do the driving. You ask some funny questions."

"Give me the keys."

"Whatcha gonna do?"

"Give me the keys."

He reached in his pocket, pulled them out and threw them to me. I caught them with my left hand, and shot him in the head.

FIVE

I LEFT HIM WHERE HE WAS IN THE CHAIR, WITH HIS prints on the glass of spilled whiskey and the smoldering cigarette on the floor. I took a miniature of cheap Scotch from the mini bar, drained it and dropped the empty bottle at his feet. My shots had all been through-and-throughs, five in total. I collected the slugs and the casings, then used Joe's Taurus to put two bullets through the knife wound in the blond guy's trachea. After that I removed four more rounds from his magazine, leaving seven.

When the cops arrived, they'd find a bunch of bums who'd shot each other up. They might scratch their heads at a few details, but they wouldn't waste the Kentucky taxpayer's dollar on these out of state low-lifes. And if they did, all they'd find would be more questions.

I stepped out into the night. It was turning icy cold. I ran across the road, taking care to keep my face covered against the CCTV cameras at the gas station. I climbed in the SUV, drove back to the motel and parked beside the

Focus, outside the room. Then I went and tapped on the bathroom door. "Cyndi, it's me, Lacklan. We have to go."

There was absolute silence for a moment, then the door opened a crack and she peered out. She was drawn and terrified. I shook my head. "We haven't got time for this, Cyndi. I need you to get a grip and react. We have to go. Open the door."

She opened the door. She was trembling badly. I pushed in past her, grabbed her case and thrust it into her hands. "Go outside and get into the black SUV. Not the Focus, the SUV. You understand?"

She stared up into my face and nodded.

"Do it. Now."

She moved toward the open door. I grabbed the bedding from the bath and threw it all over the bed. Then I grabbed the whiskey, my cigarettes and the Zippo, slung my bag over my shoulder and followed her out, leaving the lights off and the door closed. There were none of my prints and none of Cyndi's prints, none of my slugs and none of my casings. If they traced the Ford, it would lead them to Joseph O'Brien, who would soon vanish into thin air.

The sky was black overhead. The light from the streetlamps was a dead kind of yellow, and I could see clouds of condensation billowing from Cyndi's mouth as she stood staring into the SUV. I opened the back, threw in her case and my bag, slammed it shut and physically lifted her into the passenger seat up front. I put the whiskey on her lap, closed the door and went around to the driver's side. Then we were pulling out of the parking lot and accelerating through the night toward Lexington. I glanced at my watch. It was four AM.

I settled at a steady seventy, pulled my cigarettes from my pocket, shook one loose and fed it into my mouth from the pack. "Drink." I glanced at her. She was staring at the bottle in her lap. I flipped my Zippo, leaned the cigarette into the flame and took a deep drag. As I blew out I said, "It's not what your doctor would tell you to do for shock, but I never yet met a doctor who witnessed four men get killed. For me, whiskey does it every time. Take a shot, a big one. It'll help, believe me."

She was staring at me. She still looked pale. After a moment she opened the bottle with trembling hands and took a pull. It made her cough, but after a moment she took another.

I said, "Tell me when you're ready for a cigarette."

I knew pretty soon she was going to get cold and start shivering, but I couldn't give her the medically prescribed treatment for shock. She was going to have to deal with it as best she could. And in my experience, which was a damn sight more extensive than most doctors, the best way of dealing with it involved a bottle of whiskey, a pack of cigarettes and a pair of balls. Two out of three for Cyndi would have to do.

We pulled in to Lexington at half past five, and by six o'clock I had found the estate on Nicholasville Road where the car hire firm was. I had it booked to collect at seven thirty, so we had an hour and a half to kill. Google told me there was a twenty-four hour fast food café at the Tates Creek shopping center, on Tates Creek Road, not far from the car rental. So we drove there, through the cold pre-dawn, and went into the soulless, plastic desolation of the café. I sat Cyndi down, put my jacket around her shoulders and got two buckets of coffee and two burgers. I laced the coffee with whiskey and we sat in silence for ten minutes, warming up.

After she'd drunk some of the brew she seemed to relax a little.

"Do you feel up to talking?"

She sighed and nodded. "Yes. I'm OK. Talking about what?"

"Now, here's the thing, Cyndi, those men were not Omega."

She frowned. "What does that mean?"

"That's what I need you to tell me."

"I have no idea. What makes you say they were not Omega?"

"You need to try and think this through. They were there for you. The last guy told me so. They knew where we were. They came right to the motel to the room. How would anybody know where you were at that time?"

"I'm telling you, Lacklan, I have no idea."

"Did you call anybody on your phone?"

"No."

"Your husband?"

Her face flushed with anger. "Will you let up about my husband!"

"Let me see your cell."

"*What?* No!"

"I'm not going to check your calls. I'm going to check inside for a bug."

She handed it to me. It was still turned off. I slid off the back and examined the inside. There was no tracking device. I gave it back to her.

"Those guys were amateurs. They were cheap muscle for some minor associate of the Irish mob in Baltimore."

She glanced at me, then looked away and sipped her coffee.

"Does the Irish mob mean anything to you?"

"Of course not."

"McFarlane?"

"Scottish!"

I left it at that, and at seven I took the SUV, parked it at the Southern Acres Christian Church parking lot, half a mile from the car rental, and went on foot to collect my new car. This one was a Honda Civic, one of the ten most unremarkable cars in the world, and exactly what we needed.

At twenty past eight I collected Cyndi from the café and we headed off. I was pretty confident at that time that Omega did not know where we were, or what vehicle we were driving, and I wanted to put as much distance between us and Lexington as I could. That meant not using remote roads, or roundabout routes. It meant getting on the I-64 and staying at a steady seventy miles per hour through Louisville to St. Louis, and then southwest on the I-44, through Springfield and Joplin, into Oklahoma, and there find somewhere to stay the night. It was ten hours driving, maybe more, and seven hundred miles. It was not my original plan, but I figured if I hadn't known I was going to do it, neither could Omega.

And that took me back to the million dollar question.

I kept turning that question over and over in my head for the five hours it took us to get to St. Louis. Just before we got there, at ten minutes after one, I pulled into a restaurant in the town of New Baden. It was called A Fine Swine, which seemed to be a promising name. It also had a parking lot at the back where our vehicle would be out of sight. We left the car tucked in beside some dumpsters and went inside.

There was a lot of melamine pretending to be rustic wood, a TV playing sports on the wall, and a smell of good, fresh meat being barbequed. There were half a dozen tables occupied, so there were plenty to choose from. We sat away from the windows, ordered some championship pulled pork and a couple of beers from a friendly waitress, and when she'd gone away I leaned back in my chair and studied Cyndi's face. She didn't look quite so pale, and she'd had about four hours sleep in the car on the way there. I figured she was ready to do some talking. She looked away from me, toward the glare of the window we'd avoided.

"Cyndi, we are going to have to address this. We have a problem, and the longer we put it off, the more at risk you put yourself, and the rest of us."

She closed her eyes and sighed. "I don't know what you want me to say, Lacklan."

"I want you to quit feeling sorry for yourself and take responsibility for what's happening to you."

She narrowed her eyes at me. "That is harsh. That is damned unfeeling. You know what? I have just about had enough of you..."

I shrugged. "That suits me fine. I'm here doing you a favor, remember? You've had enough of me? That's fine. It means I get to go home and read all about it in the papers. What are *you* going to do?"

"You're a real piece of shit, you know that?"

"Yes, I know that. What are you going to do?"

"What's it to you?" I didn't answer so she carried on. "I'll rent a car and carry on to Albuquerque, make the meeting. I can do that without you."

"Sure you can. You going to use your credit card and ID?"

She stared at me. I could see the tears starting in her eyes. The waitress brought our beers, saw Cyndi's face and hurried away.

I went on, "Because both of those will enable Omega to locate you. These people have access to all the federal databases and the technology available to the Bureau and the intelligence services. These people operate out of the Pentagon, Cyndi, and you of all people know what that means.

"So when you ask me, what is it to me? Well, the people you are going to meet in Albuquerque, that you are so casually sentencing to death, along with yourself, are friends and associates of mine. Now you say you've had about as much of me as you can stomach, and you are going to go it alone. Tell me, exactly, how you are going to get out of New Baden and either back to D.C. or on to Albuquerque? Because the choices you make might cost my friends their lives."

She closed her eyes and took a long, deep breath. "If you knew just how much I hate you right now..."

I waited till she'd opened them again. "Are we done?"

She nodded, but there was still real hostility in her expression.

"I'm going to see if I can make you understand this. Those men who broke in last night, were hunting for you—not me—you. Do you understand that?"

"Stop patronizing me. Of course I understand it!"

"Now let's assume for a moment that I had been an obedient, mannerly officer like Major Charles Hawthorn. You would have had your room, and I would have had mine, according to your wishes, and you would have slept in your bed. And right now you would be dead. As it was, because we did it my way, I faced the risk, I killed the men who were hunting for you, and I got you out of there alive."

She had the good grace to avert her eyes.

I pressed on. "Now, remind me how much you are paying me for my services."

She didn't say anything.

I leaned closer. "I didn't hear you."

"You made your point."

"No, not yet. My point is this: I don't give a damn whether you hate me or not. You go it alone and you die. I don't. I go home and nobody knows I was here. You die. My point is also that the longer you piss around feeling sorry for yourself and hating me, the more you put all of our lives at risk. Now, you tell me you want to go it alone, as though that is supposed to upset me or worry me. Cyndi, what *you* need to be worrying about is what the hell you are going to do if I get pissed off with your attitude, get in *my* car and go home."

She went ashen. "You wouldn't do that..."

The waitress brought our food, told us to enjoy it and scuttled away.

"What's to stop me? The fee?"

"I offered to pay you. You refused."

"Now maybe you understand why. This way I am not beholden to a spoiled brat who hates me because she doesn't like the way I saved her life. So moving on. What is to stop me walking out right now? Your charming and engaging personality?"

"Please, Lacklan, stop."

"Your looks? Let me tell you, I have a beautiful home, with a beautiful woman waiting for me. And right now I am wondering what the hell I am doing here. I am laying it on the line for you, Cyndi. You get a grip, you work with me and cooperate with me, right now, or I am going to get in my car and leave you here on your own."

"Please don't do that, Lacklan."

I ate in silence for five minutes, allowing her to think. She picked at her food, but seemed on the brink of bursting into tears. I knew I had been brutal, and I hadn't enjoyed it. But time was too short and I'd had no other option. Finally I pulled off half my beer, set down the glass and said, "Omega always uses their own men. They are trained professionals. But the men who came last night were just thugs. They had no training, their weapons were cheap, and the guy I spoke to told me they were muscle for a smalltime Irish gang outside of Baltimore. So, I know you don't know who they were, or why they came, but I need you to start thinking about it. Somewhere in your head is the answer, Cyndi. One person in your circle of family, friends or associates, connects somehow with those men last night."

She shook her head. "I can't believe that."

I felt a rush of anger in my belly, but suppressed it. "No, Cyndi, you can. You can believe it. You just don't want to. You are an intelligent woman. It's time for you to start thinking. I shouldn't have to be asking you these questions. You should be asking them yourself. How did those four thugs know where you were last night?"

"I promise I will think about it."

We finished our meal. I paid cash and we left. We drove through St. Louis and then followed the I-44 south and west for the next five hours or so, until we came, at about six in the evening, as the sun was setting and the air was turning cold, to Tulsa. And twenty miles south of Tulsa, just outside the town of Bristow, we came to the Carolyn inn. It looked clean and pleasant, and best of all it had a large parking lot with secluded space at the back. I was exhausted and every part of me ached. I ached in parts of me I didn't even know I had.

I pulled in, left the car at the back of the lot, told Cyndi to wait, and went and checked us in. There was a pretty, young receptionist on duty and I told her I had been driving for over ten hours and I needed to sleep, so could she please give me a room at the back, away from the traffic. She was sweet and obliging, and gave me a double room with two single beds, at the back left hand corner.

I dragged Cyndi, her case, my bag and my body into the room and then collapsed on the bed. She closed the door, pulled the drapes and sat in one of the chairs. I checked my watch. It was seven PM. I glanced at her. She was watching me with an expression that was difficult to read.

I said, "I am going to sleep for one hour. Don't go out. Don't open the door to anybody. Do not phone anybody. Don't even switch on your cell. If you want to read, I have a dystopian thriller in my bag. OK?"

She nodded, then smiled, and I slipped into obsidian sleep.

SIX

THERE WAS A VOICE TALKING IN THE DARKNESS. I couldn't make out what it was saying, because it was speaking in hushed tones, almost whispering. I knew the voice. It was a woman's voice. For a moment I wondered if it was Marni, but then realized that that would have been a dream; and I was coming out of a dream, not into one. It was Cyndi's voice. I opened my eyes. On my left the drapes were drawn closed. There was a diffuse light coming through them from the streetlamps outside. I looked at my watch. It was eight.

I turned my head, searching the room for Cyndi. She was still sitting in the armchair on my right, watching me from the shadows. She smiled. "Hello."

I said, "Who were you talking to?"

She raised her eyebrows. "Seriously? Have a look around. I'm sitting here in the dark on my own. It must have been a dream."

I sat up. "I guess so. You must be hungry."

"I suppose I am. I need to get past the shock of last night. I seem to have lost my appetite."

We were quiet for a bit. I stood, planning to go to the shower and wake myself up.

She spoke suddenly. "Lacklan, can we please go out?"

I frowned. "Go out?"

"To dinner. Please? I can change my hair, wear jeans and a sweatshirt. I can not use makeup. I can make myself totally different. I guarantee nobody will recognize me."

"It's not a good idea."

"No. It is a good idea. Please, I ended up agreeing with you on everything. Now listen to me on this one."

I sighed and managed a small smile. "OK, I'm listening."

"I have just been through the most terrifying experience of my life. My nerves are in pieces. If I am going to get through the next couple of days in one piece, *and* deal with a meeting with Professor Gibbons and Marni Gilbert..." She trailed off, shook her head. "Lacklan, if I have understood one thing in the last two days, it is that the importance of this meeting is incalculable. I cannot get there in this state. And if I have to spend the next night without sleep, in a state of terror and anxiety, I am just not going to make it."

"How will going out to dinner help?"

She held out her hands, almost as though she were pleading with me. "I am not a soldier! I am not trained in the way you are. This is like a crazy fantasy, or a nightmare to me. To you, in some weird way, it is second nature. But to me it's madness! I need to ground myself. I need to go back, even for just a couple of hours, to the *normal* world, that *I* know."

I sighed and sat back down. I didn't want to fight with

her again. I had driven her hard and put her under a lot of strain. I needed to ease up and start building some rapport with her.

"Where? How far from the motel?"

She held up both hands. "Listen, if you really think it would be dangerous, I will accept that. But I am telling the benefits will outweigh the risks. I know this town. The place is a mile down the road, a twenty minute walk. It is a cute Mexican place, and I could really use a couple of margaritas. You'll love it. The food is great and it will help me to get things back in perspective. It will help me work through the shock."

I thought about it. There was some sense to what she said. She had experienced a very violent shock and there was a risk of her cracking under the strain. It did seem we had temporarily thrown Omega off the scent, and the bottom line was, we were no more at risk in an obscure restaurant than we were at the motel. Plus, there was another point that weighed heavily in the balance. When people are highly stressed, their frontal cortex tends to shut down and they stop thinking. If she relaxed a bit with a few drinks she might start thinking again, and I really needed her to start thinking. I needed to know why Omega had sent those thugs instead of one of their own teams.

I smiled at her. "Jeans, sneakers, sweatshirt, hair down and no make up. We'll be like a couple of college kids going on a first date."

She laughed. It was a nice thing to see and hear. "*Mr.* Walker! Are you flirting with me?"

"Give me five minutes in the shower and I might just start."

I stood under the stream of hot water for ten minutes, shaved, and by the time I stepped out of the bathroom, dressed in fresh clothes, she had become a different woman. Or, perhaps it would be more accurate to say that she had revealed the woman who hid behind the trappings of office, the woman who protected herself with the Greco-Roman columns of the Capitol and the façade of temporal power. In boot cut jeans, a Snoopy sweatshirt and her hair tied back, not in a ponytail, but in an auburn explosion of curls, she looked human. More than approachable, she looked attractive.

I smiled at her and she grinned. I said, "You have freckles."

"Don't remind me."

"With makeup, you look like a beautiful senator, without it you look like a beautiful woman. You shouldn't hide your freckles."

"Will you stop that!"

I opened the door and we stepped out into the limpid wash of streetlight. Her cashmere coat looked conspicuous, so she borrowed my black leather jacket, which looked huge on her, and wore a heavy sweater.

She took my arm. "I don't know if you are more dangerous as a grouchy soldier or a charming date."

We walked because I figured nobody would expect us to. If Omega had any inkling of where we were, they would be looking for two people hidden in a motel, or driving a car. The last thing they'd expect would be two people on a date. We were half a mile outside town, so the first ten minutes we strolled under the kind of stars you just don't see in D.C., and she spent most of the time with her head thrown back staring at the vastness of the night sky and the staggering number of ice cold sparkles of light.

"Every one of them," she said, "is a picture of the past. The light we see there left its home thousands, even millions of years ago." Then a small frown creased her brow. "Do you think we will eventually make our home out there?" I didn't answer and she looked down, watching her own feet on the sidewalk. "People like Elon Musk, visionaries, see us colonizing Mars, and from Mars spreading out to the moons of Jupiter, Saturn, and beyond. That is exciting and inspiring, but it's a shame they have no visions for our world." Now she looked at me and there was something infinitely sad in her eyes. "This poor old planet has been a good mother to us, we have thrived and prospered here—too much! And yet our visions for her are all dark."

We were entering the town, passing a magnificent, Georgian building that claimed to be the Spirit Bank, and she suddenly gripped my arm tight and gave a little hop, grinning up at me. It made me laugh. This was not the firebrand senator I had seen so often on TV. This was an excited teenager in jeans and a leather jacket three sizes too big for her.

"Hey! You know where we are?"

"Bristow? The Spirit Bank?"

She stopped dead and pointed at the road. "You are on hallowed ground, my friend. This here is the legendary Route 66." In a flash her expression had changed again. She took hold of my arm and gazed down once more at her feet, taking one step after another. Unexpectedly she said, "Humanity's last cry of 'Freedom!' before the darkness began to close in."

"The sixties?"

She nodded. We were quiet then for the rest of the way, until we came to a small, two-story red brick building with a parking lot on one side. For some reason, in that limpid light from the streetlamps, with the vast sky overhead, it reminded me of an illustration from an early 1960s science fiction comic. And inside, the 1960s theme continued. It was like Carlos Castaneda meets Happy Days, with Formica tables and burgundy vinyl seats, Mexican blankets and walls painted in yellow and lime-green chalk. It was warm, and almost full, and the smell of cooking meat and chili made me realize I was hungry. We found a table at the back, out of sight of the window, sat where I had a view of the entrance, and ordered two beers, a fajita salad to share, and beef and chicken tamales.

When the waitress had gone, Cyndi gave me a peculiar smile. "Thanks for doing this, Lacklan. I appreciate it. You're a beast, but you're a good man."

I gave her a peculiar smile back. "Hey, the country needs you, but it needs you sane."

She snorted. "That ship sailed!" The waitress came with our beers. Cyndi took a swig from the bottle, then became serious. "Tell me about Omega." She hesitated, frowned. "Not just facts and figures, your thoughts and feelings."

I leaned back in my chair and studied the dark brown glass of the bottle in my hand. I took a swig and gave my head a small shake. "That's not easy."

"Why not?"

I sucked air through my teeth. "Because what they are trying to do makes sense."

She narrowed her eyes at me. "What? I don't follow you, Lacklan. You telling me you're with them?"

I gave a small laugh. "I hope for their sake that I'm not. Nobody on Earth has caused them more damage than I have. No." I thought a little more, wondering, not for the first time, exactly what it was about Omega that I hated so much. "What they are trying to do makes sense in as much as, we have passed the point of no return." I looked into her face. "We have nearly eight billion people on this planet. The planet can sustain nine. But to house, clothe and *feed* this many people we need mass production and mass distribution, and whatever Elon Musk may say, that requires the massive burning of fossil fuels..." I smiled and shrugged. "And that reduces our capacity to produce food. So as far as that goes, they are right. Somebody has to address this problem, and there is no painless way out. It's the Malthusian nightmare meets Frankenstein's monster on steroids. We need to reduce the population of the planet to pre-Industrial Revolution levels."

Her frown had deepened. "So you *do* agree with them..."

I raised an eyebrow. "I agree with their statement of the problem. I don't agree with their solution."

"What is their solution?"

The waitress brought our salad and Cyndi stabbed into it with her fork. I took another pull on my beer and tried to set it down precisely on the ring it had left on the table.

"Their solution comes in two parts. First, let the problem play itself out: droughts below the fifty-second parallel, food shortages, famine, hurricanes and eventually the collapse of the Greenland ice sheet and half of the Antarctic. They figure that will account for most of the overpopulation. It's ruthless, but I am not necessarily opposed to ruthlessness.

"The second part of the solution focuses on the aftermath of what they call 'catastrophic change'. They figure climate change and overpopulation will reach a critical mass sometime in the near future, and then there will be a catastrophic event, or series of events. And they want to be in a position to pick up the pieces and be top dog in the new world, to create some kind of new Eden. And to achieve that they want to exercise control over people's minds and emotions."

"What kind of control?"

I smiled. "I guess it's nothing new. We've been doing it for at least ten thousand years. There is an elite that enjoys a degree of freedom through power, and then there is the great, gray mass, whose purpose in life is to sustain the elite. The difference is that until now that control has been exercised through fear, through the threat, express or implied, of violence. But what they have controlled has been not so much thought as behavior. What Omega wants is to take it to the next level. They want their populace to be happy. They want their subjects, their servants or slaves, to be content with their lot. And that..." I looked at her and realized it as I said it, "That is what I hate about Omega. We were brought up to think of Hell as a place of conflict, torment, pain and struggle." I gave a small laugh. "But that's just *life*. Hell... hell is where you lose the capacity, even the desire, to fight. Hell is not fire and brimstone. Hell is a world of social media, two-line thought-bites of inoffensively potted wisdom, and armies of people in standard uniforms of sneakers, jeans, anoraks and small rucksacks, each armed with a plastic bottle of water, because a benign government has legislated that water, unless packaged in sterile plastic, is dangerous."

She stared at me a moment, then burst out laughing. "My goodness! You *are* a dangerous man! You are a true subversive. How on Earth did you survive in the army?"

I smiled, thinking of comrades like Bat Hayes and my mentor and guide, the Kiwi Sergeant Bradley. Each one a quirky, anarchic individualist. I shook my head. "The Regiment isn't like the regular army."

"Crazy Brits, huh?"

"Something like that."

She was thoughtful for a while. Then she said, "I'm a politician, Lacklan. You are an anarchic soldier of fortune. You can afford to have radical ideas about freedom. But every politician knows that, in the words of the song, freedom is just some people talking. It doesn't exist. If we want to stay out of the caves and live in a comfortable, safe society, we need rules, laws, some kind of government control."

I leaned forward, with my elbows on the table. "Sure, but that has to come from agreement, not from threats of violence, and certainly not because I have adapted your brain so that you don't want to fight me." I shook my head and looked deep into her eyes. "We have nothing in this world, Cyndi, nothing at all—impermanence will take everything—except one priceless treasure: the freedom we have in our minds, our freedom to be ourselves. Nobody can ever take that from us, and if they try, then we must fight to the death to preserve it. It is the only thing that gives life any meaning."

She nodded a few times, but not necessarily in agreement. Finally, she said, "Boy, you are passionate about this."

"Yeah. I am. There is no greater crime, in my mind, than when one human being makes a slave of another."

"And that is what Omega aims to do."

"Allow the surplus to die, and rob the rest of their will and their individuality, that pretty much sums it up."

The waitress brought our tamales and told us to enjoy. I ordered two more beers and she went away. When she'd gone, Cyndi shook her head. "It sounds like science fiction. If it weren't for what happened at the UN, and last night, I'd have trouble believing any of it." She picked up a roll in her fingers and bit into it. As she chewed she asked me, "How, and when, do they plan to exercise this mind control?"

I watched her chew, keeping her chin over her plate, dabbing at it with a paper napkin and licking the fingers of her left hand.

I said. "You were right. The 1960s was the last cry of freedom. It will not be heard again."

"What do you mean?"

"You asked me when it would begin. When they would start to exercise their control over people's minds and emotions. Look around you!" I laughed a dry, unhappy laugh. "Orwell predicted a screen watching every person. He never foresaw that each person would voluntarily carry a screen with him everywhere he went. This isn't the zombie revolution, it's the zombie involution. It's already begun."

SEVEN

After the meal Cyndi wanted to hit the tequilas. I knew she was going to get drunk. I knew she needed to, and there was nothing I could do about it. If I got serious with her it would make the problem worse. If I gave her free rein, maybe tomorrow I would have a cooperative ally—albeit one with a big hangover. So I ordered a glass of whiskey and nursed it while she gave the tequila bottle a hard time. I told myself the restaurant closed at ten, and however stressed out she was, there was a physical limit to how much she could drink in an hour.

Still, she gave it her best shot, and by the time we stepped out and they flipped the 'closed' sign behind us, she found just about everything in the world hilarious, and I was her best buddy in that world: "Lacklan, we have not known each other long, but *man!* We had *been* there! And we have *done it!* Together! Am I lying? I mean, tell me if I am lying, 'cause I think we are friends, and we can be honest with each other, right?"

I couldn't disagree with her and I didn't, mainly because I didn't know what the 'it' was that we had been to and done together. But it was good to see her happy, so I laughed along with her and told her we certainly had been there, and done it, together, and we were certainly friends.

It was icy cold. I was exhausted and needed to get at least four hours good sleep before we set off on the last leg of our journey. The cold, the alcohol and the after effect of the shock were making Cyndi sleepy too. So we walked quickly, huddled together, with her clinging to my arm, giggling and talking incessantly, mainly about what her husband would think if he could see her now.

As we came to the parking lot at the motel I turned to her and put my finger to my lips. She made an 'O' with hers and nodded. We approached the back of the building quietly, and when we had reached the corner I told her to wait. I scanned the cars. There was nothing new. They had all been there when we went out. The drapes were as they were, and when I listened I couldn't hear anything. My gut told me something was wrong, but my brain couldn't detect what it was. So maybe it was natural caution. I pulled my Sig from my waistband, crouched down and slipped the key into the lock by very slow degrees. I turned and pushed gently. The door swung open, stretching a dull oblong of lamplight across the foot of the nearest bed. Nothing happened.

Cyndi was still seven or eight feet away at the corner of the building, motionless, watching me. I was still crouching. I half closed my eyes and focused my mind on the sounds I could hear: the far off, sporadic hiss of tires on blacktop. Nearby, in the trees, an owl. Closer, the soft creak of the hinges as the door finished its swing. The silence in the room. The silence in the bathroom. Soft breathing.

There would be one facing the door, waiting to shoot at our silhouettes as we came in, another behind the door in case we rushed. Maybe more, but at least two. I stood, keeping away from the portal, and hissed in a loud, drunken stage whisper, like I didn't want the neighbors to hear, "*You think I drove you half way across the goddamn country so we could sleep in separate beds? What kind of a schmuck do you take me for?*" I saw Cyndi gape. I went on. "*Why don't you get your goddamn husband to drive you if you're so damn in love with him?*" She was still gaping. I continued as though she had answered. "*I don't give a damn if the guests hear! I'm sick of doing what you want all the time and not getting a damn thing in return. I'm a man. I have needs like any guy! You're always showing me your damn cleavage, flirting with me, coming on to me, but when the time comes to pay up, you tell me you're still in love with your damn husband! Well maybe I should...*"

The click silenced me, as did the pressure of cold steel against my ear, and the harsh rasp of a voice that said, "Shut up and step inside, both of you."

I raised my hands and allowed my voice to tremble slightly as I said, "OK, I don't want no trouble. My wallet's in my back pocket. Just take what you want. I don't want any trouble." I looked at Cyndi. She had gone very pale. I mouthed, '*Stay there*' and said, "Cyndi, honey, just do what they say, whatever it is, and they won't hurt us."

The voice rasped again, "Get inside and shut the fuck up!"

"OK, OK, I'm doing what you say, just don't hurt me..."

I turned. The figure stepped out. He was dressed in black with a ski mask over his face. He was holding an automatic out at arm's length, pointing it at me and then at Cyndi by turns. "Inside. Get inside, both of you."

I knew if she went inside she was dead. He was six, maybe seven feet from the door, at an angle where he could cover us both. I couldn't hear anything inside, but that didn't mean a thing. Cyndi still hadn't moved. She was paralyzed by indecision and fear. I knew the guy would be reluctant to shoot outside. He wanted to make his kill in the room, where it wouldn't attract attention. He said again, "Inside!"

I stepped toward him with a pleading face. "Can I go to the john? I been drinking and the cold..." It was a fraction of a second. He looked at me like I was crazy. I took another step. "Man, I am pissing..." My next step was slightly to my left. My left hand slapped the barrel of the automatic and gripped it hard as my right hand slammed into his wrist. In an instant the gun was pointing at him. A fraction of a second after that I pulled the trigger. It was a 9 mm and blew a plume of brains and gore out the back of his head.

I knew what would happen next, and it would be immediate. I turned and dropped on one knee with the weapon held out in front of me. Whoever was inside was going to come charging out. They could not now afford to be trapped in the room if somebody called 911.

Sure enough there was a scrambling of feet and a large body, dressed in black with a ski mask over his face came barreling out. I double tapped to his chest. He tripped over his feet and fell face down.

I waited. Nothing. A team of two? Did they think, like

the thugs the night before, that it would be just Cyndi, and perhaps 'some guy'?

I stood, moved forward to the wall, held the gun six inches from the door at chest height and put two rounds through it. I heard a voice say softly, "Oh Jesus, oh no..." The door swung toward me and there was a dull thud.

The switch was just inside the door at shoulder height. I slid the barrel of the gun in and flipped on the lights. Then eased open the door. It was stopped by the weight of the body on the floor. I spoke softly. "This goes down one of two ways, pal. I call the Feds and you get driven away in an unmarked car to give evidence before a select committee about the activities of your employers, and you hope and pray that Omega never catches up with you. Or you lay down your weapon, we have a talk, and then you go on your way. You choose, pal."

He did neither. He wrenched open the door, seized the barrel of my gun in his left hand, shoved it to one side and smashed a fist like a concrete block into my face. Then he grabbed the scruff of my neck, dragged me inside the room and threw me against the wall. Blades of pain shot through my lungs, my legs gave under me and I fell to the floor.

To my surprise he didn't try to finish me. He went outside. As I struggled to get to my feet, I heard a muffled cry, and a moment later he came in holding Cyndi, with his right hand over her mouth and his left arm crushing the air out of her lungs. He closed the door with his foot and dropped her on the floor. She was half unconscious. He turned to me with the air of a man who's had enough of wasting time.

He was big. Six foot six with a barrel chest, huge shoulders, and arms like a weightlifter's legs. He was wearing a ski mask too, but you could still see the rage in his eyes. He bore down on me and grabbed my neck in his left hand, pressing his thumb against my trachea. I couldn't breathe and I knew that in a second or two he was going to crush the cartilage. Then I would die a particularly agonizing death.

I couldn't reach him with my hands. His arms were longer than mine, and he was turned sideways to me, staying out of reach. He began to squeeze. For a moment I saw Sergeant Bradley glaring at me with his huge, Kiwi face, snarling in his weird Kiwi accent, "Nivah stop moving! Be fuckin' aggrisive, and move! Move! Move!"

I swung my right arm over his wrist, pressed savagely down and at the same time smashed my right foot in a vicious kick hard into his nuts. He wheezed painfully and let go, staggering back. I couldn't follow up because I was choking. I dragged air into my lungs, wondering if he had crushed my windpipe. He stumbled, reaching for the door, and fell on his knees, clutching at his groin. I gasped again, feeling my throat easing. I would live, which was more than this guy could say. I stepped toward him with my left foot and kicked him hard in the head with my right. It was like kicking a mature oak. He grunted but didn't go over. I pulled my Fairbairn Sykes from my boot and rammed the tip of the blade two inches into the back of his neck, between the vertebrae, severing the spinal cord. He shuddered and twitched, but remained kneeling.

I opened the door, went out into the lot and dragged each of the bodies inside. By the time I'd pulled the second one in, Cyndi had got up from the floor and was looking in horror at the four dead men. I ignored her and stood on the threshold, listening. There was no sound of sirens. Nobody had heard, or nobody had bothered to call. I closed the door. Cyndi was pointing at the big hulk. She looked as though she might start crying.

"Why...? Why is he kneeling? Is he..."

"He's dead. Take your clothes off."

"What?"

"Take your clothes off."

"What are you...?"

"Do it now or I'll do it for you. Everything, including your underwear."

She began to strip. I took her clothes and threw them in her case along with her cell phone, her watch, her necklace and her earrings. She watched me do it and began to sob.

I said, "I'm sorry." I pulled some socks, a pair of jeans and a shirt from my bag and tossed them on the bed for her. "Put them on. Fast. We need to get out of here."

She started pulling on the clothes I'd given her, still sobbing convulsively and wiping her eyes with her forearms. "Why are you doing this? What..." She stopped to swallow and breathe. "What did you do that for?"

"I'll tell you in the car. Let's go."

"I need *shoes...!*"

"I'll get you shoes tomorrow. Now we have to get out of here. Right now."

I wiped everything I could think of that we had touched, including the goon's automatic. Then I pushed Cyndi out into the lot, closed the door and ran to the car. I threw the case in the trunk and said, "Get in, fast!"

I got in and she climbed in next to me. We slammed the doors, I fired up the engine and we pulled out of the lot.

Joseph O'Brien was now a man on the run, and needed to vanish. He needed to do that fast, and I needed to put a lot of distance between the motel and the car before I dumped it. As of the next day, when they found the bodies, Joseph O'Brien was going to have both Omega and the Feds on his tail.

I turned onto I-44 and floored the pedal. I could see there was woodland on either side of the road, but it was hard to make out any detail. Eventually, after about four miles, we passed under a bridge and I saw a turn, a track, on the right. I killed the lights, slowed and pulled off onto that track. It led to a smaller road which I followed to the left, and soon there was another dirt path leading in among woodland to a large pond. I stopped, killed the engine and opened the trunk.

Cyndi was watching me and asked, "What are you doing, Lacklan? You're acting crazy."

I said, "Give me a hand. Take the cap off the gas tank."

She did as I said while I carried her case over near the pond, concealed by the trees. I laid it on the ground, opened it and pulled out a cotton blouse. Then I ran back to the car where she was waiting for me. There I fed the blouse slowly into the petrol tank until it was sodden, then I pulled it back out again and carried it to the case where I put it in with the clothes, her cell and her other possessions. Then I scrounged for broken branches and pieces of wood, and piled them on top. Finally I lit a cigarette and with Cyndi watching me like I was a maniac, I threw it into the case. It gave a *whoof!* and a small jump as the gas ignited and the entire collection of her possessions began to burn.

I turned and went back toward her. "Let's get out of

here. We're six hundred miles from Albuquerque, that's eight or nine hours driving."

She didn't move. She just stared at me, standing in the clothes that were far too big for her, in socks with no shoes. She was shaking her head and began to cry. "I can't *do* this! You just *killed four men!* And now..." She held out her arm, pointing with an open hand at the burning case, breathing like she was hyperventilating, "*...now you burned all my stuff! Why did you do that!*"

I went to her and held her, counting the seconds in my head. I spoke quietly. "Get in the car. The fire department and the sheriff will be here in a few minutes. By the time they get here, we need to be long gone. Come on, Cyndi. I'll explain in the car."

She allowed herself to be guided back. I put her into the passenger seat, then climbed in the other side, slammed the door and pulled back onto the highway. I accelerated away, west, and after I had counted thirty, when I couldn't see any lights in my mirror, or approaching on the other side, I switched on the headlamps.

Cyndi was sobbing uncontrollably. I was exhausted. I had slept one hour in the last forty-eight and we had a nine hour drive ahead of us. At some point soon I would need to rest. And think. If I was exhausted I would not think straight. I would make mistakes. I could not afford to make mistakes.

After a few miles, her sobbing subsided and her breathing slowed. Eventually she asked me, "Why did you do that? It was a crazy thing to do. Why did you burn all my stuff? My phone, my *earrings* for God's sake!"

I waited a moment, then told her.

"I told you, you need to start thinking. Now work this through with me. There was no way anybody could have traced the car. It was booked in a false name and we were not followed. So the car was not traced, OK?" I glanced at her. She gave a small nod. I went on, "Nobody could have traced me. None of them—neither the gang yesterday, nor this bunch—knew that I was here. Joe told me yesterday, they expected you to be alone, or with a non-professional. So not the car and not me. That leaves only two ways they could have known we were here..."

I glanced at her again to see if she was following me. She had gone very quiet.

I said, "One, you phoned your husband and either he told them, or they tracked you when you switched on your phone. Two, there was a bug, some kind of tracking device, in your clothes, your phone, your jewelry or your case. We didn't have time for the kind of painstaking search needed to find it. That meant leaving it behind. Does that make sense?"

She took a shaky breath. "Did you have to burn it?"

"Yes. We couldn't leave Senator Cyndi McFarlane's property lying around in a motel, or in a ditch, so it had to be destroyed, burned."

She didn't answer.

I gave her a moment, then asked, "Did you phone him?"

She still didn't answer.

"Sooner or later you'll have to tell me, because we still have a long way to go, and you've seen for yourself, Cyndi, that your life is in very serious danger."

She gave another shaky sigh. "I did. I made a call. I'm sorry. It was stupid. I didn't believe the risk would be..." She puffed out her cheeks and blew. "I thought you were exaggerating."

I was quiet for a while. Then I said, "Eight men have died so far, in just twenty-four hours." I turned and looked at her. "You need to get with the program. I'm doing this for you. It's your damn program."

She nodded quietly. "So what now?"

"Now we need to get into Texas, which is about four and a half hours away, we need Joseph O'Brien to vanish off the face of the Earth, and we need to change the car. And I need to sleep."

She didn't say anything and we sped on along the endless, timeless Route 66, under the vast expanse of the sky, under a trillion cold, distant stars, toward what? I didn't know. But I knew that death was right there, riding shotgun with us.

EIGHT

We crossed the state line into Texas at four in the morning, and fourteen miles over the state line we came to Shamrock. There I slowed and pretty soon I saw what I was looking for. Set back from the road there was a motel and a restaurant, with a large parking lot between them. Both stood dark and silent, and in the lot there was maybe a dozen cars. I pulled in, killed the engine and the lights. Cyndi was asleep, but woke up and looked around with bleary eyes when I stopped.

I said, "Go back to sleep. We're going to rest here for a while."

She closed her eyes again and drifted off. I waited ten minutes to see if any windows lit up, or if anybody came out to see what we were doing. But the windows stayed dark, like dead eyes. It seemed everybody was sleeping deeply.

I got out of the Honda and took my Swiss Army knife from my pocket. Then I searched for the dirtiest car in the lot. It was an old Ford pickup. I hunkered down behind it and had a look at the plates. They were caked with mud. I unscrewed them and took them back to the Civic. I removed those plates, collected a bottle of water I had in the door, and carried the rental car's plates and the water over to a patch of dirt by the parking lot. I made some mud, caked the plates with it, and then screwed them onto the pickup. After that I put the pickup's plates on the rental car. That might give us anything from a few hours to a few days. I thought about buying some spray paint the next day and changing the color of the Honda, but then I figured it was one of the most common cars in the States, painted in the most common color, so maybe the smart thing was to leave it as it was.

I desperately needed to sleep. But I didn't want to risk sleeping in the car by the side of the road. The last thing I needed was a sheriff's deputy getting curious about us and checking out our plates. I had a long shot, but I figured I could make it. I pulled out of the service area and drove twenty miles to the next town, McLean. There I came off the highway and stopped at the Cactus Inn. I left Cyndi in the car and went in to reception. There was a young guy behind the desk, looking sleepy and watching a portable TV with the volume turned down low. He smiled at me as I approached. I checked my watch. It was half past four. I returned his smile and said.

"Help me out here, will you? We've driven here from New York, and man, it's hard to believe, but we were robbed in Oklahoma. They took my wife's suitcase with our ID cards, driving permits and credit cards. Fortunately I had the cash in my wallet."

He looked genuinely shocked. "Did you report it? Do

you want to call the sheriff? I think you need to report it in Oklahoma. This is Texas."

"Yeah, I know. We reported it, but we need to get to San Francisco, and I have been driving all night and I am exhausted. To be frank, I am a danger to myself, my wife and other road users. But here is how you can help me out. Let me have a room, for four hours so I can get some sleep. I will pay you cash in advance, and a hundred dollars on top for the inconvenience. Can I do that? My wife is pregnant and we are on our way to see her mother..."

"Uh..." He blinked a few times.

I pulled two hundred and fifty bucks from my wallet and put them in front of him. "I will be gone before nine in the morning. Do me this favor, pal."

He eyed the money, grinned and said, "Sure, of course, no problem!"

He handed me a key, pocketed the money and I walked out and drove the car around to the room. I woke Cyndi, hauled my bag out of the trunk and locked the car. Then we staggered to the room and let ourselves in. She collapsed on the bed, but before I allowed myself to sleep, I took Joseph O'Brien's documents and credit card, burned them and flushed the residue down the can. Then I fell on the bed next to Cyndi and slipped rapidly into deep, exhausted sleep. At some point in the small hours I half-awoke to find Cyndi covering us with the duvet. She put her arms around me and rested her head on my shoulder. I drifted back into slumber as she whispered, "*Don't leave me alone...*" and I slipped into oblivion.

We left the room, just as I had promised the kid, shortly before nine in the morning. We had pancakes and coffee in the restaurant and pulled out of the lot, back onto Route 66, at exactly nine thirty. We were five hours from Albuquerque, about two and a half from the border with New Mexico, we were free from tracking devices, Joseph O'Brien had vanished in the night, and our car was less than a needle in a haystack, because nobody would be searching for those plates on that car. I was feeling almost confident. In five hours I would hand Cyndi over to Marni and Gibbons, have as much of a heart to heart with Marni as she would permit, and then I would be gone, back to Independence—in more ways than one.

Route 66, the road to freedom.

The Texas Panhandle is flat, the horizon is vast and driving through it is monotonous. But that morning the sky was clear and the temperature was climbing toward an agreeable sixty-eight degrees, so we had the windows open and the fresh morning breeze battering some of the exhaustion from our brains. I glanced at Cyndi and gave her a bit of a smile.

"My first dates don't usually turn out like that."

She raised an eyebrow but didn't look at me, and changed the subject. "What do you reckon, ETA Albuquerque in five hours?"

"Yeah. We'll make a pit stop before Amarillo and get you some clothes that fit. Huntin', shootin', fishin' suits you. You could make it the theme of your next electoral campaign: Farm Girl saves the world."

Now she looked at me. "Is that an edge of bitterness I hear in your voice, Mr. Badass?"

I shook my head. "No." Then I shrugged one shoulder. "I don't know. Maybe. It's not you, it's your profession. Politics destroys people."

"Well that is about the best example of the kettle calling the pot black that I ever heard. You destroyed eight people in the last thirty-six hours!"

I nodded. "I agree, Cyndi." I looked at her. "That's why I refused payment for this job, and it's why I am quitting once we reach our destination."

She stared at me with a strange expression. "You know the thing with ugly jobs like yours and mine, Lacklan? They require commitment. Real commitment. You can quit being a bus driver, a plumber, a dentist or even a lawyer or a doctor. But what you do and what I do? That is not so easy, because what we do affects people's lives. Not one or two people, but hundreds, thousands, perhaps millions. When Professor Gibbons, or Marni Gilbert look at you and say, 'We need you,' I wonder what you will answer."

We crossed the state line into New Mexico at twelve thirty, having pulled off at a gas station with a general store outside Amarillo to get Cyndi some boots, jeans and a shirt. At Tucumcari we stopped for lunch at K-Bob's Steakhouse, stocked up on first class protein and hammered on through the afternoon, across the Cuervo Mesa and into territory that was not desert, but only just.

We passed Moriarty at one o'clock and entered the Sandia Hills. Forty minutes later we came down out of the hills and entered the city of Albuquerque, our final destination. As we entered the town and joined the traffic on Central Avenue I said, "Well, here we are, madam Senator, tell me where to take you."

I looked at her. She was staring ahead, expressionless. She took a deep breath and sighed. "Just keep going straight," she said. "I'll tell you when to turn."

I frowned. "What's eating you? We made it, and you're alive."

She didn't answer and we continued along the broad road, among the low, flat buildings under that vast, pale sky. At Carlisle Boulevard she said, "Take a right here. Keep going till you get to Lomas, then turn left."

I did as she said and after a moment I spoke quietly. "What's going on, Cyndi?"

"Marni and Professor Gibbons will explain it to you. I don't want to."

"Explain what to me?"

I turned left into Lomas and she pointed through the windshield. "Take Girard Boulevard. Three blocks up, it's the house on the corner, on the left. Pull into the driveway."

It was a two-story, brown, adobe style house. It had a small gravel yard out front with space for two cars. There was a Jeep parked there, and a Dodge Durango parked down the side, under a cane veranda. They both had D.C. plates.

I sighed. "Jesus Christ, Cyndi. Don't you people ever learn?" I drove past the house, crossed the intersection, checked my mirrors and pulled over to the side of the road. "Get out. I'm going to lose the car. I'll see you at the house in ten or fifteen minutes."

She stared at me for a moment, got out and slammed the door.

About a block away I found a university campus parking lot. I dropped the car there, took my bag, then wiped my prints from the wheel, the dash and the trunk. After that I made my way on foot to the house, keeping my collar up all the way. I knew what I was going to find when I got there, and the senator did not disappoint.

I rang on the bell and the door was opened to me by a six foot two Marine in a dark suit and dark glasses, with a crew cut, baby blue eyes and pink cheeks. I sighed at him, said, "At ease, soldier," and stepped past him straight into a large living room with mass produced furniture and a wooden staircase going up the far wall. Cyndi was not there, but I could hear a shower going upstairs.

On the sofa there were two more men in dark suits with shades in their handkerchief pockets. They looked exactly like Baby Blue, only one of them had a dark crew cut. A fourth sat in an arm chair. He was bigger than the others, and he was black. Other than that he was a clone. The other arm chair was occupied by a fifth, who had struck a blow for individuality by growing a moustache. I studied them all for a moment and they studied me back.

"Who is your commanding officer?"

The reply came from behind me. "I am."

I knew the voice. I turned. "Hawthorn. I might have guessed."

He was standing in the kitchen door with a mug of coffee in his hand. "Correction. *Major* Hawthorn. And I am not their commanding officer, I am your commanding officer, collectively."

"Where are Marni Gilbert and Professor Gibbons?"

"Where are Dr. Gilbert and Professor Gibbons, *sir?* And that is 'need to know'."

"Yeah? I need to know."

"No, you don't, Captain. I want you washed, shaved and dressed appropriately by fourteen hundred hours. You will be in car two. Understood?"

I held his eye for a moment and spoke very quietly. "I'm

not in your army, Major. Don't make me humiliate you in front of your men."

I crossed the room and climbed the stairs, following the sound of the shower. I came to a landing with a passage. There was a door in front of me and I could hear the sound of running water through that door. I opened it and went in. I saw a double bed up against one wall. The jeans, shirt and underwear we had bought outside Amarillo were thrown on the bed. Over on the right there was a door ajar onto an en suite bathroom. The water was still hissing and splashing. She had a lot of miles and a lot of blood to wash off. I crossed the room and pushed into the bathroom.

The shower was in the bathtub, and there was a plastic curtain drawn across it. I could just make out her silhouette. I didn't pause. I yanked the curtain back. She gaped down at me. She had lather in her hair and all over her body, but it did nothing to hide how good she looked. She clasped her left arm across her bosom and slapped her right hand over her private parts. I reached in. The water sprayed all over my head and back. I put my arms around her waist, heaved her over my shoulder and lifted her out of the bath. She screamed louder than I have ever heard anybody scream. She kicked and thumped. Outside I could hear feet thudding up the stairs. I threw her on the bed, scowled at her and snarled, "If you want to get wherever you're going with a full complement of men, you had better tell them not to come in. Plus, your toy soldiers are about to see you naked and humiliated on that bed."

Her eyes went wide. She leapt up, pulled the door open an inch and peered out. She grinned foolishly through the crack and gave a small laugh. "Sorry, Charles, false alarm. As you were. Yes, no, no, everything's fine. Be right down."

She closed the door, turned, glared at me and covered herself. "How *dare* you! Get me a towel right now! Give me a towel!"

"Where are Marni and Gilbert?"

"Will you *please* get me a towel!"

"Get the damn towel yourself. Where are Marni and Gilbert?"

She took a deep breath. "They will explain it to you..."

"Wrong. You will explain it to me, right now, or I will assume you are Omega and I will start breaking necks."

"Will you please *stop* this barbaric behavior! Hand me a towel, we will sit down and I will explain to you what the situation is. *Please*, Lacklan..."

I went to the bathroom, grabbed a bath towel and threw it at her. She wrapped it around herself. "Another one for my hair, please."

I studied her for a moment. Grabbed another towel and threw it on the bed. She wound it around her head, sat, looked at her knees and sighed. I interrupted her as she drew breath to speak.

"Let me just make a couple of things clear to you, Senator, before you feed me another crock. First, Major Asshole downstairs is somehow under the impression that he is my commanding officer. Clearly you have not understood anything that I have told you over the last couple of days. Second, what I have seen since we came into Albuquerque stinks of Omega. Now you have thirty seconds to convince me that I am wrong. If you don't, things are going to get real ugly around here."

She looked into my eyes and I could see that she was scared.

I nodded. "Call them up here. I'll explain it to them too."

She closed her eyes and raised her hand. "Just calm down, Lacklan. You have completely misread the situation. Marni and Professor Gibbons are not here. They never were. It was their idea, not mine. They are running this show. They didn't want anybody to know where they were, not even me. All I knew was that we would receive instructions once we got here."

She reached over to the bedside table, picked up an envelope and tossed it across the bed to me. I opened it and pulled out a note. It was printed on an inkjet and read simply, '*Corpus Christi, Texas*'.

I took it into the bathroom, set fire to it and let it burn in the sink. Then I washed the ash down the plughole. I went back into the bedroom and stood staring at Cyndi. "What about your army of clowns downstairs?"

"Can you please try to stop being so offensive?"

"No. What did he mean when he said he was my commanding officer?"

She looked genuinely embarrassed and smoothed the duvet beside her leg with her hand. "Marni and Professor Gibbons need you to come with us to Corpus Christi." She looked up at me.

I narrowed my eyes.

"I have put Major Hawthorn in charge of the security operation from this point on. You did hear me on the phone at the motel in Bristow. But I wasn't calling my husband, I was calling Charles. You are an extraordinarily brave man,

Lacklan, and I would surely not have made it here without you. But frankly, you are a barbarian. From this point on we are going to do things differently. It is just a drive, from here to Corpus Christi. It will be well ordered, well organized, and there will be no endless detours and no massacres. You are under the Major's command."

I laughed out loud. When I had finished, I shook my head. "There are so many reasons why that is not going to happen. And the first is that I do not plan to commit suicide, which is what you are about to do."

"Lacklan, please."

"If you make it to Corpus Christi alive, give Marni a message from me. Tell her I quit."

NINE

She shouted down to me as I reached the front door. I should have gone on and left the house, but for some reason I stopped. Maybe somewhere inside I felt my history with Marni deserved more. Maybe I thought the senator deserved more. Whatever the reason, I stopped with the door half open and turned back. The major and his five clones were all on their feet. Cyndi came thudding down the stairs in her jeans and bare feet, buttoning her shirt as she went, shouting, "*Lacklan! Wait!* Don't do something you will regret all your life just because you are mad!"

I raised an eyebrow at her. "Is that a threat?"

"*No! Goddamit! Will you stop this now, please!*"

I waited.

She pointed at a chair. "Please, sit down, have a drink and let's talk about this."

I was telling myself I was less than two days' drive from Independence. All I had to do was walk away, hire a car and go home. Cyndi was watching me, and she read me like a book. I was about to turn and go through the door when she spoke. “You owe it to yourself, you owe it to the world, goddammit! You owe it to Gibbons, and above all you owe it to Marni and your father. Just sit down and talk, for ten minutes, and if after that you still want to leave, then fine. You can get up and go.”

I sighed, closed the door and sat in one of the armchairs.

The major turned to his men. “You boys start loading up the vehicles. We depart on time at fifteen hundred hours.”

Cyndi sat close to me on the sofa.

I said, “Sit down, Major. I want you to be a part of this conversation.”

He wanted more than anything else to tell me to go to hell, but he knew he had no choice, and Cyndi said, “Sit down, please, Charles. I’d like you to be a part of this too.”

He sat in the chair opposite.

Cyndi started to talk. “Lacklan, I want you to know how grateful I am. I realize I could not have...”

I cut her short. “Cut to the chase, Senator. If I need an ego massage I’ll go to the local whorehouse.”

Her cheeks flushed red and I saw tears in her eyes.

The major snarled, “You watch your mouth, Walker!”

I ignored him. “We’re on the clock, Senator. Talk.”

She looked down at the carpet. I could see her jaw muscles bunching. After a moment, she said, “Professor Gilbert and Marni both stressed to me that it was of vital importance that you make the rendezvous with us. I honestly don’t know any more than you do. But I do know that they need to see you for something of the utmost importance. So much so that my meeting with them would be almost a waste of time if you did not come also.” She buried her face in her hands, ran her fingers through her hair, then looked up at me. "Look, Lacklan, I have made an absolute mess of this. I can see that now and I hold my hands up to it. But it is done! And we need you at this meeting. Marni needs you at this meeting. Please come with us."

I pulled my Camels from my pocket, lit up and put them away again. I inhaled deeply and let the smoke out slow. I knew myself well enough to know that if Marni needed me that bad, I would go. But I'd be damned if I went on their terms, and I sure as hell wasn't putting my life in the hands of Major Disaster and his gang of amateurs.

I said, "How long have you had those two neon signs outside?" They both frowned at me. I jabbed at the door with my thumb. "I'm talking about the two SUVs out there with D.C. plates and U.S. Navy Seals written all over them in neon letters."

The major's face went hard. "They have been there for two days, Captain. And there is nothing wrong with a show of force. Let them see that we mean business."

"Listen to me, Major. You can give a show of force when you know how strong your enemy is. But if you don't even know *who* your damn enemy is, a show of force is just plain stupidity." I turned to Cyndi. "Does he know anything about who he is up against?"

"Very little. None of us knows much at all."

I nodded. "That's why Marni wanted me to take you, not your own men." I turned to the major. "I know who we are up against. I know them very well. And your show of force is nothing to them, believe me. All you have done is advertise your presence. And you can be sure that they have tracked you from D.C. They know who you are, they know why you are here and they know your strength." I looked at Cyndi. "This is your well ordered, well organized military operation?"

"Ma'am, do I have to sit here and listen to this? I need to see to the loading of the vehicles."

I held up a hand. "Before you go, Major. Let's get a couple of things clear. I am not under your command. I ride with the senator, and her safety is my personal responsibility." I turned to Cyndi. "If you can't live with that, we are done here."

She nodded.

I turned back to the major. "And one more thing. What weapons have you got?"

"The men all have their own sidearms. In addition we have six assault rifles and back up ammunition."

"What route are you planning?"

"Ma'am, I don't have time for this..."

I interrupted him. "Are you planning to take the I-25 through Las Cruces, down to the Big Bend?"

His face flushed. "Yeah! Yeah, that's what I'm planning. What? Should I have run it by you first, *Captain?*"

"They'll hit you before Las Cruces."

"Take a hike!"

I looked at Cyndi. "You're going to die today."

There was panic in her eyes. She looked at the Major.

"Ma'am, you don't have to listen to this wiseass!"

I stood. "I take the Dodge. I drive. I'm in the lead. It's not negotiable."

He shouted at me, "*Screw you!*"

"Your call, Cyndi. Take it or leave it."

She stared at the Major a moment. "Charles, this really

doesn't change a thing. Captain Walker is an expert and he has a deep knowledge of the workings of Omega. He knows what he is talking about. We go in convoy as you had planned, but we will go in the lead and you will go behind. That is how we will do it."

He scowled at me. "Yes, ma'am!"

He slammed out.

I shook my head at Cyndi. "You made a big mistake." I started climbing the stairs.

She said, "Where are you going?"

"To have a shower." I stopped and looked back at her. "I'm sorry I picked you up and threw you on the bed. I shouldn't have done that. But you have to stop playing smart games, Cyndi. Politicians play games and people die. Stop it."

WE DIDN'T SET off at fifteen hundred hours. We set out at three fifteen, because at ten to three I decided to make coffee and a sandwich, and took my time about it. Major Dumbass had complained and I'd told him to go on ahead, we'd follow. It would have helped if he had. It might have saved his life, but he couldn't see that.

I took two of his boys in the Dodge. The big black guy rode up front with me, the one with the moustache rode in the back with Cyndi. I told them both I wanted them armed with assault rifles. We joined the I-25 from Coal Avenue, and straight away I accelerated to one hundred MPH. Major Disaster had told me, with a smug show of pride, that he had cleared it with the New Mexico PD, Texas PD and the Texas

Rangers, that we would be passing through at high speed with a politically sensitive passenger. That's the kind of stupid thing you can do when you have connections at the White House.

Six minutes out of town we crossed the Rio Grande and turned south toward Belen. When we were under way I said, "OK, listen up and pay attention. Senator, anything starts, you get flat on the floor, immediately. Soldier, what's your name?"

The guy with the moustache said, "Sergeant Eames, Sir."

"OK, Eames. First sign of trouble, your first task, before you fire a round, is to put the senator flat on the floor of the car and make sure she stays there. Don't be polite. You cover her at all times. Understood?"

"Yes, sir."

I glanced at the big guy next to me. "What's your name?"

"Sergeant Jones."

"All right, Sergeants, I know our enemy, and I know him very well. He is powerful and well equipped. When he attacks, he will seek to outgun us and outmaneuver us. So I am expecting him to attack while we are on the road, where our ability to take evasive action is limited. And I am guessing he will strike from the air as soon as we are some distance into the desert. That being the case, we should expect a helicopter attack, by two choppers, somewhere between Belen and Las Cruces."

Jones said, "Holy shit..."

Cyndi said, "Oh my God..."

I cut her short. "Too late for regrets. Now listen to me. Usual procedure is that the package goes in the rear car.

They will target both vehicles, but they will make a point of taking out the rear car first, because they'll figure that's where the senator is most likely to be. So, Eames, your task, having ensured that the senator is on the floor, is to neutralize the chopper that's targeting the rear vehicle. You get in the trunk, you smash the rear windshield and you take out the pilot. Short, focused bursts. Understood?"

"Yes, sir."

"Jones, the moment we are aware of their presence, you are going to open the sunroof. Don't worry. I am going to make you a very difficult target to hit. However, they are going to be using high velocity, armor piercing rounds."

"I understand."

"Don't waste ammunition on the shooters. Shoot the pilot. If you can't see the pilot, aim for the engine and fuel tank. They'll most likely be below the rotors and behind the cabin. Any questions?"

Jones gave his head a single, stoic shake. "No, sir."

But after a moment Eames asked, "Who are these people?"

"Your worst nightmare, Sergeant. Every conspiracy theory you ever read on the 'Net, and then some."

They came at us an hour and forty minutes out of Albuquerque, forty-five miles north of Las Cruces. I caught the throb of the rotors on the periphery of my hearing and snapped. "Senator! Get down now!" At the same time, I accelerated and moved into the fast lane. "Eames! In the trunk. Jones, sunroof!" I grabbed the radio. "Major! Two incoming choppers on your six. Stay with me, we'll take out the one targeting you."

The radio crackled. "What the hell are you talking about, Walker?"

I dropped the radio and accelerated to one twenty. Speed was not really an issue. The choppers would be doing in excess of two hundred miles an hour, and there was no way I could outrun them. What I needed was to go fast enough that if I weaved, I would make it hard for them to aim effectively. A twitch of the steering wheel at fifty, you're a sitting duck. That same twitch at a hundred and twenty and you have dodged ten yards across the road. Try it at a hundred and fifty and they won't need to shoot you because you'll already be dead.

I heard the rear windshield shatter, then Eames was shouting: "Two choppers! One at our six, taking position over rear car. The other coming alongside, your nine, sir!"

Then his rifle was stuttering, short bursts of four rounds, so he could keep control of the weapon.

Meanwhile, Jones had opened the sunroof, had one foot on the seat and had wedged himself in the opening, resting his weapon on the roof. He fired three short bursts, and next thing we were raked with a hail of fire that shattered a window and tore two holes through the chassis. I slammed on the brakes so the chopper overshot us, then hit the gas, accelerated to a hundred and forty, then slowed to a hundred and twenty. The chopper swung around to take its position again.

I shouted as I careened across the road, "Count of five, I'm going to hold her steady for four seconds! Take your shots!"

Another rain of fire strafed the blacktop and punched a

hole in the roof. I swung the car across the road and back again, hollering, "*One! Two! Three! Four! Five!*"

And I held the Dodge steady in a straight line for four agonizing seconds. In that time they got off four bursts of fire each, thirty-two rounds. Then I was burning rubber again, screaming across the blacktop, while Eames shouted, "*I got the mother fucker. I got him!*"

Behind us there was a screaming of brakes and rubber. Eames said, "Oh no, Lord no!" And then there was a terrible rending of metal and a massive explosion. I glanced in the mirror. The chopper had come down in the path of the Major's Jeep. He had tried to veer to the side, but had collided with the body of the aircraft and both had exploded in a ball of fire.

I barked, "Stay focused! Eames! Nine o'clock! Take that chopper down!"

"Sir!"

"Cover the senator!"

"Sir!"

But even as he replied, we were strafed again. I saw the plumes of pulverized blacktop racing across the freeway toward us like a sprinting ghost. I veered right. My windshield exploded and I heard a hard *thwack!* above my head. Jones' big body whiplashed and he slumped down onto the dashboard with half his head missing.

I heard Eames say, "Oh sweet Jesus!"

I snarled, "Stay focused! I'm taking the bridge. Get him in the belly as we go under!"

We had come to exit 51. I spun the wheel and accelerated up the ramp. I saw the chopper rise over the bridge. I hit the brakes, slid my ass into the bend and floored the gas across the overpass. Eames was half out the window, screaming like a deranged berserker, emptying the magazine into the belly of the chopper.

He pulled himself in, ripped out the empty magazine and rammed another in as we screeched onto a broad dirt track that climbed into the sierra. I hit the brakes, sliding on the gravel, and he rolled into the back, taking aim at the pilot who was fishtailing and trying to get behind us. I heard three short bursts from Eames, but I was hurtling around a bend, climbing fast and raising a big cloud of dust behind us.

He shouted, "I can't see him!"

Then we were hit by a hail of bullets and he went quiet. I floored the gas pedal again. We were at the top of the hill, and up ahead on the right I could see a canyon. I pulled off the track doing fifty and we bounced and jumped across the brush and gnarled bushes. I heard Cyndi scream, slammed on the brakes and skidded to a halt six inches from the edge of the canyon in a huge cloud of dust. I grabbed Jones' rifle and a spare magazine, hollering, "*Get out! Get out! Get out now!*"

I scrambled, wrenched open the back door and dragged Cyndi out. The dust was swirling all around us. The thudding of the chopper was deafening and its downdraft was kicking up even more dust. I dragged Cyndi to the edge of the ravine and shouted "*Lie down!*"

She fell to the ground. I dropped on my belly and, as the rotors rose over the cloud of dust, I took aim. For a second the pilot saw me and we looked at each other. We were maybe twenty yards away. We looked at each other and he knew he was going to die. I riddled his upper body and his head with twelve rounds in three steady bursts of four. The chopper spun out of control, swung in a circle, lifted its tail in the air and smashed down face first onto the hillside.

I didn't wait. I ran to the SUV, grabbed the spare gas can, doused the inside of the cab with it, then pushed it over the edge. It didn't burst into flames when it hit the bottom. Cars don't generally explode when they crash. But a hot round into the cab ignited the gasoline, and then it did explode, and it began to incinerate the two bodies inside it.

I glanced at my watch. It was five fifteen and evening was closing in. In the distance I could hear sirens. I grabbed Cyndi and dragged her to her feet.

"Come on, we have to run."

"*What?*"

"Run! Down into that canyon! Now!"

And we ran, not to where the Dodge had exploded, but further on, stumbling down into the shadows, away from the burning wreckage that would be the focus of attention of the cops.

For now at least.

For now at least, we had some respite, too. By tonight Omega would know that Cyndi was not in the rear car. By tomorrow night they would know that the lead car had only two occupants, and that they were both burned beyond identification. It would be several days, maybe more, before they discovered that neither of them was Senator Cyndi McFarlane.

So, for the next couple of days at least, our own presumed deaths would allow us to live.

TEN

THE MOON HAD RISEN EARLY AND NOW HUNG huge, three dimensional and orange over the jagged black edge of the sierra. It was cold, freezing, and we were both shivering, huddled close for warmth. A mile away we could still see the desultory flash of red and blue light over the edge of the canyon, where the fire truck, the ambulance and the Highway Patrol had arrived to try and fathom what the hell had happened there. I had no doubt the Feds were there too, and even less doubt that Omega had a man on the spot.

And while those lights were flashing, we had no choice but to wait it out. Our problems had become very complicated. Not only were we without a vehicle to get us where we needed to go, I had no usable ID, no credit card, and we were practically out of cash. Yet, looking at Cyndi, I didn't know how long we could wait. The cold was getting to her, she had low body mass, and pretty soon she would slip into hypothermia. Her teeth were chattering and she was getting a glassy look about her eyes. Sergeant Bradley, my Kiwi mentor from the Regiment, had a saying that had saved my ass more times than I could remember. I could see him now, swigging whiskey from his hip flask, with the camp fire washing his face with red and orange, making him look diabolical. "When the Devil is up your arse, mate, there's only one thing you can do. Move your fuckin' arse!"

I said, "OK, let's go." I got to my feet and pulled her up. I took my jacket and put it around her shoulders, over the top of her own.

She was trembling so bad she had trouble talking, but eventually she managed to ask, "Where are we going?"

I pointed roughly south, toward the dull glow of the freeway. "Garfield. It's about two and a half miles away."

We started stumbling and sliding down a slope into a deep ravine that threaded its way toward the I-25, a quarter of a mile away. It was a strange sight, like a bizarre, surreal stage set in the middle of the pitch-black desert: a long, dark gray strip of tarmacadam, illuminated by tall, spindly silver lamps. But I had spotted something that gave me hope. Where the road passed over the gulley, it was raised on a high bank. My bet was that when it rained, a lot of water would accumulate against that bank, so there would have to be some kind of drainage system to allow it to get through to the gully on the other side. If I was right, we would be able to cross the highway without ever being seen.

Twenty minutes of scrambling and stumbling down steep slopes, littered with rocks and shrubs, brought us to the foot of the bank, and the gaping maw of a vast tube, fifteen feet in diameter, that had been built into it. It was there to allow heavy rains and flash floods to flow beneath the interstate without damaging its foundations. Tonight it was going to allow us to do the same thing.

It was over a hundred yards from one end to the other. It was damp and full of garbage, and stygian dark. The only light we had to guide us was the dim circle of limpid blue moonlight at the far end, suspended in shapeless blackness. It told us where we wanted to go, but not the path, not how to get there.

I gave Cyndi my arm. "Hold on to me. Don't let go. It's going to be a hundred paces. We'll count them off, and then we'll be out the other side. I want you to make a noise, you understand? Don't be shy and don't be quiet. Let's go."

It was not pleasant. We could hear the rats scuttling and scurrying near our feet. They were not shy and they were not quiet. I could feel Cyndi's fingers digging into my arm and her body going rigid, quivering. I could tell she wanted to run, but I knew if she ran she could fall, and then we might have a real problem, because two got you twenty that as well as rats, there could be snakes in that tube, hunting the rats. So I told her stupid stories about pranks we used to play in the army, what the Brits call jolly japes, everything from escaping through the back windows of whorehouses while the cops stormed in the front, to adding pure alcohol to one lieutenant's intimate deodorant. I even sang her a song while she counted off the steps. The worst were from fifty to seventy five, because we'd gone too far to turn back, but we still had half way to go.

Eventually, finally, the circle of limpid blue moonlight began to swell and take shape, and we began to leave the small, poisonous creatures of the dark behind us. And then we were finally out, on the clean, dry sand and she was clinging to me, trembling violently and repeating through clenched teeth, "I will not cry again, Lacklan. I am done crying, but how many more people have to die? How much more horror do we have to go through?"

I held her tight, but I didn't answer. I had no answer to those questions.

We followed the gully for about a mile and eventually came to a narrow road. There was some kind of tree plantation there, and a yard with trucks, but nothing I would want to use. So we turned south, onto the road, and followed it toward the small town of Garfield.

After three or four hundred yards we came to the first few scattered houses and I saw the one I wanted. You cannot hotwire modern cars, anything after the mid '90s is impossible unless you have some pretty sophisticated electronic equipment. But fortunately, these days, a kid's first car is still often pre-millennium, and that was exactly what I had been looking for, and what I had just seen: a mid '90s Ford Taurus.

It was deathly quiet in the outskirts of Garfield, but through the stillness of the desert night you could hear the murmur of a TV through the lighted window at the front right of the house. The Taurus was parked at the left side, so there would be a room and a TV muffling the sound of the engine.

I took my jacket off Cyndi's shoulders, wrapped it around the muzzle of the Sig and shot out the driver's window. It didn't silence it, but it muffled it enough not to raise an alarm. I opened the door, climbed in and opened the passenger door for the trembling senator. To hotwire a car, you can mess around searching for the right wires, but they are different in each vehicle and you can waste a lot of time that way. It's much easier to smash a screwdriver into the ignition. Ideally you would use a drill to break the pins, but failing that, if you're desperate—and we were—brute force will do it.

Two minutes later, we were accelerating away from the town of Garfield and back onto the I-25, with the heater at full blast. As we hit the freeway, Cyndi was shaking her head. "Lacklan, we have almost a thousand miles to cover. How the hell are we going to do this?"

"I need to make one stop, in Socorro. After that, if you're willing to share the driving, we can make it in fourteen hours. I figure we have two days, maybe more, before Omega figures out what they are looking for and where to look for it."

She shook her head again. "This car, and any car you steal tonight, is going to be reported stolen by tomorrow morning at the latest. We can't keep doing this."

"Not any car. Now, I've told you. Are you going to keep arguing with me? Or are you going to try something different?"

She sighed and rubbed her face with her hands. "Fine. Yes, you're right. You have proved yourself right every time, and me wrong every time." She was quiet for a moment, then added, "Poor Charles, and the others."

"The others died because of Charles' stupidity and arrogance. I know his type of soldier. If you have an enemy, you throw money and weapons at him until he lies down and dies. You can't do that. You have to understand your enemy before you tackle him. That is where you and Charles, and many others, have gone wrong. You think your enemy is like you, like all the others, but he is not. He is different."

We made it in just over an hour. Socorro is one of the most dangerous cities in the Southwest. It is physically connected to Ciudad Juarez in Mexico and one of the main points of entry for Mexican heroin into the U.S.A. And it was going to provide me with exactly what I needed to get to Corpus Christi.

I took the I-10 down to a bar I knew called the Blue Flamingo. It was a mock Spanish villa set back from the road in a big, ugly concrete parking lot, and advertised itself with a big strip of neon showing a girl in a cowboy hat with her arms around a blue flamingo. It was very subtle.

I parked around back and told Cyndi to stay put. Then I crossed the lot, walked through the central patio, past the mock Louis XIV fountain, and pushed through the glass doors to the 'Adult Entertainment Establishment'. There was a plush, red-carpeted lobby with two white staircases leading up to a second floor, where all the luxury bedrooms were. I had drunk champagne in a few of them when I was younger, and less wise. A second set of doors led me into a large, plush cocktail bar with carpets so deep you could lose your life in them, and corners so dark you could forget you cared.

I went to the bar like I was in a hurry. Delroy saw me and came over to shake my hand. "My man, we haven't seen you around here in a while. How are you doing? Where's your pal, Bat?"

"Trying to stay out of jail. Listen, I'll be back to shoot the breeze and have a drink, but right now I need you to help me out."

"Sure man. Name it."

"I need to score some coke."

He looked surprised. "You? I didn't think you did that shit, man."

I shook my head. "I don't. It's not for me. I'm on a date and I think the party could get interesting if I can do this for her."

He laughed a lot. "Yeah man, sure."

"What about some 'H'?"

Now he looked unhappy. "Ah, no, man. That's bad shit."

I shrugged. "It's what the lady likes, my friend."

"Shit, man." He shook his head. "OK, you gonna cross over the freeway. It's on Bovee Road, right down by the wall." He gave me the address. "Guy's name is Slee. Don't tell him I sent you. I don't like that guy. Tell him Randy sent you."

"Who's Randy?"

He shrugged. "A pal of his. Another low life." He laughed. "You know what? Don't pay him. Break his legs instead. That piece of shit destroys lives. Think about what you're doing, man."

I gave him a wink. "I owe you. We'll have a drink and catch up."

I stepped back out into the night, through the elaborate patio and ran around to the Ford. Cyndi was still there, looking unhappy. I got in, hit the gas and accelerated away toward the underpass. I followed Horizon Boulevard, then at Bulford I came off and followed the back streets to the address he had given me. It was a single-story house surrounded by scrubland. The drapes were closed, but you could see slashes of light at the edges. I wasn't surprised to see a BMW 2 series parked out front. I tucked the Ford behind it, killed the engine and turned to Cyndi. She was staring at me like she thought I was crazy. But she also remembered she had promised to stop questioning me, so she was biting her tongue.

"I'll be ten minutes. Don't move. We'll be in Corpus Christi for breakfast."

I climbed out, pulling on the latex gloves I still had in my pocket. I walked up the path to the front porch and knocked.

A voice spoke through the door. "What?"

"Hey, Slee, man, I'm a friend of Randy. Said you could fix me up."

"What do you want?"

I put my mouth close to the door. "I don't wanna be shouting out here, man. He said you had some 'H'. Money's no problem, man. I need some coke, too. We're having a party."

He opened the door. He was tall, heavy, going to fat. He had a white vest, a baseball cap and jeans that looked like they'd been designed for a malformed hippopotamus. "Where'd you see Randy?"

I shoved the Sig into his belly. "Here."

He went pasty gray and held up his hands. His eyes bulged and a vein started to throb in his temple. I said, "Back up, do as I say, and you won't get hurt."

He backed up. He wasn't about to give anyone any trouble. I stepped in and closed the door behind me.

He was shaking his head. "Y'all making a big mistake,

man. You don't wanna do this to me. I got friends over the border, man. You feel me? You know what that means?"

I nodded. "Yup. Now, this goes down one of two ways. You give me what I want, I leave and you live. Or you give me what I want after I have blown your kneecaps off. Where is your cash? I'm going to count to three. On three I start shooting kneecaps. One..."

"No, man, I have to give that to... You know what they'll do to me if I don't pay..."

"Two..."

"No, listen to me, man..."

I shot him in the left kneecap. He gave a high-pitched squeal, did a funny, one-legged jumping dance and fell over. He was sobbing and clawing at his leg. I don't have a lot of sympathy for people who deal in heroin. I hunkered down next to him.

"You might just save the leg, Slee, if you get to a hospital on time. Your best plan now is to call the cops, make a deal and sell out your Mexican friends. But that's for you to decide. Where is the cash?"

He started shaking his head. His face was wet with tears. I pressed the muzzle against his right kneecap. His eyes started and he shook his head more violently.

I said, "One..."

"OK! OK! OK! I'll tell you. In the bedroom! In the wardrobe! In a sports bag!" I walked into the bedroom, opened the wardrobe and found the sports bag. I opened it. There must have been fifty grand in there. A testament to people's enduring stupidity. I went back into the filthy living room. There was a cell phone on the coffee table. I picked it up, went and squatted down next to Slee again.

“That your BMW outside?” He nodded. He was looking bad. He’d lost a lot of blood from his knee. “Key.”

“In my pocket. Please, gimme the phone, man. I’m dying.”

I reached in his pocket and pulled out the key. Then I looked at him and shook my head. “You’re not dying, Slee. You’re dead.”

I put a round through the center of his forehead. He didn’t deserve to be put out of his misery, but I couldn’t afford to have him talking, either.

I took the bag out, stuffed five grand in my pocket and threw the rest in the trunk. Then we spent ten minutes wiping our prints off the Ford, transferred our stuff to the BMW and took off, once again, for Texas and Corpus Christi.

ELEVEN

It was a seven hundred mile drive. Ten hours, so long as we stuck to the speed limit, and with fifty grand in a hold all in the trunk of a car stolen from a drug dealer, it made sense to stick to the speed limit. We stopped at the first gas station outside Socorro, filled her up and bought food: bread, cheese, ham and chocolate. And then we drove. We took it in turns. Five hour shifts. I took it as far as Sonora while she slept, and from Sonora to Corpus Christi, she drove while I slept.

It was a tedious, exhausting drive. But after the violence and constant threat of the previous days, it was a relief to know that we had total anonymity for the next few hours.

There was practically no traffic, and the endless, straight road under the immense, clear Texan sky was hypnotic. Occasionally a truck would pass on the westbound road. It would appear as a bright light in the distance, slowly swell, then flash past, leaving just silence in the darkened cab, aside from the quiet hum of the engine.

Towns, clusters of houses with sleeping windows and sleeping cars, motels and gas stations, they would all pass in their still pools of dull light, shut down for the dark, nocturnal hours, when only predators and their victims were abroad.

After Sonora I tried to sleep, but it wasn't easy. I knew that in the morning I would be seeing Marni. I knew that she wanted something from me, and I knew that I no longer wanted to give it to her. I knew I was going to tell her it was all over: with me and Omega, and with me and her. Because a relationship with Marni meant a relationship with Omega. And I couldn't do that anymore.

Part of my mind told me I should do one more job and give them fair notice. But I had heard the 'one last job' refrain too many times from colleagues and comrades, and I knew there was no such thing. I had already done my last job. This was it—I handed the senator over, and I was done. From here, I went home.

Home to Independence. And, maybe, even home to Weston, Kenny and Rosalia. I could visualize Abi there. She would make it a home. She would give that big, old house warmth and joy, and light.

Lights. I opened my eyes and realized I had been sleeping, dreaming. There were bright lights all around me, moving. I saw Cyndi glance over at me and smile. She said, "San Antonio," and I closed my eyes and went back to sleep.

When I opened them again, a blood red sun was leeching into a pale gray sky on the horizon. It was a very flat horizon. I had a pain in my neck, my back hurt and I was hungry. I looked at the clock on the dash and saw it was eight AM. I stretched. My joints crunched.

"We passed San Antonio. We made good time. Where are we?"

"We just left Mathis. We're twenty miles from Corpus Christi."

"Wow, I see you stuck to the speed limit."

She snorted. "This is Texas, it doesn't count."

"So now what?"

She shrugged. "I don't know. You saw the note. I guess we wait for them to contact us." She was quiet for a bit, then spoke my own thoughts. "Though, having said that, how will they know we're here?"

I sighed, then yawned. "We tell them. I need a shower and a soft bed. We go to the Corpus Christi Omni. It's big, it's on the seafront and it's as close as this town gets to a five star hotel. We book in, in my name..."

"You mean Joseph O'Brien? I thought he was dead."

"No, I mean me, Lacklan Walker. I'm through running and hiding. In any case, I don't think Omega has connected you with me yet. The last they know of you is leaving Albuquerque. Right now they're not even sure you're alive. And I haven't been on their radar for about a year. So if Marni and Gibbons are looking out for us, let's make it easy for them to find us."

We drove to Shoreline Boulevard, had the valet park our car and walked in to reception. It was beige and wood and had a feel of the seventies about it. The receptionist was as polite and pleasant as just about every other Texan, but something in his eyes told me that every one of his other guests was appropriately dressed, and we weren't. My black Amex changed that look when I laid it on his desk.

"How may I help you today, sir?"

"First of all, you can book me into your best bay view suite for the next week. Then you can tell me where the best shops are. We had our luggage stolen in New Mexico and we need to replace it."

"I am very sorry to hear that, Mr... Walker..." He frowned, like the name meant something to him. "Anything we can do for you to make up for that experience..." He spoke as he typed into his computer, but trailed off. "Actually, sir, I believe we have a message for you, from a Professor John Smith, of Oxford University...?"

John Smith is to Brits what John Doe is to Americans. The message was obviously from Gibbons. I smiled. "Oh, sure. I told John we'd be staying here. Thanks."

He handed me the note and I read it while he got me a key. It said simply:

You have a yacht booked with Fun Time Rental on the Lawrence Street pier. It's reserved for the next two weeks. It is reserved in the name of Lacklan Walker. Sail it to the following coordinates: Latitude: 26°51'34.95"N Longitude: 94°53'13.87"W Destroy this message.

That was Gilbert. He loved his James Bond games. I put it in my pocket and the receptionist had a bellhop take us up to our suite. There was practically no luggage to carry, so at the door I gave him twenty bucks and told him to bring me two hundred Camels and a liter of Bushmills. He went away happy.

The suite was large and comfortable, with a sofa and

armchairs and a small dining area with a dining table. There was also a terrace with, as the name promised, a spectacular view of the Gulf of Mexico. I gave Cyndi the note and went into the bathroom to stand for twenty minutes under the shower, letting the bruises, the stress and the aches wash away. When I finally stepped out of the cubicle and grabbed a towel, Cyndi was standing in the doorway, leaning on the jamb, watching me, smiling. It wasn't what you'd call a friendly smile. It was more insolence, with a touch of provocation.

She was still wearing the clothes we'd got her from the general store: the red plaid shirt, jeans and boots, with her crazy hair tied behind her head. She didn't look like a senator.

I dried my face and said, "What are you doing?"

She shrugged. "An eye for an eye."

"Witty. Are you going to throw me over your shoulder and toss me on the bed? I promise I won't scream."

"Have you got a boating license?"

"Yeah, of course."

"Of course you have. I'm not sure if your scars outnumber your muscles, or your muscles outnumber your scars. Has anybody ever counted them?"

She looked amused at the fact that I wasn't self conscious. I ignored her, toweled my hair, then started drying my body.

She said, "When do you want to do this?"

"We're both tired. We need a good rest and a good meal. I also don't want to stand out and draw attention. So we go shopping, get some luggage and some appropriate clothes.

We go out for dinner tonight like a regular couple. You are Mrs. Walker…"

"With all the fringe benefits?"

I raised an eyebrow at her, pushed past and went to start dressing. "Tomorrow morning we dress for yachting. We have breakfast in the dining room and go and collect our boat. We tell reception we'll be back tomorrow or the day after, we're not sure. The room's booked for a week anyway, but we don't want the coast guard searching for us."

She watched me dress for a moment without saying anything, then nodded. "Sounds like a plan."

At eleven we took Slee's BMW and drove to Macy's on S. Padre Drive. There I endured the agony of accompanying a rich woman shopping and we spent a small fortune replacing the clothes we had supposedly packed for a short spring vacation on the Gulf of Mexico, and lost on the trip there. I even bought a blue blazer and some cream pants for myself so I'd look the part the next day. Just before we left the store, at one o'clock, Cyndi went to the ladies' and changed. She emerged with exquisitely understated makeup and a six hundred dollar silk dress. She looked beautiful, but I found myself missing the general store plaid shirt, the jeans and boots.

She handed me four bulging bags of clothes and raised an eyebrow at me. "You look disappointed."

"Yeah?" I shrugged. "The surgeon said that to me too."

"What surgeon?"

"The one who delivered me. Let's go and have lunch."

The concierge seemed relieved when we returned looking like the kind of people who booked suites at his hotel. We had the bellhop earn his tip by carrying the shopping up to our room, and then had a suitably expensive luncheon in the hotel dining room.

That evening we took a cab to the Yardarm on Ocean Drive. It's not much to look at from the outside, but it's comfortable and friendly, there is lots of wood and good wine, and the food is something to write home about, if you have a home to write to. We were shown to a table with a view of the Gulf. I ordered two martinis, very dry, and while he went to get them, we looked at the menu. I saw her smile.

"You brave enough to order oysters?"

"If you promise not to have veggie pasta."

She laughed. "You have my word."

The waiter came back with our drinks. I said, "We'll have a dozen oysters, with a dry, chilled Tio Pepe. Then my wife will have the lobster Thermidor and I will have the Black Angus ribeye. You have Rioja?"

He smiled as if I had asked him if he had a full complement of fingers and toes. "Yes, sir, naturally."

"Then we'll have a cold, white Marques de Murieta for my wife's lobster, and I'll have a Marques de Riscal with my steak."

He gave a little bow and went away. Cyndi narrowed her eyes at me. "What was that little number about, cave man? I get to make decisions on whether we bomb Syria, but you order my drinks, my food and my wine?"

"Stop flirting with me. It boosts my testosterone. Next thing I'll be clubbing you over the head and dragging you by your hair into a cave."

"Is that what it is?"

"Besides, you're married, remember?"

She nodded at the table, like she was having a private

conversation with it that I couldn't hear. After a moment she said, "Am I?"

"What's that supposed to mean?"

She raised her eyes and studied my face. "Have you forgotten? You believed he was in bed with Omega. You thought he tried to have me killed."

"I haven't forgotten. I just figured you'd been through enough. We're supposed to be resting today."

"You mean I am. This is probably a walk in the park for you."

"Not really."

"Well, anyway." She sat back in her chair. "You asked me to think about who could have hired those Irish boys."

I nodded and sipped. "And...?"

"It obviously wasn't Charles."

"I'd say that's a safe bet."

"So I can only think of one person."

"Who?"

"Michael, my husband."

I scratched my chin. "That's one hell of a turn around, Cyndi."

She gave a small laugh and studied the olive in her glass for a moment. Then she looked up at me. She was smiling, but it wasn't humorous. "What? You think it would need a bigger crisis than the one I've been though, to bring about such a change? In the last—what is it, three, four days?—eight men and two helicopters have tried to kill me. That will do things to a girl, Lacklan. Maybe that's your daily bread. It's not mine. It made me think."

"What? What did you think?"

She shrugged. "You were right." She offered me an

ironic smile that was not free from bitterness. "That will come as no surprise to you. I guess you are used to being right. But I had to think coldly and unemotionally. Politicians can do that." She shook her head. There was something very sad about the gesture. "Omega has the resources for electronic eavesdropping, so it would have been no surprise to have them drop in on us at the end of our first leg. But, like you said, four thugs from a small time gang outside Baltimore? That makes no sense." I was nodding and she gestured at me with an open hand. "Of course you had arrived at this understanding of the situation within seconds of..."

I smiled. "Of seeing their weapons and their clothes."

The bitterness and the irony slipped from her expression and she laughed. "OK, Mr. Bond. But it took me a little longer. So, I asked myself, in what interpretation of the facts did it make sense for minor members of a Baltimore gang to, A, want to kill me, and B, after your long, intricate, *improvised* detour on day one, even know where I was!" She paused, staring at me. " I kept asking myself, 'OK, it's weird that they wanted to kill me, but *how the hell did they know where I was?*'"

"And then I burnt your clothes..."

The waiter appeared at my elbow and gave me a peculiar look. He placed the oysters on the table, and the wine waiter brought us an ice-bucket with the bottle of Tio Pepe in it. He poured the wine and withdrew.

We were quiet for a minute while we each squeezed lemon onto the fresh mollusks, tipped them into our mouths and let them slide down our throats.

She smiled at me, sipped the wine and nodded. "I would

have had Bollinger. I was hoping I'd hate the sherry, but it's actually a perfect choice."

I didn't answer.

She ate another, sipped again. "Yeah, then you burned my clothes. And I began to think. Who was that close? Who was close enough to bug my clothes, my suitcase, my phone...?" She paused. "But not just that. There were a couple of people close enough. But who would then use minor Irish mobsters, instead of professional Omega hit men...?"

I interrupted her. "Were you having an affair with Major Hawthorn?"

She looked genuinely scandalized. "No! Of course not!" She sighed, halfway through preparing another oyster. "Look, Lacklan. I know my behavior since this morning has been a bit..."

"Provocative?"

"Yes, I suppose that would be the word. But please don't get the wrong idea. I am a very loyal, faithful woman. You are a very unusual man, and this is a *very* unusual situation. But you can take it as gospel that I would not cheat on my husband—assuming I have one."

"He's a very lucky man."

"I used to think so. Now I am not so sure. The only person who could have got that close to me was my husband. And, despite the state I was in, it did not escape my notice that after you burned all my possessions, they lost track of us."

"But they did not lose track of Hawthorn and his men. So whoever bugged you, knew to keep tabs on him too."

"Exactly. So I had to think seriously about it." She

heaved a big sigh. "My husband is a criminal attorney. We met in college, and right back then he was a firebrand. He was very passionate about things like our ancient liberties, the constitution as a weapon against tyranny, human rights... It was what I loved about him. People would often give him a hard time because he would defend everyone and anyone, from a pickpocket to major drug dealers and the Mob. He defended Juan Alvarez..."

"Patrick Donnelly is your husband?"

"Yes."

"So he is Irish, not Scottish. McFarlane is your name, not his."

"I lied. I lied to protect him. At the time I thought you were some kind of crazy, homicidal maniac." She laughed. "I think I still do, on some level." Then the humor passed and she became serious. "I always believed he was a good man. The amount of work he has done pro bono over the years must run into hundreds of thousands of dollars, protecting the rights of those whom society has robbed. He didn't care if they were good or bad people. He always said that what he was fighting for was not his client, but his client's rights—a society where everyone, good or evil, was entitled to the impartiality of the rule of law."

We were quiet for a while, and as I squeezed lemon on the last of my oysters, I said, "A person's beliefs can change. Forty-eight hours ago you believed in your husband. What it does tell us is that, potentially, he had the right connections to send those thugs after you if Omega told him to..."

I hesitated.

She said, "Kill me?"

I nodded. "Yeah. If they told him to do that, he would have the connections to send those four thugs."

"Yes, he would. And I am quite sure he did."

"I'm sorry, Cyndi."

She shrugged. "If you play with fire, you get burned." She studied my face for a moment, then added, "You're thinking that I don't seem very upset."

"I'm not sure. Maybe."

She gave a small sigh. "The answer to that comes in two parts, Lacklan. The first is that in a strict, Presbyterian home like mine, you learn to hide and control your emotions."

I raised an eyebrow and smiled. "Unless you are being attacked by helicopters and gangs of armed men."

"We might make an exception there. Briefly. The other is that over the last forty-eight hours I have cried and screamed more than I have in my entire life. So, perhaps by normal standards I don't seem very upset, but by my Scottish, Presbyterian standards, I am disconsolate."

The waiter came and took our plates away. I refilled her glass and mine and we sat in silence, looking at each other and drinking. It was intimate, but there was no awkwardness about it. Eventually she asked me, "Is there a woman in your life? You and Marni...?"

"There is a woman, but it's not Marni."

She raised an eyebrow. "Does she know that?"

"No. Not yet."

"Not Marni..." She said it to herself. "Well, whoever she is, she's a lucky woman. I just hope she's tough."

TWELVE

It was a bright, sunny morning. There was a brisk breeze out of the southeast and enough of a swell to send the occasional shower of spray across the bow. At half past nine that morning we'd told the concierge we were going to be sailing along the coast for a couple of days, and strolled off to collect the yacht. It was a Little Harbor centerboard sloop, and was making a nice six knots tacking into the wind. Once you have tasted it, there are few feelings as satisfying as sailing. For some reason, it's about as close as you can get to feeling free.

I was at the helm, with the mainsail close hauled, casting a shadow over the cockpit. It wasn't warm, maybe a pleasant sixty-eight Fahrenheit, made fresh by the breeze. Cyndi was sitting in the cockpit, looking out at the immense sweep of the sea, drinking coffee from a tin mug. The wind was enough to make her raise her voice when she spoke to me.

"How far is it?"

She slid closer to me to hear my reply.

"Hundred and fifty miles, give or take. We'll be there for breakfast tomorrow."

"What is it, an island?"

I shook my head. "As far as I can see, it's open water. They'll be there in a boat."

"Why would they choose a place like that?"

I smiled. "Because it's inconvenient, you can see for miles around if anybody is approaching, and water makes it very difficult to eavesdrop. It interferes with electronic listening devices. So it's the ideal place to have this kind of meeting."

She gave her head a small twitch, then gazed out at the sea again. "Good to know. What do they want from me, Lacklan?"

"What do you want from them?"

She shrugged. "An ally I can trust." She turned her head to look at me with meaning. "Someone to join forces with against this corruption."

"Then I guess that's what they want from you, too. Gibbons is passionate and committed. As long as you are fighting his fight, he'll stand by you. Marni is good and honest. They'll be good friends to you if you play straight with them."

"You were in love with her."

"I probably still am. I probably always will be."

"So she broke up with you?" She was frowning.

"No. But her work, her war against Omega, that takes up the whole of her life. There is no room for anything else."

"That's sad. Are you bitter?"

I had once asked myself the same question. After a moment, I nodded. "Yeah, I'm bitter. But I haven't quite lost my humanity yet."

“That’s why you want to get out of the fight.”

“So as not to lose my humanity?” I thought about it. I thought about Abi, Sean and Primrose, Kenny and Rosalia. I thought about Independence, and my house in Weston, and I wondered what made those things increasingly important to me. Were they as close as I could get to roots? Roots that could tap into my humanity?

“Maybe you’re right,” I said at last. “You and Marni, and Gibbons, are trying to save humanity. I’m just trying to save my own humanity.”

At midday she made us hotdogs and we cracked some cold beers. We sailed through the afternoon, driving ever south of east. Evening fell and the sun set behind us, putting fire in the sky and spilling blood on the sea, until both were quenched and absorbed by the dark blue of night. Then the moon rose ahead of us, waning now, but still huge and bright, casting an eerie, almost green light over the ocean. And about her, an absurd number of stars pierced the sky.

At one in the morning Cyndi went below to sleep. At two she came out again with a bundle of blankets, and settled herself on the floor of the cockpit so she could lie and look at the stars. I gazed up at the stars with her for a while, and when I looked at her again, she was asleep.

The sun rose at seven thirty, the wind picked up and so did the swell. Soon afterwards Cyndi awoke, stretched and staggered below again with her bedding. At eight she came out with coffee and a plastic bag of stale croissants. We didn’t talk. I ate and drank and scanned the horizon.

At half past eight I spotted a large, white schooner dead ahead. I estimated her at about one hundred feet, she was Bermuda rigged and lying at anchor. Fifteen minutes later we were close enough to see two figures on deck, watching us. One was a rotund man in white pants and a blue blazer, watching us through a telescope – there was no question, he was obviously Gibbons—and the other was Marni: slight, in jeans and a sweatshirt. The schooner's name was written in large, gold letters along the prow: the Magna Carta. As we drew closer, Marni waved and I waved back. Gibbons closed his telescope and walked away to the cabin. After that, Cyndi helped me lower the sails, and we used the engine to come within ten yards.

There we dropped anchor, launched the dinghy and I rowed us across to where Gibbons had lowered a retractable ladder. I made us fast, Cyndi climbed aboard and I followed.

To say the meeting was awkward would be like saying Mount Everest was substantial, or that Genghis Khan was naughty. The four of us stood on the deck looking at each other for four of the longest seconds I have ever lived through—and I've lived through some very long seconds. Finally, Gibbons held out his hand to Cyndi and said, "Senator, it is very good of you to come and see us in these, somewhat unorthodox, circumstances."

She shook his hand and slipped seamlessly into the role of politician. "Professor." She smiled at Marni. "And you must be Doctor Gilbert. It is an honor to meet you both in person at last. I was at your ill-fated conference, you know..."

I looked at her in surprise.

"Yes, Lacklan. I hadn't told you, but I already owed you my life, even before this trip."

Marni reached out and shook her hand. "Senator, thank you so much for meeting us." Then she looked at me, but didn't hold my eye. "Hello, Lacklan."

I nodded. I felt a sudden twist of hot anger in my gut and said, "Are we done? I need to be getting back."

I saw her cheeks color and her eyes went bright. "Well, actually, we hoped you would stay and be a part of this discussion. We have a lot to talk about."

I sighed. "Have we?" I labored the question, then added, "There is somewhere I need to be."

She frowned. "Where?"

"I have a lot to talk to you about, but you're busy, so it can wait until you have time, Marni."

Gibbons interrupted. "Lacklan." He thrust out his hand. "I, um... Thank you for helping us out here. Very good of you. Um... Given that you want to talk to Marni, and we want to talk to you, can't we prevail upon you to stay for luncheon? Then we can sort out the arrangements for getting the senator home and all the rest of it."

I hesitated, then nodded. "Sure, OK."

"Excellent. Good. Well, may we offer you some coffee inside?"

It was a large, rectangular cabin above deck. Inside it was spacious, with parquet floors, Persian rugs and potted ferns. It was divided in two parts. At the far end, separated by a wooden screen, there was a dining table that seated six comfortably. At the near end there was a lounge, with leather armchairs, a couple of sofas and mahogany coffee tables with what looked like genuine art deco lamps. There was also an antique dresser and a couple of bookcases. A small chandelier hung from the ceiling. Cyndi took one armchair and I took the other. Gibbons and Marni sat on the sofa. I looked at Gibbons and he cleared his throat.

"Coffee is on its way. Albert is making it as we speak. I suggest we get straight down to business."

He glanced at me.

I said, "I'd be grateful."

"Senator, I imagine that Lacklan has told you something of what we know about Omega."

"Something, yes."

"Then it will come as no surprise that we are committed to doing everything we can to stop them."

Cyndi raised a hand, as though she were flagging down a vehicle, and smiled. "Forgive me, Professor. Let *me* stop *you* there for a moment. Who exactly is 'we'? Who are you talking about here? You and Dr. Gilbert? More people? Are you an organization…?"

He sucked his teeth for a moment. "That is a good question. May we, for now, say that it is Marni and myself?"

"No. I'm sorry. I don't buy that. And if we can't have a level playing field with full, mutual disclosure, then I don't see how we can get past this point."

I smiled to myself and saw Marni watching me.

Gibbons said, "Yes, well, I suppose that's fair enough. We are not an organization—not as such."

"What does that mean?"

"We haven't got a name, or a charter, or any kind of constitution. You can't become a member, or, for that matter, be expelled. We are simply a gathering of like-minded people, from all around the world, galvanized, if you like, by our concern for where the world is headed. Are you familiar with J. B. Priestley?"

"Of course."

"The Shapes of Sleep? The Anti-Ants?"

She shook her head. "Sorry. I mostly read reports from committees these days."

"Well, never mind, our purpose is to fight to ensure the freedom of humanity, knowing of course that such a thing is a practical impossibility, but understanding also that what counts is not the victory, but the fight. So we are, if you like, a loose alliance of kindred spirits with a common aim."

Cyndi remained expressionless. "I think I could have guessed that much, Professor. And, with the greatest respect in the world, phrases like 'fight to ensure the freedom of humanity' are so vague as to be pretty much meaningless. What exactly does 'fight' mean, for example? Campaign? Lobby? Terrorism? And what does 'freedom' mean? Freedom from what? Can we get a bit more concrete?"

He glanced at Marni. She rose, went to the credenza against the far wall and came back with two slim, manila folders. She handed one to Cyndi and the other to me. "These are," she said, "What you might call, for want of a better word, our members."

It contained two A4 pieces of paper with a list of about a hundred and something names, including Gilbert's and Marni's. I noticed mine was absent. Some of the other names were surprising. I raised my eyebrows and looked at Gibbons. I said, "Seriously? This guy owns oil wells. His family are major shareholders in the military industrial complex. He's one of your not-exactly-members?"

A spasm of irritation crossed his face. "Conforming to some subjective, idealistic notion of 'good' is not a requirement for membership of this fraternity, Lacklan. A commitment to the ideal of freedom is."

"Laissez-faire is a kind of freedom," I said, but everybody ignored me.

Cyndi was studying the list with real interest. She held it up and frowned at Gibbons. "Can you back this up? I find some of these names quite surprising. There are at least two banking moguls. These people have a lot to gain from the current state of affairs, and lot to lose if things change."

He nodded. "Oh yes, I can back it up. And I hope that we can meet in Oxford and D.C. so that I can do just that by introducing you to some of these people. Nobody was more surprised than I when, after I started my campaign, thirty years ago, these people started to approach me; first one and then another, with visions and ideas about how the world could be a genuinely better place. This group has evolved quite naturally and organically."

She looked skeptical. "These people rub shoulders with the Omega top brass every day."

Marni smiled. "So do you. And you, as a U.S. Senator, stand to lose every bit as much as those people on that list, if Omega fails."

We heard feet tramping up wooden stairs, and after a moment a man in his thirties, in a white coat, approached us with a silver tray of coffee. He set it down on the table and withdrew. Marni started to pour. Gibbons said, "Senator, Cyndi, if I may..."

"Of course, Philip."

"I make little more than two hundred thousand dollars a year." He gestured around him at the yacht. "This is not mine. I cannot afford this. I could never sustain this constant battle against Omega. I am only able to do it with the logistical and financial support of those people on that list. We share a lot with Omega. We agree on the problem, and we agree on many aspects of the solution. Only one major thing separates us. They aim to control, we aim to be as free as is possible."

Cyndi gave a small snort. "There is that word again. Control I understand, but freedom?"

He took a cup from Marni and sat back. He smiled and I was surprised to see that it was actually a pleasant, humorous expression.

"It is really the most appalling arrogance on our part, to assume, as so many of us do, that only *we* are truly good people. It is a kind of blindness. Yet if you look at history, despite the awesome power of our leaders, who have always sought control, century after century, the history of the West has been the constant pursuit of freedom, in the form of democracy, social justice and spiritual growth. I am not naïve, Cyndi. If anything I am a cynic. But there is no getting away from that fact. And it is also true that most of the prime movers towards social growth and spiritual enlightenment have been rich and powerful men." He gave a little laugh. "Even Buddha was a prince!"

Cyndi raised an eyebrow and scanned the list again, then dropped it on the table. "OK, let's move on, but with the caveat that I will need proof of these people's allegiance to your cause. What does 'fight' mean, and what do you want from me?"

He sipped his coffee carefully, as though sipping it carelessly might scare Cyndi off. He then studied it while he licked his lips.

"We want quite a lot, as it happens. We want you to join

us and work with us. To be more concrete, we would like you to present a bill to Congress…"

"What kind of bill?"

"An education bill, as a matter of fact, proposing some pretty radical reforms in the education system."

She was frowning hard by now. "What kind of reforms?"

"I'll give you a draft of the bill in a moment so that you can study it at your leisure and suggest any changes you think appropriate. But in essence, you will be proposing the exact opposite of what Omega is trying to achieve. Their goal is to control people's behavior by controlling their minds. Your bill will propose practical ways in which children can be taught to think."

She laughed out loud. Marni smiled at her. It wasn't a hostile smile. Cyndi said, "Well, in principle I like the idea. Let me read the bill and we'll talk some more."

"Good. In fact we will want you to present a number of bills over the next few years, all with roughly the same aim, to safeguard people's minds. An important one, a couple of years down the line from now, will be to curb the use of subliminal suggestion in advertising and campaigning. But we are not there yet."

"Professor—Philip—presenting a bill is one thing. Getting it through Congress, intact, is quite another."

He nodded. "Oh yes, I know that. But you will receive support from some surprising quarters, believe me. And that brings me to two more things that we want from you. A list, to be updated regularly, of congressmen and women, and lobbyists, whom you feel might be sympathetic to our cause; or, conversely, members of Omega."

She snorted. "I can do that, no problem." She made a face. "Actual members of Omega may be more difficult, but I can hazard a guess. There is something I don't understand, though. If you already have people in Congress, what do you need me for?"

He gave a fat, complacent smile, drained his cup and set it down. "Aside from the fact that you can never have too many allies, you are young, attractive and very eloquent and articulate. You are also highly intelligent and you have integrity. We have friends in a position to check, and they confirm that."

"Thank you, but I am not actually unique in these qualities. There are actually quite a lot of decent, intelligent people in Congress."

"But you *are* unique in the fact that you bring them all together in such a way as to make you a perfect candidate for high office. In eight years' time, we would like you to run for president."

She froze, put down her cup, sat back and looked around the lounge as though she were following an invisible fly.

Gibbons watched her. After a moment he said, "We have the financial clout to make it happen, Cyndi. We have people who will rally to your banner and support you."

"That is a hell of a thing to land on somebody out of the blue, Professor."

"There are just two things that you need to do."

"What two things?"

"Work closely with us over the next eight years to build a reputation as a grounded, pragmatic American patriot, who at the same time is visionary and idealistic. Bridge the

Republican-Democrat divide. Personally I think you could be one of the great American presidents."

She raised an eyebrow. "And the other?"

"Keep your nose clean. Resist the temptation to give in to any kind of corruption. Power corrupts, and Omega will go all out to present you with huge temptations; power you have never dreamed of. If you yield to them, they will own you. We need you to stay free, focused and true to your ideals."

She looked at me and I knew what she was thinking.

I turned to Gibbons. "There may be an issue with Cyndi's husband."

He didn't look surprised. "Patrick." He said it as a statement, not a question. "Yes, great people who are married to their causes often lose sight of the fact that those closest to them can become a liability."

He raised an eyebrow at Marni. I saw her cheeks color and she looked down at her hands. He turned back to the senator.

"That is why it is very unwise for people like you, Cyndi, and me and Marni, to get married." He turned to face me. His expression was blunt, but not unsympathetic. "Please don't take offense, Lacklan. I don't think anyone here, including yourself, is under any illusion about what kind of a man you are."

"Thanks. I noticed I wasn't on your list."

He ignored the comment and plowed on. "And it is for that reason that I want to ask you if you will help us with a very particular job which is, I think, admirably suited to your talents."

It hadn't escaped me that he had also ignored the issue of Cyndi's husband. I asked, "What job?"

"We intend to make a very public denouncement of Omega in the near future. We aim to expose them and prove their existence. How exactly we aim to do it is not relevant right now. What is relevant is that we will need proof, irrefutable proof, of their existence, of their plans and of their methods. We want you to get it for us."

I stared at Marni. She wouldn't meet my eye. I looked back at Gibbons and labored the irony in my voice. "You want *me* to get the proof… *for you*…"

He was unabashed. "Yes."

I gave a small laugh. "How?"

"Just a minute." It was Cyndi. "I am actually not all that clear about what their plans are."

He held up two fingers, and for a moment looked like Winston Churchill making the victory sign. "In general terms they have two objectives. One, to allow and even encourage a catastrophic event that will decimate the world's population. And, second, to use any means, including psychology, neurology, chemistry and information technology, to reduce humanity to a state of passive, un-aggressive, unquestioning compliance, so that they can emerge from that catastrophic event as the only major power on the planet."

"That sounds like science fiction."

"It is science, Cyndi, but not fiction." He turned to me, gesturing at Cyndi. "And Cyndi's reaction to what I have just said is exactly why we need proof; hard, irrefutable proof!"

"How am I supposed to get that?"

"You remember the Richard John Erickson Institute, near Maplecrest, in New York?"

"I'm not likely to forget it."

"We want you to go back."

THIRTEEN

I SHOOK MY HEAD. "NO."

He nodded, not agreeing with me, but confirming to himself that this was the reaction he had expected from me.

"Cyndi and I have a great deal to talk about before luncheon. And I believe you and Marni have things to discuss, too. May I suggest that you have some refreshment out on deck? You can settle your matters and she can fill you in on exactly what we are asking. We are, of course, in a position to remunerate you appropriately."

"I don't want your money, Gilbert. I am not your employee."

He looked at his watch. "It is now ten thirty. Shall we reconvene for an aperitif at, say, twelve?"

I stood and walked out onto the deck. Marni came after me. I rested my ass on the gunwale, crossed my arms and looked across the narrow stretch of water at my boat. Right then, all I wanted was to get on it and go home.

Home.

There was a small table with a couple of chairs. Marni sat in one of them, leaned her elbows on the table and studied her thumbs. After a moment she said, "I'm sorry about Philip. You know what he's like."

"You don't need to apologize for Philip. He's old enough to do that for himself."

She didn't look up. "Meaning I should just apologize for myself?"

I shrugged. "You don't have to apologize, Marni." I gave my head a small shake. "The fact that we discussed getting married, the fact that you know I have loved you since we were children, the fact that we lived together for six months and you shared my bed, and we discussed having children, the fact that when I took you to San Francisco airport you told me you would be in touch..." I paused, fighting to slow and control my breathing. "The fact that when you did, finally, contact me it was to give me *instructions*... All of that might merit an explanation, but I don't honestly expect an apology, not when you are clearly a great person, and all I am is a barbaric employee."

She wouldn't meet my eye. "I am sorry, Lacklan. I really am. I just didn't know how to tell you, or what to say."

"Did you meet somebody?"

Now she looked at me, frowning, surprised, shaking her head. "No! Of course not! If it was going to be anybody, it would be you. I love you, Lacklan." She shrugged and looked out at the vast blue. "But it's not going to be anybody. I have to do this, for my father, for humanity..."

I sighed. "Well, that is the mission you and Gibbons have set yourselves, and you both decided a long time ago that I was not great, unique or special enough to be a part of it." A twist of anger still burned in my gut. "Even though I've caused Omega more damage than all your fraternity put together, and you'd both be in your damned graves today if it hadn't been for me and my barbaric, unseemly ways."

"I *said* I was sorry."

"Yeah. I'm sorry too. I'm going to go now."

"Please wait. I really do need your help."

"Marni..." I hesitated a moment, then said it. "You didn't meet anyone. You are a great person and you're married to your cause. I'm not a great person. I'm just an average person. I'm not married to any cause, and I did meet someone." She stared at me without expression, but her eyes were bright with tears. "I want a home, Marni. I want somebody I can give myself to, somebody I can fight for and be loyal to. You are all that, but I also want somebody who will be there for me, that I can turn to, rely on and trust. And you are not all of that. You are not any of that. You made your choice, and I knew when you went through the security gates at the airport in San Francisco, that you were leaving me." I shrugged. "I moved on. And isn't it just symptomatic that I had no way to contact you, or tell you?"

Her bottom lip curled in. Tears spilled from her eyes, but she didn't make a sound. Eventually she wiped her eyes on her sleeve and said, "First my dad, then your dad, and now you. Every man I trust ends up abandoning me."

I shook my head. "No, Marni. You don't get to do that. I *never* abandoned you. Never, not once. You weren't there to be abandoned. You never forgave me for London, and you never let me back in.[1]"

---

1. See *Dawn of the Hunter*

I waited for a reply. She didn't say anything so I stood and walked to the retractable ladder down to the dinghy. "Goodbye, Marni."

"Lacklan."

I stopped. "What?"

"We need you."

"Not you anymore. Now it's the Great People's Club who need me. But not as a member, just as an employee to be adequately remunerated."

"Please stop, Lacklan. I never said any of those things. Stop putting Philip's words in my mouth. The only thing I am guilty of is being a coward and not contacting you when I should have." She sighed. "You're so... *intense!* Everything is either peace or war, heaven or hell. I was scared to tell you how I felt."

I closed my eyes and sighed. I couldn't argue with what she was saying. I exhausted myself sometimes, what must it be like for somebody like Marni? I said, "I'm sorry."

She half smiled and wiped her eyes on her sleeve again. "Well, now we are both sorry."

I nodded, then shook my head. "But, I have made up my mind. I have a home now, Marni, and I am going back there."

"Don't make me beg, Lacklan. I will if I have to." She spoke through her tears, with her lower lip quivering. "They can't be allowed to continue. They have to be stopped. You know what they are doing to people. You can't walk away, Lacklan. That is not who you are. I don't want... I *can't* believe that you will do that. Just do this one thing for me, and I will never ask you for anything else ever again. Go to your woman with my blessing. If you love her, she must be a great person, and you deserve a good woman. But please, I beg of you, do this one, last thing. Please."

I took a deep breath, intending to say no, but somehow, instead, I sat at the table and said, "What does it involve?"

She took a deep, shaky breath. "We killed the director, you remember."

"It's another thing I am not going to forget."

She searched my face for a moment, then went on. "They appointed a new director, Theodore Ogden. He is a Harvard neurologist, a psychoanalyst and a Master of Neuro-Linguistic Programming. He is also a ruthless, soulless sadist and a son of a bitch. They have students there, on various programs. The lower level students have no idea what is going on there. But the ones with promise are approached to see if they want to be inducted into deeper programs. Higher level students range from having some idea that something is going on, to being fully-fledged members of the program."

"You keep talking about the 'program.' What program? Not Omega, surely?"

"No, of course not." She sighed. "It is very complicated to explain, but Omega have a whole range—hundreds—of programs all over the world designed to draw promising candidates in. They cover every kind of discipline, medicine, law, politics, and psychology and neurology. More besides. But psychology and neurology are the ones that most concern us, because they are the ones that involve control of thought, emotion and behavior. And the main center for research in that subject has become the Institute."

I shook my head. "But what do you think I can do?

You've said it, Cyndi said it, Gibbons has said it repeatedly. I am a barbarian. All I know how to do is kill."

She sighed. She was quiet for a while. "Actually, Lacklan, I don't think I ever said that, and if I did, I was wrong. We need you to get inside the institute, get photographic, video and documentary evidence of what is going on there, and leave without being detected."

"That's a tall order."

"Yes..." She spread her hands. "That's why I told Philip we needed you for the job. You have the necessary skill."

"I disagree. You need someone undercover, to join one of the courses, work their way in and gather intel."

She nodded but made it look exasperated. "Obviously! And we considered that option, but it would take too long." She hesitated. "We believe there are experiments being conducted, on people. They have labs. We don't know precisely what goes on there, but we are pretty sure it has to do with what they call their 'Compliance Program'."

"The mind control."

She nodded, then made a 'so-so' face. "The term is simplistic. Even today we don't really understand how the brain works, but we do know that the brain's functions are governed to a great extent by neurotransmitters. Get the balance right, and you can achieve a state of compliant obedience. The point is, levels of neurotransmitters can be altered artificially, for want of a better word, by introducing chemicals into the body, or by inducing the brain to alter the levels itself."

I frowned. "How would you do that?"

She shrugged. "There are many ways, meditation, hypnosis, even listening to music, just going for a walk, or having a talk with a good friend can cause a slight alteration. The levels of neurotransmitters are in constant fluctuation. That's why our moods change. But deep, radical changes need to be induced in some powerful way."

"And you think that's what they are experimenting with. It's the Sun Beetles all over again."

"It's an extension of the same program, yes. But I think they're taking it to another level." She gave a small laugh, but it was a grim, unhappy sound. "We have left science fiction far behind, Lacklan. The research that is being conducted today, behind closed doors, in artificial intelligence, in mechanical-cerebral interface, is beyond what you could imagine. Science fiction can't keep up with what the nerds and the geeks are dreaming up, and all of it is being funded by multi-billion dollar corporations that have a vested interest in the technology of compliance."

I puffed out my cheeks and blew. My mind wandered away from the ugliness she was discussing. I thought of spring in Independence. The snow would be almost melted. The blossoms and the first tender leaves would be in bud on the trees. Abi would be wondering where I was, what I was doing.

"I need to call Abi..."

"Abi? Is that her name?"

"Yes."

"You know that's not wise. You could put her at risk."

"This is the last job I am doing for you, Marni. When it's finished I am going home. I need to make sure I have a home to go to."

She was quiet for a long time, looking down at her

hands. Eventually she raised her eyes to mine. "It could have been us."

I nodded. "It could have been. But now it's too late."

She didn't answer.

I spread my hands. "So what happens now?"

She shrugged. "We give Philip the good news."

I stood and walked back into the cabin. Cyndi turned to look at me and they both watched me approach. I addressed Gibbons. "I'll do it. But it's the last job I do for you. After this, you leave me to get on with my life."

He raised an eyebrow. "You'll get no argument from me."

"I haven't slept since the night before last. I'm going to get four hours sleep. Then I'll sail back to Corpus Christi. You want to brief me on the job? How do you want to do this?"

He thought for a moment, chewing his lip. "Are you going back to Independence?"

I frowned. "How do you know about that?"

"Because we're professionals, Lacklan. Are you going back to Independence?"

"Yes, I'd like to. But it depends on the briefing, doesn't it?"

He looked away, staring at the window as though he was staring at his thoughts, projected there.

"We will deliver the senator to Washington. You rendezvous with us in New York in, say, a week."

I shook my head. "No."

"I beg your pardon?" He gave me a look I figured he used a lot with impertinent staff.

"You can rendezvous with me at my house in Weston. I'll be there within a week. I'll prepare the job from there."

He sighed. "Very well. I suppose it's pointless to argue."

"Yes." I caught Cyndi's smile. I smiled back. "Goodbye, Cyndi. It's been fun."

"I hope we meet again before long, Lacklan. But no more road trips."

I nodded. "No more road trips."

Marni was waiting for me on deck. She took hold of my hands and frowned into my face, like I was an equation that had given her the wrong result.

"Lacklan." She tried a couple of times to go on, but couldn't seem to find the words. Finally she said, "I don't know how we got here from Wyoming. It all seemed so perfect."

"Are you looking for a way back? Or are you just looking for a way to feel OK about where we've arrived? We wound up here after Wyoming because you left. You went to Oxford and stayed there, and you didn't want to call. It's that simple, Marni. You left." I bent and gave her a kiss on the cheek. "Goodbye. Stay safe."

I HAD CALLED Abi from the Corpus Christi airport on a disposable cell. It rang for a while but finally she answered.

"Abi, it's me. I'm on my way back."

"Lacklan! I've been so worried! Are you OK? You're on your way? Where are you?"

I smiled so she could hear it in my voice. "I'll be in Reno

in about three and a half hours. I figure you can make it in two."

"Reno?"

"I chartered an air taxi."

"You did *what?*" She laughed out loud. "Did they pay you? Did you win the lottery?"

"Yeah, in a sense. Abi, there's a lot you don't know about me. I want to start changing that. I want you to know who I am. Everything."

"Wow. You make it sound serious."

"It is serious. I am serious. Abi, I'd like you to pack an overnight bag. I want you to come with me."

"Come with you? Where...?"

"To Boston. I want to show you my..." I hesitated. "I want to show you my other home, and introduce you to my... To the closest thing I have to a family."

"Oh, my goodness."

I could hear the smile in her voice, but I asked anyway. "Is that OK?"

"Of course it is. I'm thrilled. It's just so unexpected."

We had talked some more. Then I had hung up and boarded the small Gulfstream, ordered a martini dry, and slept for the next three hours. We landed at Reno Tahoe International at three fifteen in the afternoon. She was waiting for me with her suitcase, looking a little bewildered but happy. We hugged and stood holding each other for a long time without speaking. It was a good feeling. Then we kissed for a long time too, as the people milled around us. If we were in the way, I didn't give a damn. Finally she held my face in her hands.

"What's going on, Lacklan? What's this all about?"

We found a coffee shop and sat at a small, plastic table with two plastic cups of what tasted like plastic coffee. I took a hold of her hand and looked into her face.

"The people I used to work with, they are good people and they are doing good work. They asked me to do one more job. They didn't know that I had decided to retire. So I told them that I would do it, but that this would be my last job."

She nodded, gave a small frown. After a moment, she said, "Good. I am glad to hear that, Lacklan. I know you can't tell me about it, so I won't ask, but I hope you stand by your word. I already lost one man I loved, I don't want to lose another."

"You have my word."

She smiled. "So, why are we going to Boston?"

I nodded slowly, then returned her smile. "When the job is finished, I want to ask you a favor. But before I do, I want you to see the house where I grew up, and meet what's left of my family. The people who stood in for my mother and my father."

"You're being very mysterious. What is this favor you want to ask me? Why can't you ask me now?"

"I can, and I will, but I don't want you to answer until we get there. Can you do that?"

She frowned. "OK..."

"Abi, I would like you to marry me, and make a home with me. Will you be my wife?"

FOURTEEN

We landed in Boston at seven thirty the next morning. I'd had Kenny leave the Zombie in the parking lot for me, and we took a leisurely drive up through Watertown and Waltham onto Boston Post Road, where the scenery changed from suburban New England to the insane abundance of the New England countryside in spring. She was quiet most of the way, tired and sleepy from a seven hour flight, but entranced by the spectacle of green around her, a million miles from Nevada.

"You grew up here?" She asked it not looking at me, but looking everywhere else.

I nodded. "Till I was nineteen."

"Where did you go? To college?"

Now she looked at me, and I could see the curiosity in her eyes. We had never discussed my past. I had never wanted to till now. "I went to stay with my mother, in England, and then I joined a British Regiment. The SAS."

We followed the Post Road into Weston, then turned

right onto Concord Road. It was a strange sensation. At one time I had never wanted to return. I was happy to leave Kenny and Rosalia caring for the place. But now, cruising slowly among the rich green woodlands and parkland, I did feel I was coming home. Something had changed, but it had changed in me. I smiled at her again. "Do you like it?"

"It's beautiful. You grew up out here? You were a country boy?" She smiled, as though she liked that idea. I didn't answer, and after a couple of minutes I slowed and pulled into the driveway of the house I had not seen since my father's funeral: his house, my inheritance. I stopped and killed the engine. She sat in silence, staring at the three-story pile of Georgian red brick and stucco.

"This is your *house?*" She turned to gaze at me.

I nodded.

"You told me you had money, but *this?*" The door opened and Kenny stepped out to wait for us. Abi started to laugh. "You have a *butler?*"

The next hour was taken up with introducing her to Kenny and Rosalia, which took a surprisingly long time, showing her around the house and the gardens, and getting through Rosalia's endless stories about all the mischief I used to get up to as a boy. At long last, at half past eleven, we finally sat in the conservatory and Kenny brought us coffee and freshly made croissants.

"May I say, madam," he said, with a complacent smile, "what a pleasure it is to have you both at home."

With that he left, taking his complacent smile with him, and we sat looking at each other. After a moment I said, "Abi, don't be afraid to be honest. This isn't everybody's scene. It certainly wasn't mine. I ran. I couldn't have got much farther from it if I'd gone to Mars."

Her eyes were bright and she burst out laughing. "Are you kidding me? Lady of the manor? A butler and a cook?" She spread her hands, taking in the conservatory, the lawns outside, the house. "All of this! I love it! It's like a fairy tale! And *I'm* the princess! Look what happened when I kissed the ugly toad!" She threw back her head and laughed out loud.

I smiled through a mouthful of croissant. "You'll be closer to Primrose, we can get a good school for Sean..."

"You don't need to sell it to me." She got up, came around the table, put her arms around my neck and kissed me. "Honey, you can go back to Independence if you want to. I'm staying right here!"

In the afternoon, after lunch, Abi phoned Primrose in Boston and arranged to go and see her and Sean the next day, and give them the news that we were moving to Weston. While she was talking to them I went into my study, which I still thought of as my father's study, and stood staring around me.

This had been, for years, the private office of Omega's third in command. Now it was mine, and I was going to use it to plan their destruction. I sat at the desk and called the number Gibbons had given me to contact him. He answered in his inimitable style.

"Where are you?"

"Hello, Gibbons. Where are *you?*"

"New York."

"I'm at home in Weston. Tomorrow I will be alone for

the day and most of the next day. That would be a good time for you to visit. Get here for about ten."

I gave him the address and he hung up.

Next day, Kenny drove Abi to Boston in my Dad's old Bentley, which gave her a kick, and at ten fifteen I watched Gibbons roll up through my study window, in a rented VW. Marni was not with him. He climbed out, dressed in his green Harris tweed jacket, and strutted up to the door with the air of busy self-importance that he always wore, whatever his clothes.

A few seconds later Kenny tapped on the door, opened it and Gibbons marched in. He dropped an attaché case on the floor beside one of the chesterfields by the fire and said, "I hope you know what you're doing."

I was standing with my back to the window, watching him. "That's kind of you. Will you have coffee? Tea? Something stronger?"

"No. Later perhaps. Let's get down to business."

"Thank you, Kenny. That's fine."

Kenny withdrew and Gibbons dropped into the chair. "Omega has left you alone since the UN because you've stayed off the radar, and they have had their hands very full. But returning to your father's house, bringing a wife here. You must be insane."

"Maybe I am, Gibbons. But it seems to me that if after this long absence, I return home with a wife, adopt a high profile and make it clear, with your help and Cyndi's, that I am breaking off my relations with you and Marni, the last thing they will expect me to do is raid their Richard John Erickson Institute."

He made a face that was doubtful. "There is that, but you are putting Abi at risk."

"She was already at risk. We both know that. If anything I can protect her better here."

He shrugged. "Well, it's your business. Now, about the institute. I have some equipment for you." He reached down and put the attaché case on his lap, flipped the catches and pulled out something that looked like a Velcro headband with a small lamp on the front. "This is a camera. It has a microphone attached and an ear piece so that we can stay in communication. When you switch it on, by touching this button here, it connects automatically with a dedicated laptop via a secure feed."

"How secure?"

"As secure as is possible in this day and age. Very secure."

"Who will be viewing it?"

"Me, a senior FBI agent, a District Attorney and a judge who shall remain anonymous."

"You're going to cramp my style. I may have to kill somebody."

He shook his head. "The idea is to get in and out without being detected. However, if the worst comes to the worst, you can always switch it off if you need to. But, I do want to stress, the object is to get in and out without leaving any trace of your having been there. It would also be very useful to have a constant, uninterrupted stream of data, so that there is no question of our having tampered with it."

"I hear you, but if I need to I will use lethal force."

He handed me the camera and pulled out what looked like a small cell phone. "In addition I want you to take this high resolution digital camera. It has a vast memory and will obviously take both photographs and video. It is very simple to use. You set it to your thumb print, switch it on by placing your thumb on the 'on' button..."

"I get it."

"So, what do I want you to photograph? The ground floor, what you would call the first floor, you are already familiar with. It houses only the dining room, the recreation room, a couple of classrooms, the pharmacy and the nurses' room."

"There is also the director's office."

"No, that's been moved upstairs to the first floor. What you Americans would call the second floor. I need you to break into that office and systematically go through all the papers you can find there. We are looking for anything, anything at all, that proves that they are conducting illegal experiments on behalf of Omega, or that corroborates evidence to that effect. Photograph the documents and get out without leaving a trace. The rest of that floor is taken up with classrooms. The next floor up, the top floor, is the director's residence and the dormitories for the live-in students..."

"Live-in students will be the students who have been inducted into the program. People who are complicit."

"We must assume so."

"And the director's quarters... So Ogden lives there."

"Yes. It is imperative you do not go to the upper floor. We do not under any circumstances want to raise the alarm."

"Is Ogden one of the Omega elite? Has he got a letter?"

"We believe he is the new Gamma. He takes over your father's position. My sources tell me he was appointed shortly after the UN fracas."

"So Ben finally gave up on me."

"It would seem so. Now, before you go to the office and photograph the documents, we want you to take the lift—that is the elevator—down to the basement..."

I shook my head. "Without even looking at it I can tell you that if they are conducting illegal experiments there, that floor will be locked. I'll need a special key to get down there."

He reached in his case and pulled out a weird-looking key with a bulbous head.

"Insert this, it will override the security system and take you down. We have no idea what you will find down there, but if past experience of Omega is anything to go by, they will be conducting advanced experiments in the manipulation of consciousness. Whatever you film or photograph down there will be of crucial importance. And once you have logged and recorded what is there, *then* you will go and look for documents in the office upstairs, to corroborate what you have filmed in the basement. Does that make sense?"

"Of course."

He nodded and sighed. "Lacklan, it is really of the utmost importance that you do *not* kill anyone, break anybody's bones or blow anything up. Just go in like a ninja, gather information, and leave without leaving a trace. Marni assures me you can do that."

"Yes, I can do that. Philip, tell me something, do you know who Alpha, Beta and the others are?"

He shook his head. "Only Alpha, Beta and Gamma know who Alpha and Beta are. Gamma is their mouthpiece. Some of the others are known, but not many."

"What about Cyndi's husband, Michael Donnelly? Is he in the club?"

He thought about it. "He might be. It is difficult information to get hold of. If you can find it there, that would be very useful. A comprehensive list of the 24 members of Omega could give us an edge. Who knows? We might be able to turn some of them."

I nodded. "OK, noted. Have you a particular day when you want me to go in?"

"No, not really. The sooner the better, obviously, and no later than the next seven days."

I thought for a moment. "I need a day to make some preparations, so I'll go in tomorrow night. Have you got a friendly pilot?"

He studied me a moment. He looked surprised. "Yes. You're going to drop in by parachute?"

"They've got about four hundred acres of wild land up there. Dropping in at night is the best way to avoid detection. What about the alarm system? You any intel on that?"

He nodded. "Right, we can help you a little bit here. This..." He pulled out a black metal box about the size of an A4 piece of paper, four inches deep. It had on it two buttons, one red, one green, and a folded antenna. "This is an EMP device. It is remarkably powerful. You raise the antenna, press the red button, and it will disable the alarm system, and all other electronics, in the whole building."

"That's useful."

"Indeed. However, it is obviously advisable to go in as late as possible, preferably in the small hours, when there is no risk of people using televisions or computers. Their sudden, collective failure could arouse suspicion. When you set it off, remember to keep your cameras protected. Once you are in, switch it off before putting on your camera."

"What about guards? They didn't have any when I was there last, but they may have corrected that error. If they have guards I'll have to take them out."

He gave a small laugh. "Believe it or not, there are no guards at the institute. We believe the material there is so sensitive that the guards themselves would pose a security risk. They rely exclusively on the alarm system and the secure lock in the lift—elevator. Plus the scientists themselves are on site, on the top floor."

I shook my head. "No, that's wrong, Gibbons. I don't believe that. This is their most valuable research, I have seriously damaged it twice, and I broke out of that facility. I don't buy that they have no security."

"That is the intelligence I have."

I thought about it a moment, then shook my head again. "Then you have flawed intelligence. Be prepared. I can get in there and I can probably get out with the material you want. But I guarantee you that at some point I am going to have to take out some guards."

He spread his hands. "So be it. Ideally you get in and out without being detected. But if you have to take out some guards, well, that is a good second best, as long as the intelligence, and the evidence, is intact."

"Good, understood. OK, now, what about your pilot?"

He stood, pulled his cell from his pocket and opened my French doors. He stepped outside, closed the doors behind him and made a call. I watched him walk up and down a few times, talking in his abrupt, peremptory manner, then hang up and step back inside.

"He'll meet you tomorrow night at one AM. There is a small airfield near here, Stow..."

"I know it."

"He'll meet you there. Apparently there is a café, Nancy's Café. Obviously at that time of night it will be closed. It is doubtful there will be anyone there at all. However, the airfield is operational twenty four hours a day, and he will meet you at the door of Nancy's Café, at one AM. I will not tell you his name, but you can call him John. If he speaks to you, he will call you Mr. Smith."

"How much will he know?"

"Nothing. Just his flight plan and that you will jump. I know him well and I trust him as much as I trust anybody."

We discussed a few more minor details and after half an hour he left, got in his car and drove away. When he'd gone I called Kenny, and after a few minutes he knocked and opened the door.

"Sir?"

"You have the key to the wine cellar?"

A cloud seemed to pass over his face. "Yes, sir, of course."

He took a bunch of keys from his pocket and selected one. He took it off the ring and handed it over. I took it and looked him in the eye.

"This is the last one, Kenny. After this, we lock the room and we don't open it again unless we are under direct threat."

"Very good, sir."

The door down to the wine cellar was in the hall. It was always unlocked. I went through and closed it behind me. The steps were granite and lit by a single fifty watt bulb. I followed them down to a stone-flagged room, probably forty to fifty feet across in both directions. Wine was one of those things my father loved, and there were many racks and several hundred bottles stored down there. There was also another door, a bullet-proof metal one, that required a key and a code punched into a pad to open it.

I slipped in the key, punched in the code, turned the key and the handle simultaneously, and the door swung open. It was the gun room. It was my gun room, and, according to my instructions, Kenny had kept it well stocked, with a lot more than guns. There was a cabinet with half a dozen assault rifles, another with a good selection of sniper rifles. There were small machine pistols, like the 9 mm Uzi, the Mauser C96 and the Pistolula *Dracula*, and others. There were also RPGs, a selection of bazookas and four ground to air rocket launchers. There were other weapons too, bows, crossbows, axes, knives and swords. It was a testament, a memorial, to a life devoted to killing.

Kenny had a table and a couple of chairs there. I could see from the cloths and the stains that he spent time down in that room, cleaning and oiling the weapons, keeping them in good working order for me.

I sat and looked around, thinking about what I would need. Gibbons wanted me to insert and extract without being detected, without killing anybody. He was dreaming. I knew that was going to be impossible and I wasn't even going to try. I was going to go in, I was going to collect all the evidence he needed and I was going to get the information that I wanted. Then I was going to kill everybody I had decided to kill; and after that, when I was done, I was going to come home.

Home.

FIFTEEN

The Cessna 182 was small and noisy. We had been flying southwest for almost an hour, and had left the lights of Springfield behind us about half an hour ago. The windows were dark. There was nothing to be seen, except for a ghostly half moon and a couple of flickering pinpricks of light in a formless ocean of black. According to the instruments we were over the Catskills, one and a half miles north of Black Dome Mountain. I felt a small, hot twist in my belly. We were coming up on the target.

Kenny had driven me to the airfield in the Zombie. I had put on a black ski mask in the car, and the pilot and I had exchanged no words. Now he pointed to the door. I slid it open. He looked at me and held one finger, two, a third, then he gave me the thumbs up. I jumped into the void, counted slowly to ten and pulled the cord. A jerk and a thud, and I was floating.

The darkness below was almost impenetrable. It was a bad night for an aerial insertion, but we didn't have the luxury of choice. My calculations had been minutely detailed, and theory had it I was descending toward a clearing in the forest, seven hundred yards east of the Institute. But when you're suspended in midair from a delicate piece of silk, in the darkness of night, theory is just that: theory.

Slowly, as I descended, the ground beneath me began to take shape by the tenuous light of the moon. I was slightly due south of the clearing, dropping toward dense pinewoods. I adjusted my trajectory and descended easily into the broad, grassy clearing, as close to the tree line as I could get without impaling myself.

I gathered up the chute, ran into the forest and buried it in a shallow hole, beneath leaves and pine needles. I then took two minutes to fit my night vision goggles and check my equipment. I had my Sig Sauer p226, but I had also brought a Maxim 9, because it has a built-in suppressor, it's quiet and fits snugly into a holster. I also had the new HK 433, four flashbangs, my knife and three pounds of C4 with a selection of detonators; because you never know when you're going to need to blow something up. I smiled briefly at the thought of Gibbons's face if he could see me now.

I'm not a ninja. I'm a barbarian.

I moved quickly through the forest and soon came to the edge of the woods. There I lay flat on my belly and scanned the area. I could see the institute up ahead, thirty yards away: an ugly, concrete, rectangular dog-leg, slightly luminous in the failing moonlight, with three rows of dead, black windows. There was a tree-lined drive up to a large porch that led away to the main road, about a mile distant.

The first sign I had that I was right and things were

wrong was when my suspicions were confirmed and a figure came out from behind the building, walking at a steady pace, carrying an automatic rifle. Gibbons had received bad information, as I had suspected from the start. There were guards. Which meant Omega had some idea at least, either that we were coming, or we might be planning to come. So I now had a completely unknown quantity to deal with: how much did they know? Did they know I was coming that night? Or were they just being careful? How many guards did they have? How many on the outside and how many on the inside?

They were all questions I needed answered if I was going to pull this off the way Gibbons wanted. They were also questions I had no way of answering. So Gibbons could go to hell.

I lay motionless for twenty minutes in the shadow of the trees. What I saw answered two of my questions. During those twenty minutes, two guards patrolled past, twice. Which meant that each side of the building was left unguarded for about five minutes at a time. That, in turn, meant that though they were being careful, they had not been alerted to the fact that somebody was coming that night—and they didn't know it was me. If they had known either of those two facts, the place would have been swarming with guards armed to their teeth.

I watched the guard disappear under the porch, headed for the far end of the building, and sprinted across the sward to the corner where I knew the next guard would appear in five minutes. There was no cover. He was going to see me before he died. So it had to be quick, precise and silent.

I counted off the seconds. Two hundred and fifty. He

came around the corner and found me on one knee. He needed three full seconds to process what he'd seen, but by the end of the first he was already dead. The Maxim 9 spat and at eight feet I put the round right through the center of his throat. It shattered the vertebrae in his neck and whatever his brain wanted his hands, feet or lungs to do, they never got the message. He did manage to frown. Then he folded. I pulled him out of sight and waited another five minutes for his pal. It was the same story.

I sprinted to the main entrance. At a distance of seven feet from the plate glass doors, I dropped and lay flat in the shadows, looking in. There was one, dim ceiling light burning. I knew there would be at least one guard. What I needed to find out was whether there was more than one, and, if so, what their rounds were.

After another twenty minutes I knew it was only one guy, and he did the rounds of the first floor every six minutes. I waited for him to pass and disappear down the passage toward the pharmacy, then I fired the EMP and killed the alarm system. Gibbons had believed I would then use some cunning ninja technique to open the door. I smiled, removed my night vision goggles, took the Maxim 9 and put a round through the lock. That was my ninja technique.

I brought the EMP inside, switched it off and sprinted toward the passage where the guard had disappeared. He was running back toward me. He'd heard the impact of the slug on the lock and was coming to see what it was. He burst into the lobby and took both rounds of a double tap, one in the mouth and the other in his throat. It was ugly but it was effective.

I was in no doubt by now that there would be heavily armed guards in the basement, protecting their experiments. I had to expect at least four of them, possibly more. I had only one form of ingress, the elevator, and the noise would give them advance warning of my arrival. I had a problem.

But it wasn't insoluble.

The elevator was on the first floor. I opened it and measured it. The entrance was four feet across. On either side of the door I had about thirty-six inches of space. It was enough. I stepped in, inserted the override key and turned. The doors slid closed. I knew by the time I got down they would be ranged across the entrance, seven to eight feet back, probably kneeling, with their weapons trained on the door. I took a flashbang, hunkered down against the left wall, below the panel of buttons, and waited for the elevator to come to a halt. It stopped and the doors started to hiss open. When I had a six-inch gap I tossed out the flashbang and flattened myself against the wall.

The detonation in the confined space was massive, but I was protected by the elevator. I stepped out, with the HK at my shoulder. There were six of them. They were too stunned to react and at eight feet it was impossible to miss. They were all headshots, but with their ears ringing, they didn't hear any of them.

So far the operation had gone smoothly, not according to Gibbons's wishes, but according to mine. But my gut told me it had gone too smoothly. My brain told me Ogden, the director, had been expecting something, but he didn't know precisely what. So he'd had guards, but the nature of the installation—ostensibly an educational establishment—had precluded the use of heavy, military style security. That made sense as far as it went, but it didn't satisfy my gut. My gut was still worried.

I took a couple of seconds to assimilate my surroundings. It was pretty much the same layout as the first floor. I was in a kind of lobby, maybe thirty feet square. On the right there was a passage with doors on either side. Behind me, running back from the elevator, there was another passage, also with doors facing each other. So the basement followed the same basic dog-leg pattern as the building above ground.

I pulled out the headband camera Gibbons had given me, switched it on, fit it to my forehead and inserted the earpiece. Immediately I heard Gibbons' voice.

"Where are you?"

"Basement. Don't talk."

"What is your status? Why are you delayed fitting the camera? Give me an update!"

I removed the earpiece and moved down the passage at the rear of the elevator, doing three steps backward and three forward. I was pretty sure I had taken out all the guards, but it pays to take nothing for granted. There were four doors, two on either side of the corridor, and they were all locked. So I left them and made my way to the other corridor. Here there were also only four doors, two on either side, widely spaced. They too were locked. I chose the far door on the left and blew out the latch with the Maxim 9.

I eased it open and flipped on the switch. There were no guards. There was a lot of electronic equipment. I wasn't familiar with any of it, except one long, metallic tube that looked to me like a CAT scanner. There were also screens that looked like computer terminals. I put the earpiece back in and spoke quietly. "Gibbons, when I say don't speak, don't speak."

"Will you kindly just try to follow instructions! Where are you now?"

"One of the labs in the basement."

I took the camera from my pocket and started filming, taking close ups of all the digital displays. I scanned the whole room. He asked me to close in on a couple of details, which I did.

Finally, I said, "You got everything you need here?"

"Yes. But Lacklan, I asked you to leave no trace. Couldn't you have picked the lock, for God's sake?"

"That ship sailed, Gibbons. There were guards outside, on the first floor and down here."

He sighed. "I suppose you killed them."

"No, I sang them lullabies and they went to sleep. Of course I killed them."

I crossed to the door opposite and gave the lock the same treatment. This room surprised me. There were four rows of eight desks all facing the far, right hand wall. It looked like a classroom, but instead of a blackboard, there was a gigantic TV screen, ten or twelve feet high, twenty feet across. Each desk had a screen incorporated, and a set of earphones.

"What the hell is this place, Gibbons?"

"It's a laboratory for manipulation of neurotransmitters via audiovisual stimulation. They probably also use it for the development of neural pathways."

I scanned the place and filmed it. Then I moved on to the next door. Here, there were thirty-two gurneys made up like beds. Each one was fixed up with a kind of rubber cap dotted with what looked to me, at a glance, like four or five hundred electrodes, each connected by a slim wire to a column set into the floor at the head of the gurney. Each column appeared then to be connected to a bank of computers that lined the far wall. I filmed the whole thing, and then Gibbons had me go over each of the computer terminals in minute detail.

I made my way finally to the fourth room. I blew the lock and pushed open the door, but when I flipped on the switch my stomach lurched. Here there were six gurneys, but they were not made up like beds. They were cold, bare steel. Four of them were against the wall on my right. The other two were at the center of the floor. The floor was tiled in white, and between the two gurneys there was a plug hole, like you might see in a shower, only bigger: more like an abattoir. On the gurneys there were two naked human bodies, one male, one female. The tops of their skulls had been taken off to expose their brains, one of which had had a slice removed.

There was an abundance of electronic equipment. Some of it was mounted on mobile trolleys, the rest was on benches. I asked Gibbons, "What is this stuff?"

I walked over to it and examined it closely. I heard his voice, "Mainly electronic microscopes by the look of it. The bench-mounted equipment is for examining slices of the brains post mortem. The mobile stuff must be for examining it pre-mortem or perimortem. I would love to get my hands on those hard drives."

"What the hell for?" I snarled.

"There is no way you could even begin to understand. Move on to the next room."

I left the lab and made my way to the other passage. I

had a nasty feeling about what I was going to find there. I took out the first lock and found what I expected to find. It gave access to one, long room with a second door at the far end. It was a dormitory. There were sixteen bunks, occupied by sixteen people, eight men and eight women of mixed races. They were all asleep, lying unnaturally flat on their backs. They mostly seemed to be aged between eighteen and twenty-five, though there were a couple who seemed older and a few who looked younger. They all seemed impervious to any noise that I made.

I filmed them and examined each one of them in detail. They had all been shaved, and many of them had scars on their heads from recent surgery. Several seemed to have had the top of their skulls removed. Gibbons sounded excited.

"There we have it! As I thought! There will be records relating to each of these subjects in the office upstairs. I am certain of it! You must find them, Lacklan. You understand?"

"I understand, Gibbons."

The door across the passage held no surprises either. It was another dormitory, but this one held young adolescents and children. I examined each one in turn, and each one had the same scars as the adults across the way. I could feel a hot, smoldering rage swelling in my gut.

I said, "Have you seen enough, Gibbons?"

"Yes, we've seen enough. Go up to the study now." He paused, then added, "Lacklan, given that you have killed the guards and shot out all the locks, it is now of the utmost importance that you find documentary evidence to support what you have shown us here."

"Yeah, that was what was worrying me, too, Gibbons."

I made no effort to hide the sarcasm, but he either didn't hear it or didn't care. At the elevator I stopped. "Gibbons, you have a judge, a Fed and a DA there. You have seen enough. Why don't you just send in the cavalry and seize all this stuff?"

He sighed. "Just trust that I have good reasons, Lacklan, and get me the documents."

I was about to step inside and go to the second floor, when a sixth sense made me stop and look back. There was a woman. She was standing in the middle of the passage in a white nightgown, staring at me, frowning.

After a moment she said, "Do you know where I am?"

I took a few steps closer to her. "What's your name?"

She blinked a couple of times. "I don't know where I am. I don't know..." She didn't seem able to finish the sentence. "Do you know?"

I took hold of her arm and led her back into the dorm. "You go back to bed. Get some sleep, and I'll be back for you, OK?"

I heard Gibbons' voice in my ear. "You will not. You get out of there when you're done and you leave things as they are, do you understand?"

She climbed back into the bed, lay down and closed her eyes. I made my way back to the elevators. The hot rage in my belly was turning wild. I smiled to myself. "Don't worry, Gibbons, I know exactly what you want. That's why you picked me for the job, right? Because you knew I was obedient and subtle. And above all, restrained."

"Lacklan...!"

I didn't hear the rest of it, because I had removed the earpiece again.

SIXTEEN

I STEPPED OUT OF THE CAR ON THE FIRST FLOOR, because an enclosed place, like an elevator, is a bad place when people are trying to kill you. I stepped into the lobby and ran up the steps, keeping my back to the wall and the HK trained on the stairs and the landings ahead of me. There was no one there.

The layout on the second floor was identical to the first and the basement. It was carpeted in beige, the walls and ceiling were cream and there were occasional steel-framed seats upholstered in blue. I found Ogden's office where his predecessor's office had been before, only one floor down. I blew out the lock and stepped inside.

There was a large, antique oak desk with a big, black leather chair behind it. Against the wall by the window there was a bank of filing cabinets. The top left drawer in the desk yielded to my knife and inside it I found the keys to the filing cabinets. I spent the next hour working methodically through the documents contained in them. Practically everything was useful, and the more I worked through the records of experiments, and correspondence relating to them, the more convinced I became that this was a stupid exercise. I had here several thousand documents that would prove, over and over again, what this institute was and what it was being used for, and there was no way in hell I was going to be able to photograph all of them. This stuff needed to be shipped out in bulk and examined by the County sheriff, the FBI and the world press. It was the only way.

Besides, there was one piece of information that was missing; and the more I thought about it, the more I realized it was the only one I was really interested in. I looked at my watch. It was just before four in the morning. I said, "I have a situation here. You'd better get a search warrant and storm this place. Do it now."

Gibbons sounded alarmed. "What are you talking about?"

"I'm getting some interference, Gibbons. Get that warrant. Do it."

I heard him say, "Wha...?"

I switched off the camera and put it and the earpiece in my rucksack. Then I took a couple of fistfuls of the most relevant documents and put them in too, along with the camera. I slung the backpack over my shoulder and went up to the top floor.

The layout here was, once again, similar to the lower floors, except that the corridor ahead of me was shorter, and ended in a door. Odds were good that that was Ogden's suite of rooms. The rest of it would be dorms for the scientists and students, and bathrooms.

I stood for a moment listening. There was absolute

silence. I thought about the best way to breach the door. I approached it and felt it. It was wood, not metal. There were only two other doors in the shortened passage. They were, as I had suspected, bathrooms. I pulled the Maxim from its holster and blew out the lock. It made a noise, but I was pretty sure it was not enough to rouse the dorms. It might rouse Ogden, but that was OK. I wanted him roused.

I pushed through and closed the door behind me. I was in a short corridor. It was dark. At the end I came out into a broad living room with a dining table set by a large window on the right, and a comfortable sitting area on the left, by some plate glass French doors onto a broad terrace. There was a sofa and a couple of armchairs set around a coffee table, some bookcases and a sideboard. Beside the sideboard there was a small workstation with a laptop and a printer. On the far wall there was three doors, one was open and I could see it was a small kitchen. The next I figured was a bathroom, and odds were that the one on the far left was the bedroom.

I took two steps toward it and the door opened. There was a man of about fifty in pajamas and a silk dressing gown. He looked confused, alarmed, scared.

"Who the hell are you? How did you get in here? What do you want?"

I showed him the gun and put my finger to my lips. Then I approached him, keeping the weapon trained on his chest. When I was six feet away I said, quietly, "Move or make a noise and I will shoot you in the belly. I know from experience that it is one of the most painful ways to die."

He raised his hands. "OK, just take it easy. I won't do anything. Just tell me, who are you? What do you want?"

"Get in the bedroom."

He hesitated, looked at the gun, turned and went into the room. The light was off. I switched it on and said, "Lie face down on the floor."

"Are you going to kill me?"

"Not if I don't have to. I want information. If you don't give it to me I will hurt you a lot. Lie down."

He lay on his belly and I took his shoe laces and tied his wrists behind his back. I pulled him to his feet and propelled him back out into the living room. There I pushed him into one of the armchairs, with his back to the entrance. I sat with my back to the French doors, where I could see him, and the entrance behind him.

I said, "You're Gamma."

He looked genuinely astonished. "What?"

"You replaced my father. The position was offered to me, I refused it. They kept it open till I blew the operation at the UN and killed Dr. Banks, your predecessor at this institute." I pulled the ski mask off. "I'm Lacklan Walker."

He stared at me for a long moment. "Jesus Christ."

I shook my head. "No, Lacklan Walker. He and I are very different. I don't turn the other cheek, and I sure as hell don't love mine enemy. I want just one thing from you, Ogden, and you and I both know that there is no point in your refusing to give it to me."

He was frowning, like he didn't know whether to be in awe or terror. "What?

"The list."

"List? What list?"

"The list of names, Ogden. Who is Alpha, who Beta... Who are the rest?"

He smiled, then laughed. "You have got to be joking. No way, never."

I frowned back, genuinely surprised at his response. "You do know who I am, Ogden? You know what I will do to you?"

He nodded. "I've heard about you. Alpha really likes and admires you. I thought—*we* thought—that you had pulled out after the UN disaster. He even discussed letting you live."

I nodded. "I plan to. This is my last job. If you don't die tonight, you can tell Alpha that. Now, Ogden, give me the list."

"No, I'm sorry, I can't do that."

I stared at him for a moment, nonplussed. I thought about the people in the dorm in the basement. I thought about the woman asking me if I knew where she was. I thought about the second dorm, with the children. I picked up a cushion from the sofa.

He started to say, "No, wait, what are you...?" but I smothered his face with the cushion before he could finish the sentence, and I blew off his left kneecap.

He screamed into the cushion, thrashing and jerking helplessly. I put away the Maxim and pulled my Sig. His scream ended in a sob and then he started to suffocate. I removed the cushion and, as he gasped for air, I shoved the muzzle of the Sig into his mouth. I said, "Shut up."

He was croaking as he struggled to breathe, and trembling badly. It was easy to see that he was not a man accustomed to pain or violence. I put my finger to my lips. He nodded. I said, "Have you got a better understanding of the situation now?"

I removed the Sig from his mouth so he could answer. He was still gasping for breath, holding his thigh and staring, goggling at the shattered bloody mess that, only a few seconds earlier, had been his knee.

"Ogden, look at me. Look at me and listen to me. You can still come out of this with just an attractive, interesting limp. But the next time you say no, or make any kind of negative statement, you lose both your legs from the knee down. That won't be attractive or interesting. It will be pathetic. I want you to think about that for a moment." I paused.

He stared into my face. He looked yellow and he was sweating profusely. He nodded.

I said, "You are going to give me the complete list of twenty-four names."

His face crumbled and he began to sob. I stood, took hold of the laptop on the workstation and carried it over to the coffee table. I opened it and switched it on. I said, "Password."

He stared at me, sobbing, hesitated and I pointed the Sig at his right knee. "No! No, wait, please, capital 'G' gamma, oh, eight, oh one, nineteen sixty eight."

I tapped it in and got through to the desktop. I opened Word and put it in front of him. "Write the list."

He stared at me. "How do you know I'm not going to lie?"

"I don't. But I already have one list, Ogden. The one my father gave me just before he died. If I compare them, and they are different, I will take you downstairs to your lab, extract your brain from your skull and shove it up your ass."

He was half-crying, shaking his head. "If you already have a list, what the hell do you want another one for?"

"Because I can't be sure that he was telling the truth, can I? But when I compare his list to yours, then I can be sure. Start writing, Ogden, I am running out of patience."

"For God's sake, Lacklan. The pain. I can't..."

I took aim at his right knee and he started typing, sobbing and grunting as he did so. When he had reached the end, I said, "Don't save it. Print and delete."

A moment later the printer hummed and spewed a sheet of A4. I got up, took it and examined it. I went cold from head to foot. It was so obvious: so obvious that I had missed it all this time. I heard myself whisper, "Holy shit..."

Ogden's head had flopped back. He had lost a lot of blood from his knee. It had saturated the chair and the rug under his feet. He looked feverish. I took the laptop from him, switched it off and stuffed it in the backpack. Then I shot him in the head, scratched his name off the list, folded the piece of paper and put it in my back pocket.

I pulled back the French doors and stepped out onto the terrace. The first traces of dawn were turning the eastern horizon gray, but the sky overhead was still a deep blue-black. I thought long and hard about what to do next. Then I saw the lights. There was a line of them. Three vehicles moving fast, maybe half a mile away or a little more, coming down the driveway toward the house.

I pulled the headband camera back out of the backpack, switched it on, fitted it in place again and inserted the earpiece. I went and looked down at Ogden. I heard Gibbons say, "*Jesus Christ, Lacklan! What have you done?*"

I said, "We can discuss that later, Gibbons, right now we

have a situation. There are three cars approaching down the driveway. They will be here in a matter of seconds. I am going to call the Sheriff's Department. I suggest you and your friend from the Bureau get off your asses and get here on the double, with a search warrant, because I have information you do not want our visitors to retrieve. Get here. Over and out."

I switched off the camera, put it back in the backpack and went out to the terrace again, to look over the parapet. Below there was a fringe of garden, with shrubs and bushes. They looked like bougainvillea. I swung the backpack over and dropped it into the nearest bush. Then I went back inside, made two quick phone calls, one to the sheriff, and put something in Ogden's pocket. After that I sat and waited for them to arrive.

It didn't take long. I heard the boots tramping up the stairs, voices shouting and then eight men with body armor and assault rifles burst in. They took a moment to assess the situation: Ogden lying in his chair with what was left of his head thrown back, gaping at the ceiling. Me sitting opposite him, with the HK433 across my knees, watching them.

They trained their weapons on me and waited.

Then two more men came in, these wearing suits. One of them I knew: Ben. For the first time in all the years that I had known him, I could see true rage in his eyes. He was fighting hard to conceal it, but it was a losing battle. He said simply, "You killed Gamma."

I nodded. "You told me once I couldn't hurt you, Ben. Do you remember that? You said the most we could do was cause you an annoyance. I'm curious. Do you still feel that way?"

He didn't answer. His eyes were bright. I knew he was struggling to make a rational decision about what to do next. He wanted to kill me. He wanted that very badly. But he knew that if I was sitting there, talking to him, it was for a reason. I had some kind of insurance policy.

I said, "Who's your friend?"

I was looking at the other guy. He was well-dressed, blond hair with a hint of copper. Blue eyes, a faint spray of freckles.

I smiled. "Let me guess. It's Michael Donnelly, champion of the underdog, fearless warrior, protector of our ancient liberties. Am I right?"

The guy frowned. Ben said, "Give me one reason why I shouldn't have you killed right now."

"There are quite a few to choose from, Ben. The first and most obvious is that you don't know what I have done with all the footage and photographs of your labs in the basement, the people you have been experimenting on and the documents you kept in the office downstairs, that corroborate the experiments."

He snapped, "Take him down to the basement! The operating theatre." Four of the guys in body armor advanced on me and dragged me to my feet. One of them snatched my weapons. There was no use resisting at that point, so I allowed myself to be shoved across the room. Meanwhile Ben was shouting at the other four men, "You two, get this damn place cleaned up! You and you, confine the students to their dorm, and get Dr. Patel! I want him down in the basement in ten minutes! Do it!"

We moved down the corridor while the two gorillas started the cleaning up job on Ogden. I had only used a quarter of a tablet, stuffed into his back pocket, but it was more than enough for the job. It was a simple detonator, set to be triggered when they lifted his body. It took out the room and killed the two men, which was two less for me to kill, but more than that, it gave me the opportunity I needed.

The detonation was loud, the explosion shook the top floor of the building. The four guys escorting me, Ben and the guy I guessed was Donnelly, all cowered and covered their heads with their arms. I didn't waste the opportunity. I spun and smashed my instep into my nearest guard's crotch. As he doubled up I took hold of his head in an arm lock and twisted savagely until I heard his neck snap. As he went down I took his sidearm and shot the other guy in the face. Then I vaulted the banisters and ran down the stairs, taking them four at a time. I scrambled into the elevator, turned the key and watched the doors slide closed as Ben and his remaining thugs came rattling down the stairs after me.

As I went down I tried to plan ahead. If I wedged the door open, they would not be able to recall the elevator. That meant they couldn't get to me, but it also meant I could not escape, and sooner rather than later, they'd override the safety mechanism, recall the elevator and come down in force—with body armor and automatic weapons. It was not an ideal situation. But as Sergeant Bradley was fond of saying back in the day, "It could be worse, lads! We could be fuckin' French!"

I stepped out, dragged one of the dead guards halfway into the car to obstruct the doors, and set to work. I had a lot to do.

SEVENTEEN

My first priority was the labs. I pulled all the mobile—and movable—scanners and pieces of IT hardware into the lab where the CAT scanner was and piled them on top of each other. Then I ran to the operating theater, pulled one of the unoccupied gurneys to the middle of the floor, locked the wheels and jumped up on it. I did some work on the ceiling, which I calculated to be beneath the dining room, jumped down, and pulled the two occupied trolleys into the corridor.

There I tipped them on their sides at an angle to the elevator doors, with one of the bodies laid in front. It wasn't as good as a barrage of sandbags, but it was something. I set up the other body behind the gurneys, apparently holding an automatic weapon. Again, it wasn't perfect, but it might fool them for a few crucial seconds. Then I collected up all the dead guards' automatic weapons and stashed them in the operating theater. Finally I dragged the bodies of the dead guards over and laid them in front of the elevator doors, so anyone attempting to exit in a hurry would have a difficult, unstable surface to walk or run on. That was going to be my primary killing field.

By the time I'd finished, fifteen minutes had passed, and there was nothing to do but wait. But I didn't have to wait long. Ten minutes later I heard the elevator winch kick in and the car began to rise. The body I'd laid across the entrance, to keep the doors open, slipped off and fell with an unpleasant thud onto the other corpses below. The doors stayed open.

I took up a position in the corridor, slightly to the rear of the elevators. I heard the winch stop. Then the tramp of feet entering the car on the next floor. I estimated four pairs of boots. That left two, plus Ben and Donnelly. The engine kicked in again and the car began to descend. I had a pretty good idea what they were going to do. I figured they were hunkered down with their weapons ready, and as the floor of the car descended below the ceiling, they would open fire and spray the area with bullets.

I wasn't wrong. They opened up in a hail of fire, and it didn't take them long to see the gurney barricade, and the body holding the automatic rifle. So the random spray became focused on that target. When they were three feet from the ground, I pulled the pin on the flashbang and dropped it on the bed of corpses, just outside the doors of the elevator. It detonated as the elevator stopped.

I heard shouts and screams. I stepped out and sprayed a burst into the car. I heard another scream, this one of real pain, and somebody shouted, "*Mother fucker!*" I jumped behind the gurney, let off two more bursts and backed into the corridor. I could hear one voice whimpering and swearing.

Then the charge came. Three guys piled out. I took one of them with a double tap to the head, but as his head exploded, the other two dropped to their knees and opened fire. I backed up along the corridor with bullets whining and spitting around my head. I emptied my magazine in a long, unfocused burst, felt a searing, burning feeling in my shoulder, and fell through the door into the operating theater. I was hit.

There was no time to think about the pain. I pulled the pin on another stun grenade and tossed it into the passage, then grabbed one of the guards' weapons. The grenade detonated. I leaned out and opened up with a short burst. There was nobody there. I heard the winch start up again and the elevator began to rise. I had taken out one, maybe two of them. There were four more upstairs, and I was hit. That was bad news. I was in trouble. My plan was not panning out and I had very few options.

I stepped across to the lab opposite, dropped to one knee in the doorway and lined up my sights on the corner where I knew one of them was waiting. I heard the elevator stop and boots tramp in. I was expecting two pairs, but there were four. They were all coming down. Logic dictated that as soon as the elevator stopped, the two guys down here would open fire into the corridor to cover the occupants of the car as they poured out. It was a standard beachhead operation. I had one chance, and one chance only.

The elevator stopped. I had two grenades left. I lobbed one at the elevator door and rolled the other toward the gurneys, where I knew the two guys were hiding behind the corner of the passage. I heard the shouts of, "*Stun grenade!*" a second before the explosions. I opened up with two controlled bursts but there was still nobody there.

Then two men rolled out of the elevator across the corpses, but before I could take aim the two who were waiting at the head of the passage leaned in and opened fire at me. I ducked in just in time, because next thing, all four of them were raining fire down the corridor. My rifles were in the other lab, across the passage, and my magazine was half empty. I was as screwed as the virgin at a pagan solstice.

The firing stopped. I had a half empty M16 and I was up against six men with automatic rifles, an unknown amount of ammunition and absolute tactical superiority.

I heard Ben's voice. He was close.

"Lacklan, I will not pretend that my love for your father carries any weight anymore. What loyalty I felt towards you on his behalf died when you betrayed my trust after the United Nations fiasco. I will be honest with you, as I always have been. I want you dead, more than I want anything else at this point."

I called out, "The feeling is mutual, Ben."

"However, we may have some room to negotiate."

I laughed out loud. "Really? I don't think you have anything I want anymore."

There was a moment's silence, then his voice, with a smile in it. "What about your life?"

I shrugged. "I can take it or leave it. And you know very well, Ben, that if I die today, I will make damn sure you come with me, all the way to hell."

"I have five men here who say that isn't going to happen, Lacklan. And three dozen more in the dorms upstairs who are prepared to back them up if needs be. You are, finally, out of options."

I was quiet for a bit, backed up against the wall, trying to think. I could see Sergeant Bradley in my mind's eye, with the firelight on his diabolical face, and the Afghan night behind him, saying, "You're never out of options. All you ever run out of is imagination."

That I had run out of, too. I called out, "OK, Ben, what have I got that you will exchange for my life?"

I heard the shuffle of boots moving down the passage, then Ben's voice again, a little closer this time.

"Information, Lacklan. It's always information, isn't it?"

I trained my gun on the door. Whoever came through first drew the short straw. "What information, Ben? I have a lot of information, you know that."

"Well, that's exactly what I need to know, precisely what information do you have, and, with whom you have shared it?" There was a moment's silence. Then he went on. "This soldier beside me, Lacklan, he is holding a grenade. It's not like your grenades, that make a lot of noise and light, but don't actually kill people. This is a real grenade. He has extracted the pin, and, as soon as I give him the nod, he will toss it against the wall facing you. It will explode and you will be dismembered, and the whole Lacklan Walker legend will come to a sticky, messy end."

"You have my attention."

"An armed man is going to step in now. If we hear gunfire, a grenade will follow. And make no mistake, Lacklan, I have grown very, very weary of you. I really want to kill you. So my advice? Don't offer me an excuse."

A guy stepped through the door with an automatic rifle

at his shoulder, trained on me. I dropped my weapon. He looked out through the door and nodded. Another guy came in, also training an automatic rifle on me, then two more, then Ben and Donnelly.

Game over.

Donnelly stood leaning against the doorjamb, frowning at me. Ben looked around for a chair, found one and pulled it over. I was sitting on the floor, with my back to the wall. Ben narrowed his eyes and shook his head.

"I have really, *really* grown to hate you, Lacklan. There was a time when I felt a kind of family love, as though we were estranged brothers. I hoped that you would one day grow to appreciate that, and take your place in Omega. But that has gone, long gone. I hate you deeply. You are violent, bloodthirsty, grotesque." He looked around and smiled. "But I have to say, I retain a kind of awed admiration at how fucking *destructive* you are!"

I smiled at him. It was the first time I had ever heard him swear. I eased myself into a slightly more comfortable position. The pain in my shoulder was beginning to throb in my head. Ben went on talking.

"You're like an incarnation of Kali. You destroy everything in your path. You destroyed your home, you destroyed your father. You destroyed the only woman you ever loved, Marni. If you had made a home with her when she proposed to you in London, none of this would ever have happened. Now you have destroyed Senator McFarlane's home too, and Senator McFarlane." He paused, staring at me in apparent fascination. He gestured at Donnelly, still leaning on the jamb. "She and her husband were happy, they had a good life and a good future. They had a position secured for them and their children in the New Eden, whenever that may come. But you, in your relentless destructive rage, have destroyed their lives and their future." He spread his hands, looking around him. "And now this! You are incredible! You *have* to be destroyed! *For the good of the world!"* He leaned forward, his eyes wide, half smiling. "You have to be destroyed because if you are not, Lacklan, you will destroy the last best hope of humanity!" He sat back and laughed. "I mean, what are you *like?* Everything you touch, Lacklan! *You destroy everything you touch!"*

I sighed, "What can I say, Ben, we all do what we're good at. I'm good at destroying things."

He smiled, then chuckled. "You are very, very good at what you do, Lacklan. And it is a shame we wound up being enemies. You can't deny I tried, and I was very patient. But you have pushed me too far, much too far."

"So where do we go from here? You going to bore me to death?"

"I know what you're thinking."

"Really?"

He sighed. "Yes. You are thinking that the one thing—the one *person*—I have not mentioned in the list of things and people that you have destroyed, is Abi... Abi and her two children. The very attractive Primrose and the boy, Sean."

I snorted, "The whore from Independence? You have to be kidding me."

He stared down at the floor for a moment. "The whore from Independence. A little lame, Lacklan, considering that you have moved her into your house in Weston. Were you really that confident that you'd thrown us off? That we were *that* shaken by the UN fracas? You thought you could lie low for a few months in Nevada and then come trundling home with your new love?"

"Again, Ben, what do you want?"

He chewed his lip for a moment. "What does Gibbons want with Senator McFarlane?"

I shrugged and shook my head. "I have no idea. Gibbons hates me almost as much as you do. He broke me and Marni up and tells me squat. That's basically why I am out of the game."

He nodded several times, with labored irony, and gestured around him. "Yes, I can see that you are out of the game."

I closed my eyes and blew through puffed cheeks. "Wake up, Ben. Gibbons wanted me to come in, get info and get out without leaving a trace. That wasn't my plan. My plan was to get enough information on you, and cause you enough damage, that you would leave me and Abi alone. Gibbons told me that Gamma, my father's replacement, was in charge of the Institute. I figured if I could make him talk I would have a hold over you. But I guess before he talked he telephoned..."

He nodded. "You made so much noise coming in that he called me. Unfortunately he didn't call me in time. So what information did you manage to transmit to Gibbons?"

I didn't answer. I stared at his face, thinking, calculating. Finally I said, "Enough."

"You'll have to do better than that."

I sighed. "I already told you that Gibbons and I are not bosom pals. I sent him what he needed to know for his purposes. You've got some bills coming up in Congress you won't be so happy with. But the real information, the readouts from your scans, your work on neurotransmitters..." I smiled. "And above all, the list I got from Ogden after I blew his kneecap off..."

"List?"

"Yeah, the list, Ben. You know, Alpha, Beta, Gamma, Delta, Epsilon, Zeta... all the way through to Omega."

His face was rigid. "He gave you that list?"

I laughed a little, enjoying myself. "Well, let's see, Ben. Mr. Donnelly here, he'd be Omicron, and that evil genius who created social networking, he would be Theta. The number of Hollywood superstars came as a bit of a surprise, though perhaps it shouldn't have. But the big shockers were Alpha and Beta. Shall I go on?"

He shook his head. "What have you done with this information?"

"I'm a crazy barbarian, Ben, but I am not a stupid one. Maybe I sent it to Gibbons, maybe I sent it to Marni. On the other hand, perhaps I sent it to Abi, or somebody completely different. Maybe I'm just bluffing."

Donnelly looked at Ben, shrugged and said, "Torture him."

I put a smile I didn't feel on the left side of my face, where it looked ironic. "Really? That's your answer? The least reliable form of interrogation? Sure, do that, because I have never been tortured before. Who knows, I might just break."

Ben jerked his chin at me and said to nobody in particular, "Take him to the operating theater."

I said, "Wait. What do you plan to do with me in there?"

Ben chuckled. He looked at Donnelly and they both laughed. Ben said, "I guess, as you won't tell us what we need to know, we'll just have to look inside your head and see what you have in hidden in there."

I closed my eyes and sighed. "OK, I'm going to stand up. Don't do anything crazy." I held up my hands and struggled to my feet. "You can see I'm unarmed. I'm just going to reach for a piece of paper in my pocket. It's something you need to see. Are we good?"

Ben narrowed his eyes at me. He said, "If he breathes in the wrong way, cut him in half."

They all trained their weapons on me. I reached in my back pocket and slowly pulled out the list Ogden had given me. I took it in my left hand. Ben's eyes were fixed on it. Still moving very slowly I put my right hand in my right front pocket. This was not the way I had planned it. It was not the way it was supposed to pan out, but it was as good as it was going to get.

The next moment all hell broke loose.

The walls shook. Donnelly was hurled across the room in a billowing cloud of dust. Ben went over backwards in his chair. Plaster fell from the ceiling and the walls. Everybody was cowering, coughing and gasping. I'd known it was coming and had my sleeve over my mouth. I shoved the paper back in my pocket, sprang across the room and smashed my instep into one of the guards' crotch. His coughing turned into a wheezing scream. I wrenched his M16 from his hands and sprayed the doorway. I couldn't see a damn thing through the dust and smoke. Somebody screamed. Feet ran. I let off another burst and listened. Nothing. So I ran forward through the door and let off another burst down the corridor. Somebody swore.

I ran then into the operating theater. There was a pile of

rubble in the middle of the floor and a gaping hole in the ceiling, through which sunlight was streaming, and the dust and smoke were escaping. I grabbed one of the gurneys I had left in the room, stashed it on top of the rubble, locked the wheels and clambered onto it.

Out in the passage I could hear voices shouting, one screaming in pain. Ben was bellowing, "*Get in there! Get that bastard! I want him dead! Dead! Kill that mother fucker now!*"

I reached up and pulled myself into the dining room. I positioned myself where I could see the doorway into the operating theater, expecting them to come in after me, but they didn't. In the confusion, with all the dust and the smoke, they thought I was still in the lab, with the CAT scanner and all the other computer equipment. I smiled and gave them a few seconds to get in. Then I backed up and pressed the other detonator. It was one and a half tablets of C4, in an enclosed basement, and it made one hell of a bang.

EIGHTEEN

The blast wave, channeled through the open doors and up through the hole in the floor, was enough to throw me sprawling on my back. It was a good thing that it did, because a moment later the walls separating the labs collapsed and the floor where I had been standing caved in.

I lay a moment, looking up at the ceiling above me. The pain in my shoulder was excruciating. By gradual stages I pulled myself into a sitting position. A slow, almost motionless mushroom cloud of dust and smoke lingered over the gaping hole in the floor. It was like a nuclear explosion trapped in a time warp. I told myself I should go down and confirm the kills, at least Ben and Donnelly, but I knew I couldn't. Not yet. Not with my shoulder in the state it was in.

I waited ten minutes, sitting on the floor with my back against the wall, until the dust cloud had started to clear. Then I got to my feet, put the M16 to my shoulder and inched toward the hole. I knew the chances of anyone having survived were minimal, but minimal was not zero, and overconfidence in this kind of game is as big a killer as C4, maybe bigger.

The gurney was a mangled wreck. Everything down there was a mangled wreck. There were no bodies visible, because all you could see was rubble. I decided that, even if anybody had survived, they would not be getting out any time soon. I could afford to go and collect my backpack.

I slung the M16 over my shoulder and limped and groaned my way to the main entrance. On the way I glanced at my watch. It was still working. It was a few minutes after half past seven. I pushed out into the cold, bright morning air and made my way along the front gardens until I came to the Bougainvillea bush that stood below the top floor terrace. My backpack was there. I picked it up and slung it over my other shoulder.

I stood then for a moment, peering at the southeastern sky. I wondered for a moment if it was my imagination. The sun was an inch above the horizon, and in the molten glow of its light I thought I could see a small, black speck. The more I looked at it, the more certain I became that it was a chopper, and it was coming my way at speed. And that could be either really good news, or really bad news.

I hobbled my way, a little faster now, back toward the entrance to the building. It was when I was halfway there that I started to hear the distant wail of sirens. Then I started to laugh. I leaned my back against the wall, dropped the M16 and slid to the ground.

The chopper arrived a little before the sheriff, coming in low and fast over the trees, making them bend and bow and toss against the downdraft. It slewed to the right, reared slightly and then slowly settled onto the lawn. I was pretty sure by then it wasn't another wave of Omega agents. If it had been, they would have riddled me with 50 cal. rounds from the chopper. So if it wasn't Omega, that meant it had to be Gibbons and his pals, hopefully with a search warrant.

I wasn't wrong. He jumped down, hunching into his shoulders, and ran toward me on his small, strutting legs while his green tweed jacket flapped around his thighs. I looked for Marni, but she wasn't with him. I didn't blame her.

The helicopter turbines whined and the blades slowed. Behind Gibbons, two men climbed out. Both wore expensive suits, one was charcoal gray, and the man wearing it was well groomed and in his fifties. I figured he was the DA. The other one was blue, and the man wearing it was younger by maybe ten years. He had wayfarer shades on and FBI written all over him.

They approached while Gibbons stood a couple of feet in front of me and shouted, "What in the name of all that is holy have you been doing? Are you completely *insane?*"

I threw the backpack at his feet. "The sheriff is about to arrive, Gibbons. You better get your DA and your pal from the Bureau to establish jurisdiction. You have everything you need in the way of evidence in what I sent you, what's in that sack, and in what's left of the labs downstairs. Did you get a warrant, like I told you?"

He ignored my question. "What do you mean, 'what's left of the labs'?"

I laughed again. "Go take a look." I struggled to my feet. He watched me and for a moment, I saw real rage in his eyes.

He looked down at the backpack, picked it up and looked at me again. "What have you done?"

The two suits drew level with him. Blue suit said, "Are you Lacklan Walker?"

I nodded.

He pulled out a badge and showed it to me. "Special Agent Denis Mason."

I looked at the gray suit. "And you must be the DA."

He nodded, "Ed Chavez."

"I'd like to take you gentlemen on a tour of the Institute..." I jerked my head, indicating behind them to where a line of four silver cars from the Green County Sheriff's Department was approaching at speed down the drive. "But I think we'd be well advised to wait for the deputies. I'm not sure there isn't somebody still alive down there."

Gibbons had turned puce. "I swear, Lacklan... I swear..."

The cars pulled up and seven deputies and a sheriff, all in the dark brown uniforms of Green County, climbed out and approached us. The sheriff was a big man with blue eyes and a mustache. He was frowning hard and said, "Is one of you gentlemen Lacklan Walker?"

"That would be me, Sheriff. These gentlemen here are Professor Philip Gibbons, District Attorney Ed Chavez and Special Agent Denis Mason. I think you'll find that the Feds have jurisdiction here, but I may be wrong."

He stuck his thumbs in his belt and raised an eyebrow at Mason. "Why don't we just find out what happened here first, and then we can decide who has what?"

I nodded and looked at Gibbons, then at the DA. The DA looked deeply troubled. Then I turned to Mason, who was trying hard to maintain a poker face.

I said, "What has happened here is that Dr. Theodore Ogden has been conducting some experiments on living human beings. Some of those experiments involved vivisection in the form of cranial and cerebral open surgery. You'll find somewhere in the region of thirty-two of his victims downstairs in the basement, in a dormitory."

The sheriff was looking at me like I was insane. "Holy shit!" He turned to his deputies, who had gathered behind him. "Get down there and take a look..."

I raised a hand. "Sheriff, there is a lot of bomb damage down there. There are also maybe a dozen corpses, perhaps a few more, including..." I paused and looked at Gibbons. "Including Michael Donnelly, Senator McFarlane's husband. You are going to need a couple of forensics teams."

The DA raised both hands. "I have heard more than enough. This clearly falls within the jurisdiction of the Federal Bureau of Investigation. I hope, Sheriff, that you will cooperate fully."

The sheriff didn't say anything. Mason was already on the phone to the New York field office. Gibbons was looking at me and the expression in his eyes had graduated from rage to something close to hatred. When he spoke, he spat the words at me. "Have you *any* idea of what you have done? Have you any conception of the damage you have caused? You *deliberately* destroyed this place!"

Chavez said, "Now hold on a minute, Gibbons..."

I interrupted him. "I didn't do a damn thing, Gibbons. You want to watch where you throw rocks. You might damage your precious greenhouse."

The sheriff was peering at me curiously. "What exactly was your role in all this, Walker?"

"Sheriff, I want to cooperate, but in view of the accusations that are flying at the moment, I think I might be well advised to wait until I have spoken to my attorney."

Chavez said, "Wise words. You'd do well to heed them, Gibbons."

Mason returned, switching off his phone and slipping it into his pocket.

I said, "The bomb damage is in the basement, in the south wing. You are going to find victims of Ogden's experimentation in the north wing, in a dormitory. It should be undamaged by the blast. From what I saw last night, I would say that these people are in urgent need of medical care."

The sheriff turned to Mason. "I'm going to call the ME and have him arrange medical assistance and some ambulances."

Mason nodded and the sheriff walked away toward his car. I continued. "Upstairs, also in the north wing, you are going to find a similar number of people, confined to their dormitory. But these are not victims. They were participants. I don't know how much they were aware of, or to what degree they participated, but at least one Dr. Patel was involved with the vivisections. Before the bombs went off, he was going to carry out open brain surgery on me."

He narrowed his eyes at me, then turned to stare at Gibbons. The look was eloquent. Finally he turned and walked away, toward the sheriff and his deputies. He was pointing at the building and talking loudly. "...position your men at the entrance and at the top floor. I don't want anybody leaving this place until backup arrives."

I looked at Gibbons, who was still staring at me with

hatred in his eyes. He said suddenly, "I should never have listened to Marni. She is blind to your true nature."

Suddenly I was sick to my back teeth of him. I shook my head. "What the hell is the matter with you, Gibbons?"

He scowled at me.

I went on. "You got everything you wanted and then some. This damned operation has been blown wide open. With your contacts and the DA's you can have the press and the media crawling all over this like flies on shit. And you know as well as I do that the one thing Omega fears above all else is exposure. What I have done here could well cripple them."

He seemed not to have heard me. "I can't believe that you would *deliberately* destroy this..."

Before I could answer, Mason came back. I was still frowning at Gibbons, trying to make sense of the intensity of his reaction. I'd known he'd be mad, but I hadn't expected this. "You sent me here, Gibbons, assuring me that there were no guards. There were eight guards, plus Ogden and twelve men who turned up later, including Donnelly and Ben. And every goddamn one of them was trying to kill me!"

Gibbons said, "Ben? Ben was here?"

"You'll find his body in the rubble in the basement, along with Donnelly's."

Mason was staring hard at me. Suddenly he said, "Lacklan Walker, I am placing you under arrest on suspicion of terrorism, murder in the first degree and theft of state secrets. You do not have to say anything, but anything you do say may and will be taken down and used in evidence against you. You have the right to an attorney. If you cannot afford one, the court will appoint one for you. Please turn around."

I looked at Gibbons. He was still scowling.

"Really?" I said. I looked at Chavez. He seemed even unhappier than before.

Mason said, "Please turn around, Mr. Walker. Don't make me use force."

I gave him my best ironic smile. "*Really*, Mason? I'll come with you, but you can shove your cuffs up Gibbons' ass."

He nodded once and turned to call to the sheriff again. "Sheriff! A team from the Bureau are on their way. They'll be here in about half an hour. Secure the area. Don't touch anything. Don't let anybody in or out until the agents get here. Understood?" He turned to me. "Come on, Walker, let's go."

I didn't move. I said, "Are you Omega, Agent Mason?"

He shook his head, "No, Walker, I am not."

I turned to Gibbons. "Are you?"

He narrowed his eyes. "No, of course not. Don't be absurd!"

I looked at my watch. It was twenty minutes past eight. I nodded, pushed through them and crossed the lawn toward the chopper, wondering whether or not to throw Gibbons and Mason out over the Catskills.

I'D BEEN WAITING three hours in a large office overlooking Broadway from the 23rd floor of 26 Federal Plaza, in New York. It wasn't the kind of office you'd expect your run of the mill Special Agent to have. In my book it would have been more like a AD's office.

Mason eventually showed up at just before one. He dropped a paper bag in front of me with two roast beef sandwiches in it, and put a large plastic cup of coffee on the desk. Then he lowered himself into his black leather chair. He did it with care, like he was worried he might break.

I raised an eyebrow at him. "Long night?"

"You could say that."

I gave a single nod. "Yeah, me too. You're an AD, right?"

He leaned back and nodded. "Yes. So how about you tell me what happened last night? Let's start with the part where you explain what the hell the deal is between you and Gibbons, and why he sent you there?"

I bit into a sandwich and watched him while I chewed. After my second bite I said, "Do you remember the tactical nuclear device that was defused at the United Nations, the morning Professor Gibbons and Dr. Marni Gilbert were supposed to give their address on climate change and overpopulation?"

"Of course I remember."

I took another bite and stabbed my finger several times at the floor while I chewed. "Less than a week before that, I came here, to this field office, to warn you that there was going to be a terrorist attack on the UN. I spoke to Special Agents Harrison Mclean and Daren Jones. First they wouldn't listen to me. Then, just like you, they tried to arrest me."

He spread his hands. "I just told you, I'm listening, talk to me."

I nodded, stuffed the last piece of sandwich in my mouth

and pulled the other one out of the bag. "Do you know who defused that bomb?"

"Go ahead, amaze me."

"Me, I did. You know who arranged to put it there?"

"Has this *anything* to do with what you were doing at the institute?"

"Everything."

"Fine, go ahead."

"Ben Smith. You should find his body in the rubble, if you haven't already. I don't know what his real name is, but he was my father's assistant for years. He masterminded the attempted bombing of the UN, and from the time of my father's death, until just after I defused the bomb, he consistently tried to recruit me."

"Into Omega?"

I nodded and bit into the second sandwich.

He sighed. "And you have a background in special ops, so you thought you'd just go in there, take the law into your own hands, and start killing people."

I gave a small laugh, stuffed the last of the second sandwich into my mouth, chewed and started in on the coffee. "Attractive as that proposition sounds, Mason, no. Gibbons asked me to go on a fact-finding mission. That's why he fitted me with a camera and a mic, and invited you, the judge and the DA along, remember? Killing these guys is like trying to kill cockroaches. You can't do it. If you'll forgive the obviousness of the metaphor, you need to clean the environment, then the infestation dies on its own."

He leaned forward and put his elbows on the desk. "Lacklan, you murdered a leading doctor, the head of a major institute. You murdered a leading attorney from D.C., the husband of a senator, for Christ's sake! You *slaughtered* God alone knows how many other men down there, not to mention those three men guarding the premises."

"Murder is a technical term that you are going to have to prove. I, and my attorneys, are going to argue that it was in self-defense. When I do that, it will emerge that my presence in that building was sanctioned by the Federal Bureau of Investigation, the District Attorney and a New York Judge."

He sighed and sank back in his chair. "You were expressly told not to destroy property or kill people."

"Come on, Mason! I was also told that there would be no guards. By now you have seen those poor bastards with the scars on their heads! You've seen the two corpses in the operating theater! You think the people who did that would balk at killing me? Now how about you tell me the real reason you have me here?"

He turned his head away and stared at the window.

I waited but he didn't say anything. So I went on. "I figure it has to be one of two things. Either you belong to Omega, or you think Gibbons does."

Now he turned to look at me. After a long moment he said, "Do you?"

I got to my feet and walked over to the window. There I stood looking down at the human infestation, the millions of tiny cells swarming over the sidewalks, spilling into the traffic, dodging the cars—those larger metallic cells that swarmed through the city's arteries, spewing poison into the air, transporting the human infestation over the face of the Earth. I shook my head. "I don't know, Mason." I turned to face him. "I was surprised at the violence of his reaction when he discovered I had destroyed the institute's research. I got the feeling he was more interested in getting his hands on it than exposing Omega. I might be wrong. He's never liked me. We have bad chemistry."

Mason shrugged. "He's not easy to like. If he hates you so much, why'd he choose you for the job?"

"He was acting on advice from somebody who knows my background."

He nodded. "Why'd you agree to do it? Why were you there? What was your agenda, Walker? I'm damned sure it wasn't the same as Gibbons's agenda."

I took a moment before answering. "OK, Mason. I had two objectives, neither of which was homicide. First, I wanted to destroy their research. What they are doing has no positive application and is not worth preserving. Second, I wanted to get information, an insurance policy. I want out of this game, and I wanted to get Ben Smith and Omega off my back. I figured if I could get enough information, I could use it as insurance." I shrugged. "If at the same time I could help Gibbons to bring them down, so much the better."

"But you told Gibbons you'd get in and out without causing damage."

I shook my head. "No, I didn't. I told him it probably couldn't be done. But he only listens to what he wants to hear. He assumes people are going to do what he tells them to do. He's an asshole."

He smiled. "I can't argue with that. I think he is now also your enemy."

I thought about that for a moment. He was probably right. I said, "Frankly, Mason, I don't care. I'm through. This is not my fight anymore." I returned to my chair, dropped into it and sighed. "I want to talk to Senator

McFarlane. I killed her husband last night and she deserves an explanation."

He frowned and gave a small laugh. "You're under arrest, remember?"

"Bullshit. A, you can't make it stick. B, two gets you twenty the DA has already told you you can't hold me, you have to release me. C, you never intended to hold me anyway. You just wanted to talk to me away from Gibbons."

He smiled. "You'll be a loss to the cause. You're smart."

"Maybe. The cause didn't want me, and now I have a different cause." I crossed my arms, studying Mason's face, wondering about him. "Gibbons was a good man, but power corrupts good men just as much as bad ones. Honestly, I don't know if he is in bed with Omega. If he is, he's playing a very deep game. If he's not, there is nothing to stop him turning his own, weird fraternity into something just as ugly as Omega. Either way, you should keep an eye on him. Now tell me something, Mason."

"What?"

"Is this you, or the Bureau?"

He took a moment to think about the question, and his answer. "Both. It's an official investigation, but the part that relates expressly to Omega is need to know only, and I am very careful about who needs to know."

"Talk to Dr. Marni Gilbert, away from Gibbons. You should also know that Ben Smith interviewed me twice, trying to convince me to join them. He interviewed me at an office in the Pentagon."

He sat forward, frowning, "*In the...* Jesus Christ!"

"On the second occasion, former President Dick Hennessy was part of the conversation."

"Holy shit, man..."

I nodded. "And the office where he died, in that explosion...?"

"Don't tell me, that was the office where you had the meeting."

"Yes. I'm telling you this because you need to know how far this infection has spread. I believe we have allies in Dr. Marni Gilbert and Senator McFarlane, and maybe still in Professor Gibbons, but the bottom line, Mason, is that people..."

I trailed off. I couldn't think of an adequate adjective to describe people. He snorted and gave a small laugh, then smiled at me.

"Don't be too judgmental, Lacklan. The word you're looking for is 'human'. People are basically human."

He had a point. I returned the smile. "I'm going to go."

He handed me a card. "Stay in touch. If Gibbons contacts you again, please let me know. If anything comes up I think you should know about, I'll contact you."

I stared at the card for a long moment, not wanting to take it, not wanting to stay involved. Finally I reached out, took it and put it in my pocket.

"You know where McFarlane is?"

He nodded. "She's with Gibbons, and Marni Gilbert." He wrote something on a piece of paper. "That's her cell."

NINETEEN

She agreed to meet me at Columbus Circus, by the USS Marine Monument. She was already there when I climbed out of the yellow cab at two PM. She watched me approach with no expression on her face and for a moment I felt self-conscious, aware that I looked a wreck. I was unshaven, dirty and had a wound in my shoulder that had been patched up by paramedics, but not yet seen by a doctor.

I stopped in front of her, with the crowds milling around us. After a moment she said, "Same old Lacklan. You look awful."

"I don't feel great, if that's any consolation."

She shook her head. "I don't blame you, if that's what you mean."

"You want to grab a coffee, or some lunch?"

"Let's go to the ball fields."

We started to walk. It wasn't cold, but it wasn't warm

either. Spring was trying to assert itself, but winter hadn't quite let go yet. I shoved my hands in my trouser pockets and watched my feet as we walked. "I don't know where to begin, Cyndi. It was not my intention..." I stopped, hesitated, then started again. "I didn't go there with the intention..."

She interrupted me. "I'm going to be honest with you, Lacklan. I am conflicted." She looked at me, watched me a moment while we walked. "You saved my life—I've lost count of how many times. I came to rely on you, emotionally, in a way I have never relied on anybody. Not just that, I watched you, day after day, put your own life on the line to protect me. That has a deep impact on a person."

I nodded. "And then I round it off by..."

I trailed off. Neither of us finished the sentence. We walked on in silence, skirting the softball fields. Eventually she said, "I want you to tell me exactly what happened, how he died."

So I told her, not exactly, not in every detail, because there were things I did not think concerned her, but I told her about Ogden, about the fact that he had made a phone call when he heard me blowing out the lock in his door, and that the call was to Ben and her husband. I told her that they tried to take me down to the basement, and what they intended to do to me down there. And finally, I told her how her husband had died, in the blast from the C4 I had placed on the ceiling.

By the time I'd finished we had arrived at the café. I sat at a table outside and she went in and got a cappuccino and a quadruple espresso for me. When she returned and sat, she shook her head and said, "I have to say, Lacklan, I don't understand why you destroyed all the computers. You took weapons with you. That I understand because your experience and your instincts told you to expect armed guards. But you also took C4 with you, and that tells me you intended to destroy what was there."

I smiled a lopsided smile and frowned at the same time. "I'll answer your question, Cyndi. But first I'd like you to answer one of mine. Your husband died last night. You're sitting in front of the man who killed him, and after I told you the story of how I did it, your first question is, why did I destroy the computers? Not, was his death quick? Did he suffer? Am I certain that he was actually with Omega? None of that..." I trailed off.

She sat staring at her cup.

"Cyndi, what's the deal with you? Are *you* Omega?"

She closed her eyes, sighed and shook her head. "No, Lacklan, I'm not Omega, and neither is Gibbons." She opened her eyes and drew breath, like a mother trying to explain math to a stupid child. "Not everybody is like you. For you everything is simple, clear cut, straightforward: Kill or be killed, live or die, tell the truth or lie. But for the rest of us it is all a million shades of gray. I'm a politician. I loved my husband. I will miss him, and when I am alone tonight I will cry for him, as I did last night, and the night before, and every night since I discovered that he tried to have me killed.

"But as a politician I can also see that there is a hell of a lot more to this—a *hell* of a lot more—than just my personal loss." She stopped, watching me carefully to see if I had understood. "Yes," she said suddenly, "I need to process the fact that probably for years my husband had been lying to me consistently. I need to process the fact that he was probably instructed to marry me because I was a potential threat to Omega." She leaned forward, her eyes wide and bright. "I have to process the fact that the man I loved ordered my assassination!" She sat back again. "But that is *my private life*, and I am a Senator of the United States, and my first duty is to my constituents and my country."

It was a convincing speech and I was inclined to believe her. I sipped my coffee. "OK, Cyndi. You're right. I took the C4 with intent. I told you when I agreed to take you to the meeting with Gibbons that I didn't work for you. I don't work for Gibbons either. I don't work for anybody. That is something that Gibbons has trouble understanding. He seems to think the whole damned world is there to serve his vision. He told me expressly not to kill anybody, to leave no trace of my having been there, et cetera, et cetera, et-fucking-cetera." I shrugged. "In his mind, and in yours, that meant that that was what I had to do. But not in mine. I answer to nobody but myself, Cyndi. And myself told me that there was one supremely important thing that had to be done in the John Richard Erickson Institute that night, and that was to destroy all the research that they had done. Because that research is not useful, Cyndi, to anybody. There are no 'right hands' for that research to fall into, only wrong hands."

She drew breath. I cut across her and raised a finger. "That research serves only one purpose: the purpose of enslaving human minds. There was only one thing to do with it: destroy it. And that's what I did."

I sipped my coffee and set the cup down again. I watched

her a moment, then said, "People who see things in a million shades of gray can convince themselves that, for example, when obedience leads to the absence of suffering, control of a person's mind is justified. I like you, Cyndi. I actually like you a lot. But it is not hard for me to imagine a situation where you would put that research to use, for the good of humanity. It's even easier for me to imagine Gibbons doing it. So I went there, to the institute, with the intention of destroying that research so that it would never fall into your hands or his."

She stared at me for a long time. "You think it is better to suffer than to be obedient?"

"The only thing we have is the freedom of our minds. If you take that away, you take our souls, our very existence. I said it to you once before, Cyndi, on Route 66, when we were talking about humanity's last cry of freedom. It is better to rule in Hell than to serve in Heaven."

She frowned. "I remember. You were quoting John Milton. But those words were uttered by Satan, Lacklan, when he was cast out of Paradise."

I gave a small shrug. "Lucifer, the Bringer of Light. Let's not get into a theological argument. What's in a name? I hate Omega not because they are called Omega, but because they intend to rob humanity of its freedom. No..." I shook my head. "That isn't it either. What they plan to do is to rob Joe, and Pete, and Mary, and Sarah of their individual freedom to be themselves and make their own choices about who and what they want to be and do. You know? When you start talking about groups and classes of people, like the French, Americans, Blacks, Whites... or even Humanity, you dehumanize them. You can talk about what's good or bad for them like they have no say in the matter. But when you bring it down to the individual, to the man or the woman whose brain you are going to cut open, program and alter, whose freedom and humanity you are about to steal, then it changes."

"Isn't that exactly what you did when you decided to destroy that research?"

I laughed out loud. "I stole Humanity's right to choose to lose the right to choose? Only a politician could come up with reasoning that twisted, Cyndi." I shook my head. "Take my advice, before you become one of Them, take some of those shades of gray and make them black or white. Sometimes you have to be absolute. Sometimes you have to define a limit beyond which you will not go. Some things are just not acceptable."

We were quiet for a long time, listening to the sounds of early spring around us. Eventually she said, "You think Gibbons wanted to get his hands on that research to use it?"

I shook my head, then shrugged. "I have no idea. He seemed pretty mad that I had destroyed it. But I can't pretend to know him that well."

She heaved a big sigh. "I have to go." But she didn't get up. She remained sitting, looking at the trees. "Lacklan, can we be friends, please? You are like this primal, bestial being, so absolutely certain of what you know. I think, if I have you there, to reach out sometimes, you could keep me grounded."

I smiled. "I'd be honored to count you as a friend."

She stood, gave me a kiss on the cheek and walked away. I didn't get up. I didn't move. Because I knew that he would show before long, and he did. He came walking toward me up the path, with his vigorous little legs pumping at the ground under his big, tweed jacket. He had an angry frown on his face, but that didn't mean much. He always had an angry frown on his face. He stopped in front of my table. I smiled at him.

"Hello, Gibbons. I wondered if you'd show yourself. I've been aware of you hiding in the bushes. What do you want?"

"Was it you who alerted the press?"

"You know that I did. I called them last night when I called the sheriff."

"You destroyed the labs, you called the sheriff and you alerted the press."

"Yes, Gibbons, and if you were not such an egomaniac, you would have known from the start that that was exactly what I was going to do."

"They are all over the site, filming from the air, with vans set up. And now somebody has leaked the experiments to them..."

I smiled and wondered if that was Mason. I said, "And isn't that a good thing, Gibbons? I'd ask you to explain why that's a bad thing, but I'm afraid you would, and I really don't give a damn anymore."

He narrowed his eyes at me like I was the embodiment of some paradox. "Have you no conception of how badly you have set back our fight?"

I leaned back in my chair and laughed up at the blue sky. "No, Philip! I have no idea, and I don't give a rat's ass, either. You got lost, pal! You know the warning in Japanese Budo?" I sat forward and stared at him. "The Zen masters tell you, 'Don't look into your enemy's eyes, lest you become your enemy.' Do you understand that, Gibbons?" I pointed at him. "What you're fighting against has become more important to you than what you're fighting for. What the fuck is wrong with you, Philip? You're complaining that the press are nosing into Omega? Can you not hear how *stupid* that is? You're complaining that research they were doing into how to enslave people's minds has been destroyed? That is, to you, a bad thing? These are your *problems*? You better take yourself away and do some fucking soul searching pal, because there is something seriously wrong with your vision."

He pointed a trembling hand at me. His voice was shrill. "That research could have been invaluable in our struggle! We could have used it against them! For the first time in decades it would have given us the upper hand over them! And you, with your barbaric, animal stupidity, you have set us back years!"

I frowned at him. "Does Marni realize how far gone you are, Gibbons? You need help. You seriously need help. You've lost the plot, pal."

He shook his head and half screamed, "Stay away from me! You stay away from me! And stay away from Marni!"

I stood, and the chair fell back behind me. I stepped over to him, grabbed him by the scruff of his neck and dragged him up to within an inch of my face. Then I snarled at him, "*Stop! Stop telling me what to do! Stop telling people what to do! Now fuck off out of my sight, you clown!*"

I shoved him. He staggered back, fell on his ass, scrambled to his feet and ran. Several people were staring at me. I flapped a hand at them and walked away. I was going home. At long last, I was going home.

I made my way first to the apartment I had in Manhattan, on Riverside Drive. I ordered a rental car, and while I waited for it to be delivered, I had a shower and a shave, changed the dressing on my wound, and put on some fresh, clean clothes. Then I went down, collected the car and drove the two hundred miles back to my house in Weston. On the way I called Abi. She sounded happy but worried.

"I'm so relieved to hear from you. Are you OK?"

"I'm fine. It's over. Really over this time. I'm on my way home. Are you there or are you still in Boston?"

"I'm home, we all are."

I smiled. "Primrose and Sean are with you?"

"Yes. They can't wait to see you."

She hesitated a moment.

I said, "What is it?"

"Nothing. They love the house. They are thrilled at the news."

"Glad to hear it. I'll see you in a couple of hours."

By the time I pulled into the drive and parked, there was already light in the windows, and the sky was turning from dusky gray to a darker blue. The door opened as I climbed out of the car and Abi ran to greet me. We kissed and when I looked up, Primrose and Sean were in the doorway, looking sheepish. I gave them each a big hug and Sean said, "This house is so cool! You must be really rich!"

Primrose gave me a private smile and said, "I have lots of news for you, Lacklan."

"I can't wait!" I said, and we stepped inside. I closed the door behind me. "But I am starving and exhausted. I need a drink and I hope Rosalia has something amazing up her sleeve for dinner."

Abi grimaced and took hold of my lapels. "Lacklan, I'm sorry. You have a friend here. He turned up on the doorstep and I didn't feel I could turn him away. I haven't asked him to stay to dinner, but he did want to wait till you got home to say hello. I hope you don't mind."

I frowned. "A friend?"

"He's in the drawing room." As I moved across the hall she added, in an undertone, "He looks as though he's been in an accident or something."

I pushed open the door and stepped inside. Abi and the kids came in with me. Ben was sitting in my father's chair in front of the fire holding a glass of whiskey. His face was badly bruised, cut and grazed, and his left arm was in a sling. He smiled at me like we were old friends and raised his glass. "Lacklan. It's so good to see you. Your taste in whiskey is as good as your father's was. I hope you are well. As you can see, I have been in the wars."

I stared at him for a long moment. Every instinct inside me told me to kill him there and then. But another voice, a new voice, told me that I should not bring that kind of violence to my family.

I said, "It looks like you lost." I sat in the chair opposite him. "I'm afraid I can't invite you to stay, Ben. I've been in the wars myself." I turned to Abi. "Would you be a sweetheart? You and the kids go and tell Rosalia I'm back, and I am going to need a cow pie for dinner, at least."

She hesitated. "I think she's..." She caught my look, smiled and said, "Of course! C'mon, kids, let's go talk to Rosalia."

They left the room and closed the door behind them. Ben was watching me. He said, "Did you win?"

I made a question with my face.

He explained, "You said you were in the wars. Did you win?"

"There are no winners in war, Ben. You know that. I withdrew. I retreated. Now I'm like Switzerland, rich and neutral."

He nodded for a bit, examined his whiskey, rich and amber in the firelight. "You didn't look so neutral last night."

"Yeah? Was that around the time you were planning to extract my brain?"

He gave a little snort. "As I recall, by that time you were already there, killing my men."

"I was there looking for insurance, Ben. I never wanted to be a part of this damned war. My father asked me on his deathbed to look after Marni. Then you wanted me to join Omega. I never wanted any goddamn part of it. Now Marni doesn't need me, she has Gibbons. And you and Gibbons can go to war with each other, fight for which one of you gets to eat Humanity's brains and control the world. I don't want anything to do with it."

"It's not that simple to walk away, Lacklan."

"Wrong. It is that simple. You know how dangerous I am, Ben. Look at you, look at the state you're in. Look at your damned institute. Look at your organization. That's what I did trying to get out. If I come after you with intent, Ben, I will burn your towers to the ground, I will kill every one of you, from Omega all the way up to Alpha. And, Ben, I know who you are."

He studied my face or a while, then said, "You tortured Ogden." He was quiet for a moment, nodding to himself.

"That was your insurance policy, so that you could retire with your wife and your stepchildren."

"Amongst other things. Now, you go away, you don't ask me any more questions, and you leave me and my family alone. In exchange, I will not kill you. I will not make you tell me who got you out of the institute, who helped you escape. I don't care. It's none of my business anymore."

He thought for a moment, gazing at the flames. Then he took a deep breath. "You are not a threat?"

"I am the biggest threat you will ever face, Ben." I paused. He frowned. I sat forward. "If I get even a remote feeling that I am not getting through to you tonight, that you are thinking about reprisals, I will come over there and I will break your back and your neck and throw you in the furnace in the basement. I will destroy you and your organization completely. But if you are willing to leave me in peace, then I will leave you in peace. Ben, I want to retire. Leave me alone."

He nodded. "I want to kill you, Lacklan. I want to kill you very much. But I want you out of Omega's hair even more. So you have your truce. But if I ever discover that you have returned, I will not come after you. I will come after them..." He pointed at the door.

"Don't threaten me, Ben. We're done here. We have discussed everything there is to discuss. Get out of my house and stay away from my family."

He got to his feet with difficulty, pulled his cell phone from his pocket and sent a message. Then he limped painfully toward the door. I followed him. He stopped, hesitated before opening it, and turned to look around the room one last time.

"I loved your father," he said. "I miss him. I loved you too, Lacklan. I wish..." He paused, gazing at the floor. "I wish I could make you grasp the enormity of the tragedy. If you had taken your place among us..."

"Get out, Ben. Go away."

He opened the door and hobbled across the broad hall. He looked oddly like a crippled old man. I followed him. Outside, a waning, sickle moon hung low over the treetops. I heard the sound of tires on gravel and two headlamps flooded the drive with light. A dark blue Audi pulled up. The driver got out and opened the back door for Ben. He climbed in and the driver closed the door. For a moment I saw his face, pale and ghostly, looking at me through the window. The driver climbed in behind the wheel, slammed his door and I watched the two red lights, like the red eyes of a demon, recede into the darkness among the trees.

I stepped back into the hall and closed the heavy, oak door behind me. Was it over? Was it really over? I looked around me at the magnificent hall that had once been my father's. I searched for him in the house, with my mind, but could not find him. Maybe his soul was finally at rest. But somehow, in some part of my mind, I knew it wasn't.

Then Abi was there, at the top of the stairs that led down to the kitchen. She was smiling. "Has he gone?"

"Yes, he's gone."

She crossed the hall to me and placed her hands on my chest. "Are you OK?"

"Yeah. I'm OK. I'm better than OK. Where are the kids?"

"Playing cards with Kenny and Rosalia, in the kitchen. Sean is a cheat."

"What's she cooking?"

"Steak and mushroom pie, with roast potatoes and Brussels sprouts."

Later that evening we sat around the dining table and talked and laughed. Primrose was excited because she had decided to do Marine Biology and had received a conditional acceptance to the University of Massachusetts. She was also excited because she had met a boy she liked, and she was pretty sure he liked her. Sean was excited too, because we hadn't found a school for him yet, and that meant a few weeks of nothing but playing in the woodlands, going fishing, and exploring his huge, rambling new home. He made me promise to teach him how to shoot a rifle and a bow, and I promised him I would.

Then we told them our plans to get married. There was a moment of stunned silence, followed immediately by squeals of joy and a lot of running around and kissing and hugging and laughing and tears of joy. Finally I called Kenny and Rosalia and told them to bring up a bottle of our finest Bollinger, and to have a glass with us.

It was a happy moment in a happy evening.

Outside the sickle moon rose higher over the trees into a darkening sky, and touched the black slate rooftops with silver light. An owl in the church bell tower called out, and its solitary cry was answered by a distant echo, deep among the shadows of the New England forests. And far, far away to the south, a dark blue Audi sped through the black night toward Washington, D.C., toward that great seat of temporal power, and in the back, Ben Smith wept like a child with twisted, tortured rage.

Later that night, as Abi prepared for bed, I stepped into

my study and opened the safe. I knew in my gut I had not seen the last of Ben. I knew, as I slipped that sheet of paper into the safe and locked it away, that if Abi and the kids were ever going to be safe, I was going to have to hunt down each one of the surviving twenty-three, and I was going to have to kill them.

Don't miss KILL: ONE. The riveting sequel in the Omega Thriller series.

Scan the QR code below to purchase KILL: ONE.

Or go to: righthouse.com/kill-one

NOTE: flip to the very end to read an exclusive sneak peek...

DON'T MISS ANYTHING!

If you want to stay up to date on all new releases in this series, with this author, or with any of our new deals, you can do so by joining our newsletters below.

In addition, you will immediately gain access to our entire *Right House VIP Library,* which includes many riveting Mystery and Thriller novels for your enjoyment!

righthouse.com/email

(Easy to unsubscribe. No spam. Ever.)

ALSO BY BLAKE BANNER

Up to date books can be found at:
www.righthouse.com/blake-banner

ROGUE THRILLERS

Gates of Hell (Book 1)
Hell's Fury (Book 2)
Ice Burn (Book 3)
Judgement by Fire (Book 4)

ALEX MASON THRILLERS

Odin (Book 1)
Ice Cold Spy (Book 2)
Mason's Law (Book 3)
Assets and Liabilities (Book 4)
Russian Roulette (Book 5)
Executive Order (Book 6)
Dead Man Talking (Book 7)
All The King's Men (Book 8)
Flashpoint (Book 9)
Brotherhood of the Goat (Book 10)
Dead Hot (Book 11)
Blood on Megiddo (Book 12)
Son of Hell (Book 13)
Merchant of Death (Book 14)
Extinction C-14 (Book 15)

HARRY BAUER THRILLER SERIES

Dead of Night (Book 1)
Dying Breath (Book 2)
The Einstaat Brief (Book 3)
Quantum Kill (Book 4)
Immortal Hate (Book 5)
The Silent Blade (Book 6)
LA: Wild Justice (Book 7)
Breath of Hell (Book 8)
Invisible Evil (Book 9)
The Shadow of Ukupacha (Book 10)
Sweet Razor Cut (Book 11)
Blood of the Innocent (Book 12)
Blood on Balthazar (Book 13)
Simple Kill (Book 14)
Riding The Devil (Book 15)
The Unavenged (Book 16)
The Devil's Vengeance (Book 17)
Bloody Retribution (Book 18)
Rogue Kill (Book 19)
Blood for Blood (Book 20)
The Cell (Book 21)
Time to Die (Book 22)
The Reaper of Zion (Book 23)

DEAD COLD MYSTERY SERIES

An Ace and a Pair (Book 1)
Two Bare Arms (Book 2)
Garden of the Damned (Book 3)
Let Us Prey (Book 4)
The Sins of the Father (Book 5)
Strange and Sinister Path (Book 6)

The Heart to Kill (Book 7)
Unnatural Murder (Book 8)
Fire from Heaven (Book 9)
To Kill Upon A Kiss (Book 10)
Murder Most Scottish (Book 11)
The Butcher of Whitechapel (Book 12)
Little Dead Riding Hood (Book 13)
Trick or Treat (Book 14)
Blood Into Wine (Book 15)
Jack In The Box (Book 16)
The Fall Moon (Book 17)
Blood In Babylon (Book 18)
Death In Dexter (Book 19)
Mustang Sally (Book 20)
A Christmas Killing (Book 21)
Mommy's Little Killer (Book 22)
Bleed Out (Book 23)
Dead and Buried (Book 24)
In Hot Blood (Book 25)
Fallen Angels (Book 26)
Knife Edge (Book 27)
Along Came A Spider (Book 28)
Cold Blood (Book 29)
Curtain Call (Book 30)

THE OMEGA SERIES

Dawn of the Hunter (Book 1)
Double Edged Blade (Book 2)
The Storm (Book 3)
The Hand of War (Book 4)
A Harvest of Blood (Book 5)

To Rule in Hell (Book 6)
Kill: One (Book 7)
Powder Burn (Book 8)
Kill: Two (Book 9)
Unleashed (Book 10)
The Omicron Kill (Book 11)
9mm Justice (Book 12)
Kill: Four (Book 13)
Death In Freedom (Book 14)
Endgame (Book 15)

ABOUT US

Right House is an independent publisher created by authors for readers. We specialize in Action, Thriller, Mystery, and Crime novels.

If you enjoyed this novel, then there is a good chance you will like what else we have to offer! Please stay up to date by using any of the links below.

Join our mailing lists to stay up to date -->
righthouse.com/email
Visit our website --> righthouse.com
Contact us --> contact@righthouse.com

 facebook.com/righthousebooks
 x.com/righthousebooks
 instagram.com/righthousebooks

EXCLUSIVE SNEAK PEEK OF...

KILL: ONE

CHAPTER 1

Pitch black. The painful rasp of breath searing in my throat and my lungs. The crashing and stumbling of my feet running blindly over uneven ground. Twigs like claws tearing at my face and hands. Invisible branches whipping and lashing at me. Behind me, to left and right, the baying and howling of the pack, closing in on my scent. Running blind, it had to happen and I knew it would. My foot hit a rock. My ankle twisted. Shafts of pain stabbed through my leg and I hit the hard ground. Sharp stones bit into my hands.

And then they were all around me. I could not see them in the blackness, but I could hear them and smell them. And feel them. Their presence grew in intensity until they were almost like shapes made of black light: six before me, six behind me, six on my right and six on my left, sniffing the air, tasting my fear, closing in for the kill. My skin crawled, my body arched away, sensing the long, hard steel blades, knowing the terrible killing was about to start.

And then in the darkness I saw the eyes.

I sat up with a gasp.

It was dark, but not impenetrable. I could see the pale oblong on the window on my right. Moonlight was leaning in, soft turquoise beams that lay across the foot of the bed. A cool breeze touched my skin and I realized I was sweating, my heart was pounding and I was breathing hard, as though I'd been running. An owl called out, lonely in the woods, and I half expected to hear the baying and howling from my dreams echoing across the night in response.

I swung my legs out of bed and crossed the wooden floor to the window. The moonlight hung almost like a mist over the lawns. Tall narrow shadows seemed to look back at me from among the trees in the woodland. Invisible, undefined beings, half dream, half premonition, seemed to linger in the air, waiting for their moment to become real. I listened to the house. It was silent.

And in that silence there was knowledge: a kind of truth. I knew with absolute certainty that they would come, and there was only one thing I could do to stop them. I had to kill them first, every single one of them.

I turned from the window and looked back at the bed. Abi was sitting up, with her arms on her knees. The moonlight lay across the foot of the bed, but her face and her eyes were in darkness. Her voice, when she spoke, seemed disembodied.

"You OK?"

I nodded, realized she probably couldn't see it and said, "Yeah."

"That's why you're standing staring out of the window at four in the morning."

I smiled. "I do that every morning at four, didn't you know that?"

"Talk to me."

I thought of all the things I wanted to tell her, all the things I would have told Marni without hesitation. But it was somehow different with Abi. I wanted more than anything else to protect her—not just keep her physically safe, but protect her from the darkness. It was an imperative need in me to protect her innocence, hers and her children's, from the ugliness, the ruthlessness and the killing that had been my life for the past twelve years. I had to end it. I had to kill the pack, but I had to do it far away from her.

"I may have to go away for a while, on business."

She was quiet for a while. "How long?"

"I'm not sure."

"It's not over, is it? You said it was over."

"I don't want you to think about it, Abi. It doesn't affect you. I'm a businessman, going away on business..."

"Don't lie to me, Lacklan. Don't patronize me."

I sighed. "You, Sean, Primrose. You are the only good, wholesome things in my life. You are untouched by..." I hesitated. "Untouched by my past, by my father. I want it to stay that way. These people—this *pack*—they sully everything they touch. I don't want you to know about them."

"I already know about them."

I smiled and shook my head. "No, you don't." After a moment I added, "I have to finish it, Abi. If I don't finish it, it will never end. If you..." I struggled to say it, but forced myself. "If you feel this isn't what you signed up for, if you feel you want to leave..."

"What I signed up for is standing by your side, for better

for worse. I'm not a quitter. I'm not going anywhere. What do you need from me?"

I went and sat beside her on the bed and took her hands. Now I could see the pale luminescence of her face, and her eyes watching me. "I need you to stay wholesome and sane. I need you to be something I can hold on to, and come back to. You can't know about it."

She was quiet for a long while, staring at me. Finally she smiled and said, "About what?" I kissed her and she whispered, "Come back to bed, I have a going away present for you..."

ABI AND ROSARIO had set themselves a project to create an orchard and a herb garden at the back of the house, outside the kitchen. A local gardener had been recruited from Weston and, after breakfast, the three of them had gathered on the large stretch of lawn that separated the house from the forest at the back and started pacing up and down, standing around gazing with their hands on their hips and pointing at where they visualized plum trees and apple trees in neat, shaded rows, and nearer to hand, rosemary, sage and thyme, ready in good time for Christmas.

I withdrew to my study which, since I had rearranged all the furniture, I was now beginning to think of as *my* study, and withdrew from my safe the documents I had taken from the Richard John Erickson Institute, including the list of the Omega cabal, and sat at my desk to study them.

It began to dawn on me as I worked through the papers that, though I probably knew more than anyone alive, outside the cabal, about Omega, I actually knew very little about them, about their structure and workings. All I knew was their purpose and their objectives—and even that I knew only in the most general terms.

I took the list of members that Michael Donnelly, Senator Cyndi McFarlane's husband, had printed for me before I killed him and studied it with care for the first time. There were twenty-four members of the cabal, each designated with a letter from the Greek alphabet. This much I knew. My father, before he was killed, had been Gamma. They had offered his seat to me, and when I had refused and declared war on them, they had given that place to Donnelly. That place was now, as far as I knew, vacant.

What I hadn't known till now was that the cabal was divided into six groups, and each group had a geographical jurisdiction and what they called a competence. The first group was designated Omega Alpha. It appeared to be different from the others. Its geographical jurisdiction was the United Kingdom, New England, New York, the District of Columbia and Virginia, California and Belize. I sat for a while thinking about this, then had a look at its 'competence'. It said 'Oversight and general administration'. Its members were only three, Alpha, Beta and Gamma. Beside their titles in the cabal were their actual names. Gamma, as I said, was deceased, Alpha I knew well and Beta was a household name within the IT industry.

The other five groups were numerical: Omega 1, 2, 3, 4 and 5. Omega 1 covered Canada, USA, Greenland, the Caribbean, Australia and New Zealand. I had a look at its competence: free market capital, mass production and mass distribution, technological R&D in non-biological fields, IT, social cohesion, tension and conflict. Its members were the same as Omega Alpha, with the addition of Delta (Saul Cohen) and Epsilon (Aaron Fenninger).

Omega 2 covered the European Union plus Turkey, Norway and Iceland, Omega 3 covered Latin America, Omega 4 covered Africa and the Middle East and Omega 5 covered Russia, the Far East and the islands of the Philippines and Indonesia. Their competences seemed to cover everything from the movement of capital—free market, central planning and black market—as well as research and development in all areas of technology, but especially what they listed as 'behavior and motivation management' and 'unregulated biological and genetic IT interface'.

It was beyond science fiction. But as I read through it I was haunted by the images that George Stevens had filmed on entering Dachau, and Hitchcock and his British team's record of Belsen. That was not science fiction. It had happened, seventy years earlier. It was a reality: a program to exterminate an entire race of human beings. And it had been organized by a small cabal of people who, for no good reason, considered themselves somehow superior, and reinforced their fantasy with classical and pseudo-occult trappings. The parallels with Omega were striking.

But where the Third Reich's agenda had focused on Jews, homosexuals and 'short-legged Mediterraneans', Omega did not discriminate on the basis of race. They were more politically correct than that. They were happy to exterminate everybody who wasn't in the cabal, or serving the cabal as a happy slave.

That right there, I told myself, was the reason for the second amendment. I didn't want to preserve the second amendment. I wanted to abolish a world that made it necessary. Until then, I would keep my right to bear arms.

And use them.

Twenty-four men and women who believed themselves somehow superior to the rest of humanity, whose objective was... I paused in my thinking and realized that I did not really know, precisely, what Omega's objective was. My father had begun to explain it to me, though at the time I had hardly listened. It was based on Malthus' proposition: population grows exponentially, resources grow arithmetically.

Basically, population grows more, and faster than energy and food production. Of course, the Industrial Revolution meant that we were able to produce food on a scale that Malthus had never dreamed possible, and capitalists crowed that Malthus had been proven wrong, that production could keep pace with population.

But the very scientific revolution that was generating food on such a vast scale was also doing two other things: it was providing medical advances that were wiping out disease, increasing longevity by almost fifty percent, and simultaneously creating the greenhouses gases that would change the climate and bring drought and famine where before there was super-production.

The bitter twist was that by the time the droughts struck, the population would have grown from seven hundred million when Malthus was writing, to over seven billion, six hundred million today—and growing exponentially. Edward Wilson, one of Marni's most powerful influences at Harvard, had said that, "the constraints of the biosphere are limited," and that the Earth could sustain no more than nine or ten billion, and that was without factoring in climate change.

Omega had factored in climate change and decided that seven billion people needed to die, and the remaining six hundred million had to have their minds and their behavior controlled. That was, in essence, the Omega Protocol: the final protocol.

Were they wrong? Humanity was well on its way to becoming a plague of parasites—if it hadn't already become one—you couldn't argue with that. But if their assessment of the problem was correct, it didn't mean their solution was.

I checked the clock on the wall. It was five past twelve. The sun was over the yardarm. I stood and poured myself a Bushmills, pulled a Camel from my pack and lit up, standing by the window, looking out at the lawn and the trees beyond. I had no solution for the world. I had no solution for humanity. But I did know two things: if human beings had anything of worth it was the freedom of their minds; a freedom that gave them the potential to be more than the sum of their parts. To convert human beings into slaves, into biological machines as Omega intended, was nothing short of an obscenity. And beyond that, whether Omega were right or wrong, I knew that sooner or later they would come after me and my family. And that meant simply that I had to go after them first.

I sat at my desk and looked at the list. It was clear it had to be one of the five members of Omega 1, in North America. I smiled: correction, four members in North America. Gamma was dead. Alpha and Beta could not be reached yet.

They were too well protected. That left Delta, Samuel Cohen, and Epsilon, Aaron Fenninger.

I smoked and considered the names. I knew practically nothing about Samuel Cohen except that he was a financier from a very powerful family of bankers. But Fenninger I knew more about. Most people did. He was a writer, a director and TV and film producer. He'd started out twenty years earlier with a teen fantasy series that had not only made him fantastically rich, but had had a profound effect on teens and pre-teens. Thinking about it I began to see why Omega had opened their doors to him: Silicon Valley had created the delivery system, a man Fenninger's talent and skill could create a culture be delivered to an entire generation.

Wasn't that exactly what Goebbels had done in Germany, without the benefit of IT? Wasn't it what the U.S. and U.K. governments had tried to do using the cinema? How much more powerfully and effectively could Omega do it using the vast, global IT network?

I put my finger on his name and said, "Aaron Fenninger: Kill One."

A couple of calls found me his address in Malibu, and his office on Sunset Boulevard, in the heart of Hollywood. At first glance the Malibu mansion seemed to offer the best options, but I'd need a couple of days to scout around and make a plan.

I went to the gun room and thought about what weapons I would need. The essence of this operation would be silence, stealth. I smiled to myself. I wouldn't be blowing anything up this time. Just move in the shadows, I told myself, find his rhythm and his routine, take him out and leave. Then move on to Delta, Beta and, finally, Alpha.

I selected the Maxim 9. It's a damn ugly gun, but it has an integrated suppressor so it's nicely balanced, it fits in a holster and will take any kind of 9mm rounds, sonic and sub-sonic in a 17+1 magazine. I also selected my two Sig Sauer p226s, and my fighting knife, the Fairbairn & Sykes, the best fighting knife ever made. As an afterthought I added my night vision goggles and my orange osage take down bow, with twelve aluminum arrows.

I then chose a selection of bugs, a couple of which had been sent to me by Philip Gantrie, the IT genius nerd my father had recommended to me before he died. I didn't know his story, I doubted that anybody did, but he seemed to hate Omega as much as I did, and he had helped me several times in the past. They were micro-bugs, almost invisible to the naked eye, and used advanced cell phone technology to communicate with a cell you could install in your laptop, tablet, pad or phone. Something told me I might need one of them.

Then I sat and thought for a while about the different ways the job might play out and decided to take along a new addition to my arsenal: an especially adapted drone I affectionately called the Emperor.

When I had assembled my kit I went up to my room and packed some clothes, including the jeans and sweatshirts I used for working on my cars. I thought about renting some anonymous vehicle for the trip, but I decided in the end that anonymity was not as important as not being traced, so I decided to take the Zombie 222. It had the chassis of a 1968 Mustang Fastback, in matte black. But under the hood it had two electric engines delivering eight hundred bhp, one thousand eight-hundred foot-pounds of torque direct to the back wheels, instantly, driving it from 0-60 in just over one and a half seconds, with a top speed of 200 MPH in total silence. And that was what this operation was all about, I reminded myself. The silent kill.

Finally I went downstairs and stashed everything in the trunk of the Zombie, along with a set of fake, magnetic plates, and went to find Abi at the back of the house. She was standing in the kitchen doorway watching the gardener making a start on the orchard. Rosalia was chopping stewing steak with a large knife and there was a smell of warm olive oil, thyme and frying onions on the air. She had a small TV playing and she glanced at it as she worked. It was the news. There had been a bombing in New York, a new terrorist group calling itself the FMW. The reporter was talking into the camera and behind her I could see the offices of the Union Broadcasting Corporation with thick smoke billowing from its windows. She was saying, "...believe it or not, the group claiming responsibility are calling themselves the Free Mind Warriors, and claim that..."

I turned away and put my hands on Abi's shoulders. She turned to face me and smiled. Her eyes searched my face for a moment.

"Are you going already? I thought maybe a day or two..."

I gave my head a small shake. "This is business that needs to be attended to straight away."

"How long, do you think?"

I made a face like I was calculating how many board meetings I was likely to attend. "A week, not more than two."

She nodded. "Call me, let me know how things are going, and when you're on your way back."

I kissed her and made my way to the hall. Kenny had brought the car to the front of the house and was waiting for me. He handed me two hundred Camels and a bottle of Bushmills.

"I thought these might come in handy, sir."

"I'm pretty sure they will, Kenny."

"We look forward to having you back soon, sir."

"Yeah, me too."

I went outside and climbed behind the wheel. The Zombie moved swiftly and silently out the drive and onto Concord Road, toward Weston, and from there west, toward California and the City of Angels.

CHAPTER 2

I LEFT THE ZOMBIE ON THE TOP FLOOR OF THE USC Shrine Parking Structure on Jefferson Boulevard at eight thirty AM. I took my kit bag and made my way down to the street in the elevator. At that time of the morning it was already bright and growing warm. I hailed a cab and told him to take me to the El Toro Guest House on Juniper Street, in Watts. I settled back for the half hour drive and watched the vast, sunny sprawl of long, wide avenues, palm trees and people who worked real hard at looking like they never worked hard at anything.

The driver looked at me in the mirror a couple of times. "From back east, huh?" She was young and small, in a denim shirt, chewing gum.

I smiled. "Yeah, how can you tell?"

She waved her fingers around her face. "The pallor. Don't worry. You'll soon pick up a tan. New York? How about them terrorists, huh? Crazy motherfuckers."

I shrugged and shook my head. "I heard something..."

"In New York, they wanna destroy the TV networks, and the movies and the Internet. Like life ain't bad enough, now they wanna take away the fuckin' TV. They bombed the fuckin' UBC building. Crazy motherfuckers..."

I snorted. "Life without TV and Facebook, imagine."

"Only things that shut my mother up. All I fuckin' need. No TV..."

She kept up the monologue for another twenty minutes, until I started to wonder what would shut her up.

Juniper Street, like most streets south of downtown L.A., gave me the feeling it had never quite shaken off the desert. The road was wide, and the houses were widely spaced, surrounded by trees and palms that grew any old how and any old where. The buildings were low and broad, with corrugated tiled roofs and lime-washed walls in white and terracotta. They had the look of haciendas under a broad, blue sky.

El Toro Guest House was just one such building. There were no windows out front, only a heavy wooden door with a Mexican blanket hanging in front. On the left there was a tall, iron fence and beyond it a yard with tall palms shading an area of rockery, cacti and yucca.

I pushed past the curtain and inside the Mexican theme continued. There was a rough-hewn wooden reception counter on the right. The walls were salmon and yellow, uneven and hung with pictures that might have served as covers to the books of Carlos Castaneda. There was a rough pine coffee table, a few armchairs and a TV that was now dark and silent. The only thing out of place was the guy behind the counter. He didn't look Mexican at all.

He looked up as I stepped in and his face had 'I'm a son

of a bitch' written all over it. He was maybe six feet or six one, strongly built and in his late thirties. His hair was sandy and balding on top, which made him look like a Franciscan monk with a bad attitude and a broken nose.

I didn't bother to smile. I said, "I need a room for a week. Maybe two."

"Seventy bucks a night, up front."

I nodded and looked at the pictures on the wall. "Yeah, here's the thing. I lost my ID and my driver's license. The replacements are in the post. I don't mind paying extra." I fixed him with my eye. "That's no problem at all."

He gave me a once-over, made a mental calculation and said, "Hundred and fifty bucks a night, up front."

As I reached for my wallet I let him see the Sig in my waistband. I counted out a thousand and fifty bucks and as I put them on the counter in front of him I smiled. "Two things a man should never be without: a reliable weapon and reliable friends. I am fortunate to have both. If anybody should ever ask you, I was never here."

He took an old fashioned Yale key with a paper tag attached to it by a rubber band. It had the number 32 written on it in thick black ink. He handed it to me. "Pal, I forgot you already. Out on the left, behind the yucca."

I made my way through a patio tiled in broken terracotta with a small, unenthusiastic fountain splashing listlessly in the center. On the other side, beyond a potted yucca, I found a door that stood with my number on it. I let myself in, threw my kit bag on the bed and pulled up a slatted roller-blind to let in some light. Then I sat on the bed and called a number I had memorized before leaving Boston. It rang three times and a woman's voice answered.

"Archer's Private Investigations. How may I direct your call?"

"I need to talk to Mr. Archer."

"May I ask your name please, sir, and what the call is about?"

"No."

There was a brief pause. "Please hold. I'll see if he's free."

After a minute a man's voice came on the line.

"Archer."

"Mr. Archer, I can't discuss anything with you on the line. I need to come and see you this morning. This job pays well."

He hesitated a moment. "It's urgent, then...?"

"I need to see you this morning," I repeated in a dead voice.

"Say, eleven o'clock? You know where we are?"

"I'll be there."

I stowed my stuff under the bed and made my way back to reception. He was still at the desk, reading a tabloid. I leaned on it with my hands. He didn't look up. "I need a car: hire, buy. I don't care. But I don't want to waste time with documentation."

He sighed and raised his face to study mine. "You gonna cause problems for whoever gives you the wheels?" I shook my head. "He picked up the phone and dialed. "Joe, it's Don, from El Toro... Yeah, you too. Listen to me. I have a gentleman here." He eyed me as he said it, like I wasn't really a gentleman. "He urgently needs a car, but he ain't got time to mess about with papers, you know what I'm telling you...? You got it. Now he is prepared to pay above the odds...." He stopped talking, listened, then jerked his chin at me. "How long?"

"A week."

"A week..." He jerked his chin at me a second time. "Thousand bucks deposit, five hundred for the week. Two hundred finder's fee."

I raised an eyebrow at him. "Done. Don't keep bleeding me, Don."

I gave him two hundred bucks and he pointed past me. "Second on the right, past the church. Four doors down. Red Silverado. Joe'll be there."

I stepped out into the California sunshine, walked past the big, Spanish church and found Joe leaning on the hood of his truck, smoking a rollup. As I approached, he watched me with yellow eyes set behind tangled hair in a black, leather face. When he spoke it was like slow bubbling nicotine.

"This gonna cause trouble fer me? I don't need trouble."

"You don't talk to anyone, you don't get no trouble. Only cash."

He studied me a moment through a trail of smoke, then gave a bronchial laugh. "Talk 'bout what?"

I gave him his money and he handed me the keys. "You get your truck back, Joe. I get my deposit back."

He shrugged. "I told you, I don't need no trouble, mister."

I climbed in, slammed the door and fired her up. She sounded OK and I set off on the ten mile drive back toward downtown Los Angeles.

Archer's Private Investigations was, despite the impression they tried to give you on the phone, a one man operation run out of a seedy office on the fifth floor of the only attractive building left on West Olympic Boulevard. It was a nice, eleven story granite block that looked like it belonged in a 1930s movie. It had a dark wood elevator, with shiny brass fittings and a concertina door, that rattled me all the way to the fifth floor. By the time I got there I was almost surprised to find that Archer's Private Investigations did not have a door with frosted glass and gold lettering. Instead it had a fire door with a plaque on it that said 'keep closed at all times'. It was propped open with a rubber wedge and inside I could see lots of sunlight and part of a melamine desk.

I stepped through into a small office with wall to wall beige carpet, a couple of steel filing cabinets, a door, and an attractive woman with intelligent, humorous eyes. She was sitting behind an unattractive desk that was trying to look like wood, and failing. The woman gave me a humorous, intelligent smile and I said, "I was hoping for slatted blinds and soft focus."

"That's extra, Mr...?"

"Eleven o'clock."

"Mr. Eleven O'Clock? What are your given names, Al Pass?"

I moved the smile to the side of my face and said. "Mind your own business." I nodded toward the door. "Archer in there?"

"Sure, ask him to lend you some manners while you're there."

"I'll do that."

I knocked on the door and went in. It was like a replica of the other room, only behind the desk there was a man in his fifties smoking a cigarette. He had the hard, steady stare of a cop. Behind him there were two large sash windows with views of Olympic Boulevard. I looked for a wooden coat stand and a hat, but there wasn't one.

He stood and reached his hand across the desk. I took it and said, "Are you Archer?"

He shook his head and gestured me to a chair. "Archer retired and sold me the business. I kept the name. I'm Ted Wallace. I was a homicide Detective with the LAPD for twenty years. Do I get to learn your name now that you're here, or do you want to keep playing the mystery game?"

I shook my head. "I don't mind giving you a name. Will John Smith do?"

He smiled. "Sure, what can I do for you, Mr. Smith?"

"I want to put twenty-four hour surveillance on somebody."

He looked a little startled. "Twenty-four hours...?"

"Have you got somebody reliable who can do shifts? I need to know if the target has a routine, and if he has, what it is."

He thought about it a moment. "Yeah, I can do that. I got a guy who can do the late shift. If your target leaves his house, you want him followed?"

"No. I want you to stay on the house, note what time he leaves and comes back. It's the house I'm interested in."

"Sure..." He said it like I was crazy but he was too polite to say so. "How long you want me to sit on this place?"

"Maybe a week. I'll want daily reports. I won't give you any contact details. I'll come to you."

He sat back in his chair and sighed, watching me with narrowed eyes. "I'm a cop, Mr. Smith. I don't want to get involved in anything..." He spread his hands.

"I don't expect you to break the law, Mr. Wallace, and I don't expect you to abet me in breaking it. All I want is to know the household routine, who comes in, who goes out and when." He didn't look satisfied so I sighed, like he was forcing the information out of me and said, "I have reason to believe he might have my sister there, and he may be holding her against her will." I shrugged. "Maybe I'm kidding myself, but I need to know."

"Have you told the cops?"

"I have nothing to tell them yet, that's why I need a detailed breakdown of the comings and goings of the household, day by day."

He gave his head a little sideways twitch and picked up a pen. "Good enough for me. Who is the subject?"

"Aaron Fenninger."

He laid down the pen again and stared at me. "*The* Aaron Fenninger? The Aaron Fenninger who just got back from visiting the President at Camp David? The Aaron Fenninger who was just awarded an Oscar for best director?"

"Is there another?"

"You think Aaron Fenninger is holding your sister against her will?"

"You were twenty years on the L.A. police force. Are you going to tell me Hollywood celebrities don't commit serious crimes?"

He opened his mouth to speak, but nothing came out except a long sigh, at the end of which he said, "No. I'm not going to tell you that."

I shrugged. "If you don't want to risk upsetting the aristocracy, I can take my business elsewhere..."

"No." He shook his head. "I'll take the job..."

I studied him a moment. "I don't want him to know you're there. And I'm not going after him through the courts. This is a confidential report. You're safe."

"No problem. I'll do it. When you want me to start?"

I tossed a thick manila envelope on the desk. "That's expenses and a week's pay at above your going rate. Discretion is important. Start as soon as you can, today. I'll need a report every evening. You know where he lives?"

He spread his hands and made a face that was ironic. "Everybody knows where he lives. He has a mansion in Malibu."

I nodded once and stood. "I'll be in touch."

He looked inside the envelope and his eyebrows said he was happy. I left his office and his secretary showed me a face that said she didn't want to like me but did anyway. I smiled at her. "He taught me to say please and thank you. Now I'm going home to practice. If I get really good, will you give me a sticker?"

She said something that wasn't polite, but she smiled as she said it.

I took the I-10 down to Santa Monica and then followed the Pacific Coast Highway for fifteen miles, with the windows open and the salt air of the Pacific slapping me in the face. It was twelve thirty by the time I parked on Wildlife Road, and I was surprised to see that my twenty year-old Chevy Silverado wasn't as conspicuous in Malibu as I had expected. I was a hundred yards from Fenninger's gate and there wasn't a Bentley, a Cadillac or a Ferrari in sight. I guessed they were all in high-tech garages.

On the way I had bought myself a hamburger and a newspaper, and now I settled down to eat and watch.

After half an hour a Buick sedan turned into the road from Selfridge Drive, then turned into Fernhill and parked. In his mirrors he would have a clear view of Fenninger's house. I figured that was Ted Wallace. Half an hour later the gates rolled open and a white Jaguar F-Type rolled out. It slipped past me and, through the open window, I saw it was Fenninger at the wheel. I made a U and followed at a discreet distance.

At the intersection he turned east onto the Pacific Coast Highway and began to accelerate. Fortunately he stuck to the speed limit and I was able to settle six cars behind him and follow at a steady sixty-five miles per hour. At Santa Monica he took the Santa Monica Boulevard toward Hollywood.

It was a good ten mile drive through Beverly Hills and West Hollywood, until we finally came to Cahuenga, where he turned left, then right onto Sunset Boulevard, There he pulled up outside a steel and glass tower opposite the Pacific Cinerama, gave his keys to a boy in uniform and went inside. The boy took the car down a side street. I figured he was going to park it. A sign outside the building told me that Fenninger Productions had its head office on the sixth floor. I drove on by and parked outside the Caviar building. I gave the wing mirror a twitch and sat for half an hour watching the door. Nothing much happened.

I sat for another couple of hours and a lot more of nothing much happened. Finally, at three o'clock his car came back and another boy in uniform handed him his keys when he came tripping out of the front door. He climbed in the Jag, did a U-turn and accelerated past me, going east. I took off after him. At the bridge he turned right onto the

Camino Real Freeway and headed south at speed, back toward downtown L.A.

Eventually he turned south onto the Harbor Freeway and came off at South Beaudry Avenue to cross under the bridge and park at the lot on 8th and Figueroa. I parked at the other end of the same lot, climbed out and crossed the road behind him to the Ernst and Young Plaza. I followed him into the lobby and watched him step into one of the elevators. There was a woman there with a cleaning trolley. I smiled at her apologetically and said in my best Hugh Grant English, "Excuse me, but, wasn't that Aaron Fenninger?"

She gave me a look that was on the sarcastic side of ironic and said, "Yup."

I laughed. "I'll never get used to Los Angeles. I suppose he must be going up to..."

She raised an eyebrow at me. "Ten bucks and I'll tell you." I gave her ten bucks and she said, "Intelligent Imaging Consultants. He's a consultant. Top floor. And boy? Your English accent sucks."

I walked away laughing, shaking my head and saying, "You Americans!" like I thought she was funny.

I went back to the truck and sat for a long while, drumming my fingers on the wheel and thinking. Intelligent Imaging Consultants. It had Omega written all over it and Fenninger was a consultant. My purpose here was to take out Fenninger. I could see Sergeant Bradley in my mind's eye, his big Kiwi face, his stringy beard and his cold blue eyes staring at me. "Stick to the mission, stick to the plan. Everything else is called fuckin' suicide, sir."

He was always right. But he wasn't here to slap me around the head if I got it wrong. And there was nothing to be lost, I told myself, by finding out a little about Intelligent Imaging Consultants. I climbed out of the truck and crossed the road again, but this time I went into the FIGat7th shopping center. There I bought myself a disposable pay as you go burner and called Ted Wallace.

"Was that you in the red Silverado?"

"No. Listen. I want you to find out everything you can about a company called Intelligent Imaging Consultants. Fenninger is a consultant for that company. Can you do that?"

"Sure. No problem. It wasn't you?"

"No."

"OK. Catch you later."

At seven thirty Fenninger came out with three men and a woman. The woman was dark, possibly Hispanic. One of the men looked Japanese, one was white and the other looked Arabic. Fenninger was talking a lot, gesticulating. The others were laughing. They crossed the road, dodging the slow moving traffic, into 8th Street, and pushed their way into the Brazilian steakhouse there. I sighed, went and found myself a burger and a bottle of beer, and settled in for a long wait.

At half past ten they came out, said their farewells on the sidewalk and Fenninger returned to his car. I watched him climb in and followed him all the way back to Malibu, where the white gate rolled open and he pulled into his drive.

Ted Wallace's sedan was gone, but there was a Ford Fusion in its place. I was tired and my body ached, and I needed to think. I could hear the bottle of Bushmills Kenny had given me calling to me, so I turned around and made my way back to Watts, and the Toro guest house.

I left the truck around the corner and pushed through the Mexican curtain. Don wasn't there. There was a woman behind the counter. There was a look about her that said she was Mexican. Physically she could have been from anywhere in the Mediterranean or Latin America, but there was something in her eyes that said she was Mexican. The look she gave me said Don had told her I was trouble and to stay clear of me. That suited me fine. I nodded and said, "*Buenas noches.*"

Her eyes narrowed and her left eyebrow arched. "I speak English. Good night."

I met her stare but didn't answer. I went to my room, poured myself a large whiskey and opened the window to have a smoke and think about what I had learned. I decided I'd learned enough to complicate things, but not enough to know why.

CHAPTER 3

Aaron Fenninger was Epsilon, number five in the Omega hierarchy. That made him a man with a lot of power, and it meant that everything he did in his professional life was part of his work as a leading member of Omega. More than that, it meant everything he did in his professional life was an *integral* part of his work for Omega, and more precisely Omega 1. That meant that if he was consulting on the board of Intelligent Imaging Consultants, the work of that company was, somehow, directly relevant to Omega's plans.

Outside my window the fountain made little wet noises. I examined the amber spirit in my tooth mug, sucked on my cigarette, inhaled deeply and let the smoke out through my nose. I closed my eyes and in my mind I recited the competences of Omega 1: free market capital, mass production, mass distribution, technological research and development in non-biological fields, social cohesion, conflict and tension.

There was no immediate, obvious link with Fenninger. Except...

Hollywood, the world's most powerful propaganda machine. So Omega had learned from the Third Reich, and Fenninger was their Goebbels. I took a swig and let the smooth burn run down my throat and warm my belly. It made some kind of sense, but when I remembered the sophistication of the research I had come across, both at the sun beetle farm in Colorado, and at the John Richard Erickson Institute[1], it was hard to believe that any of that was being applied in Hollywood. For one thing, the United States had never been less united, had never had a more divided, confused sense of purpose. The kind of chaos and division which was afflicting the US was not the product of anodized, neutralized or standardized minds.

What was it the product of? There were plenty of theories out there, most of them made party political points; few of them, if any, stood up to intellectual scrutiny. Perhaps chaotic disunity was an essential part of human nature, and there was more of it now than ever before because there were more people now than ever before. If that was the case, then Fenniger's work as Omega's head of propaganda wasn't very effective.

I drained my glass and dropped my cigarette butt into it. It gave a small fizzle and died. One thing was clear in my mind. It was about the only thing that was. I had to get inside Aaron Fenninger's offices and see what he was about —before I killed him. When Fenninger died, his work had to die with him, otherwise there was no point.

---

1. See *Dawn of the Hunter* and *To Rule in Hell*

I slept badly and at eight the next morning, after a work out and a shower, I called Ted Wallace. He was at his office, his relief was on duty at the house. So I got in the truck and drove downtown to talk to him. As I stepped in, his secretary looked at me like I wasn't the nicest thing that had happened that morning. She smiled with her mouth but left her eyes on scowl duty and said, "Good morning, Mr. Nine O'Clock."

I smiled with all my face and said, "I would tell you my name, but then you might steal my soul."

She raised an eyebrow. "My God," she said without feeling, "A man in L.A. who has a soul." She looked back at her computer and jerked her thumb at the door. "He's expecting you."

He had a pot of coffee on the desk and a paper bag full of fresh croissants. There were two cups, a carton of milk and a box of sugar. He said something that sounded like "Mng-ng!" gestured with his chin at the cup he wasn't holding, and added, "H'llash'llf!"

"Thanks." I sat, poured mine black and grabbed a croissant. "What have you got?"

I bit and chewed while he drank and swallowed. "Not a lot, to be honest. The house is gated and walled, so it's impossible to see what goes on on the inside, unless you want to start getting into expensive electronic surveillance, and even if you did, I'm not sure how successful you'd be. These guys employ the best and can afford the best." He sighed, bit, chewed. "One thirty PM he left the house in his Jaguar, but you already know that because you weren't waiting for him in your Chevy Silverado and you didn't follow him.

"Three PM his wife came out..." He opened a file and dropped a couple of large photographs on the desk. They showed an attractive woman in her thirties, in jeans and a white blouse. She was holding hands with two children, about eight or ten, a boy and a girl. "She walked two doors down to the Reeds' residence, stayed there until six PM and returned. Nobody arrived and nobody left until around midnight, when Fenninger returned. The exact time is in the report, but you know that because you were not following him in your not a Chevy Silverado."

He poured himself more coffee and stuffed half a croissant in his mouth.

I asked, "How about Intelligent Imaging Consultants?"

He looked at me and blinked, then looked at his watch. "What I've been able to find out since last night is that it is basically a think tank set up with money from various corporations..."

"Media?"

"All visual media, TV, video, cinema, IT obviously, and their main function seems to be to advise or make recommendations on what shows or movies to produce, promote or axe."

I frowned. "So I have a movie I want to produce..."

He shook his head. "Mh-mh..." He swallowed and sipped coffee. "No, you are a corporation that produces maybe a hundred and fifty shows, covering everything from news to sci-fi to comedy to drama, et cetera. Now, once a year you need to decide what gets axed, what goes on for a new season, and what new projects get the green light. Correct?"

I nodded. "OK."

"So sometimes that is a tough call. *Often* it's a tough call. In the old days you did it on a mixture of gut feeling and ratings. These days it's market analysis, what's trending on Twitter or Facebook—all that shit. So these guys went to the big corporations and said, 'we have the expertise, we can look at your shows and tell you which ones to axe, which ones to keep and promote, and which projects to green light.' And they give them this advice based on market analysis."

"And they have a consultant who is a TV and cinema producer. No conflict of interests there."

He smiled. "This is Hollywood. There are no conflicts of interests, only interests."

I thought about it for a minute. "That's a hell of a lot of work and research for four people."

He sighed. "I have more digging to do. As well as run a detective agency, I also have a life that includes a wife and kids."

I offered him an ironic face. "I heard that some people do that."

"Yeah. My guess, they have a team of freelance researchers trawling through social media and reports from market research companies. They distill all that research and show it to their consultant. He ignores it and makes his recommendations on what he wants to see axed, promoted and green-lighted. That has always been the way it has worked in Hollywood."

It was what I had imagined, and it meant that Omega got to choose what dominated the media. In classic Omega style, they had a conspiracy in which millions colluded without ever realizing it, while one conspirator pulled the strings.

I nodded. "Good work."

He looked surprised. "It is?"

I smiled. "Sometimes you just need a pro to confirm what you suspect. Stay on the Fenninger residence. If I don't see you tonight, I'll drop in tomorrow morning. Tomorrow the croissants are on me."

In the outer office, on my way out, I smiled at his secretary as I passed. "What's your name, by the way?"

She didn't look up from her computer. She just said, "Seriously?"

THERE WAS a surprising stillness and quiet on Sunset Boulevard. It was half past two in the morning. Listless aluminum streetlamps painted the blacktop with a sickly sheen of yellow light. The shops were closed, the offices were closed, the pizza parlors and cafes were closed. All the buildings had darkened windows, like dead, closed eyes, and black doors like gaping mouths. Only the night watchmen were awake, sitting behind their dimly lit desks, watching small TVs in their towers of steel and glass, while outside, empty streets echoed with distant sirens under a black, invisible sky.

I'd had the Emperor sitting in the back of the Silverado with the controls on my lap. Take off had been uneventful and I was now using the onboard cameras to come in for a gentle landing on the roof of the small, six story tower where Fenninger had his offices. The landing was good and I deposited the payload, then brought the drone out of range, back to the truck. When it had settled safely I triggered the powerful EMP generator I had deposited on the roof, then pulled on a woolen hat and a pair of heavy shades, and made my way across the road to the main door. I could see the guard inside messing around with his screens and his computer, trying to work out what had happened. I rapped on the glass and held my home made FBI badge against the glass. I'd had to return the one I'd 'borrowed' from Agent Harrison Mclean during the UN fiasco[2], but I'd managed to produce a decent copy before doing so, with the advantage that it had my photograph in it instead of Mclean's.

The guy in the uniform inside scowled at me, hurried over and looked at the badge. Then he opened the door. I stepped in, waved the badge at him again and said, "Special Agent Mclean, your IT out?"

He nodded. "Yeah."

"Cameras?"

"Uh-uh, everything, all out. What's going on?"

"You got anyone patrolling the building?"

"No."

I scowled at him like it was his fault. "Why not?"

"We ain't got valuables here. It's only six floors and we just got documents, film scripts, that kind of stuff. I take a walk every couple of hours. If we have trouble we call the cops."

I grunted. "OK, stand by. Do nothing. Call no one. We have this covered. I'm going to have a look upstairs." I held out my hand. "Keys."

He hesitated. If he refused I was going to have to knock him unconscious. But it wasn't necessary. I was the FBI, and

---

2. See *The Hand of War*

everybody trusts the Feds. He handed me a bunch of keys and said, "They're numbered. It's an office per floor."

I walked toward the elevators pressing my finger against my ear, and muttered, "Alpha one, be advised I am proceeding to investigate upper floors. Be alert. We may have hostiles."

I rode the car to the top floor and stepped out into a small but luxurious reception area, with a mahogany reception desk, parquet floors and leather armchairs set in nests around heavy, dark wood coffee tables. There was a door on the far right, and another behind the desk and slightly to the left. I went for the one on the far right, and my hunch proved to be correct. Once I'd identified the key and opened the door, I found myself in a large, airy office overlooking the boulevard. The walls were paneled in wood and hung with what seemed to be genuine Picassos. The floor here was also parquet, and strewn with Persian rugs. A sideboard on the right held the obligatory silver tray of decanters and a genuine 1960s soda bottle. On the left there was a nest of black leather chairs and couches. A huge oak desk that appeared to be antique sat with its back to the curved windows.

This was where Aaron Fenninger created his shows and his movies. Or was it where he played Goebbels and decided what propaganda to package as Hollywood entertainment, and feed to the Western world? I stood a moment taking in the room. It reeked of power, and yet somehow it wasn't convincing. There was something that didn't gel: something that didn't quite ring true.

I sat at his desk, pulled on some surgical gloves and went through his drawers. All of them were unlocked. There were a dozen film scripts and a stack of contracts, none of which was of any interest. There were ink cartridges, paperclips, elastic bands, pens, paper and blank notebooks.

I got up and walked around the room, looking behind the paintings. I found the safe behind a geometrically challenged woman with both breasts on the same side of her chest. I grimaced. It was a decent safe, but it wasn't a super-safe. I took my driver's license from my wallet and slipped it into the fine crack on the right side of the safe door, then began to slide it down slowly till I found the reset button. A little pressure depressed it and I punched in the new code, 123456. I pulled out my license, punched in the code again and opened the safe.

It really is that easy.

There was not much to see other than a stack of papers about two inches deep. I took them to the desk and sat to look through them. The title sheet said simply, 'INTELLIGENT IMAGING CONSULTANTS' and underneath, '*Five Year Project*'.

I was aware I didn't have long before my guy downstairs started getting antsy, so I photographed the first ten pages and put the rest back in the safe. Then I placed a micro-bug in one of the carved curls on the side of his desk and another under his coffee table, and made my way down in the elevator again, removing my gloves. As I stepped through the sliding doors I was pressing my ear again and muttering, "All clear, Alpha, stand by."

The security guard was staring at me fixedly. I frowned at him and said, "I think we must have scared them off. You better call your tech guys to check out your equipment and your cameras." I drew a deep breath and studied his face a moment, like I was thinking. "My advice." I shook my head. "I wouldn't talk about this. Nobody got hurt. Let's be thankful."

He nodded, uncertain and a little scared. I stepped into the street and made my way back across the road.

I climbed in the Chevy, slammed the door and sent the drone to collect my hardware. Once I had it in the truck and safely under a tarp, I started a leisurely drive back toward Watts, going over what I had seen. There was no indication, apart from the contents of the safe, that Fenninger's office was used for anything other than writing and producing his shows and his movies. Apart from being eighteen karat politically correct drone fodder, I didn't think there was anything especially sinister about his movies or his TV shows.

So that meant that the part of his work that was directly related to Omega was handled, albeit unwittingly, by Intelligent Imaging Consultants. I thought briefly about paying them a visit and nosing around in their offices, but I decided I was more interested in talking to them than looking at their papers. I wanted to know what was inside their heads, more than what was inside their safes.

On the way back to El Toro I pulled into an all night Walgreens and printed the photographs. They were clear and sharp, but I didn't stop to look at them. I went back to the desolate parking lot, climbed into the truck and drove back through the broad, empty streets to the guest house. There I left the truck around the corner and went inside. The same Mexican woman was standing behind the reception desk. She stared at me as I came in. I said, "Good evening."

She said, "Are you drunk? We don't want any trouble."

I shook my head and smiled. "No, I'm not drunk. And I don't want any trouble either."

Her face registered no reaction, but she said, "You been smokin' in your room."

"Yeah. Is that a problem?"

"I left you an ashtray on your bedside table. Don't smoke in the bed. We don't want a fire."

"I won't." I went to move on but stopped and hesitated. "You always on night duty?"

"Yes. Why?"

"You ever get trouble at night?"

She scanned me quickly with her eyes, then shrugged. "Sometimes."

"Your husband on hand if you need help?"

"He's not my husband. No, I call the cops. Sometimes they come, sometimes they don't."

I nodded. "Well, I won't give you any trouble. If you need a hand, shout."

She didn't say anything and I went to my room to look at the pictures. I poured myself a stiff whiskey, threw myself on the bed, poked a Camel in my mouth and lit up. Obedience was never my strong suit. I read slowly through the ten pages of documents.

Intelligent Imaging Consultants was composed of three men and a woman: Ahmed Musa, Erick Dunbar, Elena Sanchez and Izamu Suzuki. The document I had photographed—partially photographed—was a proposal that might or might not have been written by Fenninger, suggesting how and why Intelligent Imaging Consultants could and should shift from passive analysis to a more aggressive role in actually driving the direction of what it called 'popular visually-based culture'.

The text then took a very rapid and unexpected turn, and started talking about child psychology. It began by stating that, "It has been clear since Albert Bandura's development of social cognitive theory in the early 1960s that children learn behavior by imitating role models, and that television can become a very powerful delivery system for such role models. Later work by Hill, Eggen and Kauchack and Eden have shown that modeling of this type can continue in later life, where the social environment is conducive to retarding adulthood and discouraging self-reliance.

"It is proposed here that our society is eminently well suited to this kind of modeling, in that the visually-based media occupy a central role in social life and social interaction, and provide us with a wide range of ready-made celebrity role models from the earliest age. These models have already assumed a large part of the role traditionally reserved for parents and, to an even greater extent, that reserved for priests and other spiritual guides who both prescribed and proscribed particular types of behavior..."

The next few pages were in a similar vein. Then I came to a passage that stated, "The Omega Behavioral Research Team has conducted a number of experiments over the last forty years in which the potential of television, IT and cinema as tools for behavioral conditioning have been explored. Certain limitations have been identified, but the power of these media not only to promote, but to *dictate* behavior as diverse as eating habits, violence, aggression and sexual orientation, has been established beyond any doubt. It is proposed therefore that..."

That was where the photographs ran out. I didn't need to read any more. I knew what they proposed. They were like the Wile E Coyote, constantly trying out new methods from the endless ACME store of mind control devices. With the one big difference that instead of the Roadrunner they were successfully preying on almost eight billion people who were, steadily, according to Omega's plan, turning into quasi-zombies.

I sat for a while, indulging in my proscribed behavior, smoking on the bed and drinking whiskey, and wondered what our ancestors would have made of the world their descendents had created for themselves. I tried to think back and identify at what point we had entered this dystopian nightmare without even realizing we had crossed through the portal from sanity to madness. Was it, as Senator Cyndi McFarlane had suggested, in the 1960s? Or was it earlier, when we made the first steam engines and trains? Or was it when the Romans started standardizing things and spreading their empire, their culture of citizenship, of all roads leading to one place, one God. I remembered reading an old Viking saga where they described the spread of Romanized Christianity across Europe as a black tide.

And that made me think of Malthus. Because that was pretty much what he had predicted for a humanity: a black, unstoppable tide, where the victim is the disease itself. Only it was so much worse than anything he had ever predicted.

Made in the USA
Coppell, TX
04 March 2026

73234542R00163